VACATIONLAND

MAN PLANS, GOD LAUGHS

NAT GOODALE

Final Editor and Designer: Bob Avery (bobavery@umich.edu)

Cover Design:
Wesley Walker and Anna Goodale (artista_01@yahoo.com)

Publisher:

Bowditch Press
Dba Bowditch Boats, LLC
c/o Dark Harbor Boat Yard
Seven Hundred Acre Island
P.O. Box 25
Lincolnville, ME 04849
USA

Printed in the USA

First Edition, 2013

ISBN 978-0-9898406-0-6

Fiction   Contemporary   Adventure

For

Lily

Acknowledgments

I tip my hat to the following:

- first and foremost to Lily, my sweet wife, who lent me unending support and encouragement;

- to my mother for her continual enthusiasm for this project;

- to Kathrin Seitz, writing mentor and guide, and the ever insightful writers in the Jack Grapes group;

- to Wesley Walker and my daughter Anna for their cover design;

- to my editors **Deke Castleman**, Dusty Relique, and Bob Avery;

- to Major Alan Talbot of the Maine Marine Patrol;

- to Mike and Lynn Hutchings, Dana Berry, and the rest of the Lincolnville lobster gang, always bright lights shining through the fog;

- to Martin Crowe for his legal advice;

- to Mariah Ackley for her stern woman expertise.

Thank you all for your part in this collaboration.

Prologue

October 20

*P*ot *Luck*, a 31-foot wooden Willis Beal lobster boat, slipped through the fog at a slow and steady pace doing close to three knots. She headed straight for the shore without deviating or slowing and ran up on the rocks beneath the shrouded spruce trees and a lone maple, its leaves glowing a dull red, on the northwestern tip of Seven Hundred Acre Island. Nobody was aboard.

With her momentum, she rode up smartly on the slippery seaweed. Her bow rose and her planks splintered. She came to rest listing severely to starboard.

The jolt caused all the fishing gear to slide forward. The bait trays crashed into the engine box and tipped over, spilling chopped herring onto the deck. The lobster tank ripped loose and dumped its contents into the herring slurry.

The propeller remained free and continued to turn. Her engine ran steady at a thousand revolutions per minute. The wet exhaust no longer muffled the noise. Her only through-hull fitting, which normally brought cooling saltwater to the engine, was now sucking air. The 275-horsepower Chrysler gasoline engine began to overheat. Within fifteen minutes, the engine shuddered, seized, and went silent.

The tide continued to recede. Small waves lapped at the shore. A gentle breeze blew through the evergreen trees. The only thing moving, besides the squirming lobsters, was the sweep of the radar in the display over the helm. It went around and around until the battery went dead four hours later.

It was noon. The tide had turned, and the fog lifted. Shelly called the Marine Patrol to report Donny overdue and missing. At the same time, Wally was just leaving the mainland docks in Lincolnville for a run at his own traps. He looked across the now-clearing three miles of Penobscot Bay and saw *Pot Luck* on the shore. He headed straightaway toward the island, running flat out.

Chapter 1

Earlier that year...

April can be a very nasty month on the coast of Maine, like an unwelcome visit from an unfaithful wife. With the wind sweeping raw rain onto the open ground, Donny Coombs was trying to remain optimistic as he hefted his toolbox and trudged through the mud around his abandoned pickup truck to his lobster boat. It stood proudly in his yard, up on blocks and balanced by six jack stands, three to a side.

The ladder leaned on the starboard toe rail. He climbed one-handed, weighed down by the tools. His boots left mud on the rungs and tracks on the deck. Donny set the toolbox under the pilothouse, away from the rain. He stood under the roof and dug under his foul-weather gear through the neck of his thick sweater to his breast pocket and took out his cigarettes.

He fired up a Camel straight, no filter. His father had always said smoking filtered cigarettes was like sucking on a nipple through a flannel nightgown. He looked out at his house and beyond to the busy construction site in the brown and gray field next door.

Donny remembered playing in the field as a little boy, running with the family dogs. His house had been built by his great-great-grandfather. Back then it was part of a major tract of family-owned land that ran along the coast and looked down on west Penobscot Bay and the islands. Over the generations, the land had been divided and sold off piece by piece to raise enough money to move away.

A taint of wood smoke came from his chimney.

His half-acre and the original homestead were all that remained. The house needed some new wood and paint. He'd get to that later when his boat was in the water.

The house was snug on Route One, which went all the way down to Key West. In the old days, it was a sleepy two-lane road — and who wanted to plow a driveway anyway? A filthy semi-truck whizzed by spewing up grit and whirlwinds of road grime, sounding sticky on the wet pavement.

Donny's new neighbors had set their house right up to his property line but down closer to the water away from the road. First thing they did last fall was pave the driveway right up to the foundation of their three-car garage. They obviously looked forward to having their curvy driveway plowed. They'd planted a row of ornamental cedars along the road as a noise break.

Smoke trailed the pitched cigarette into the mud. He could probably get the plowing job.

He unlatched the engine box and raised it out of the way. Today's task was to accomplish what he'd neglected to do last fall. It seemed that once *Pot Luck* was hauled and up in his yard, the job of laying up the engine and winterizing the boat gave way to drinking beer. The fishing was over, and it was time to relax. Who worked when you had money in the bank?

The engine had to be run to stir up the old oil, though only for a bit without ocean water to cool it. He turned the key, hit the starter button, and nothing happened, a thought unspoken. Swearing, he buttoned up his slicker and made his way down the ladder to fetch the battery charger and power cord.

Two trucks could fit in his garage, in theory at least. In reality, there was hardly enough room to get to the back wall for the charger. He stepped around a stack of lobster traps. They were the last batch, about twenty. The other four hundred were neatly piled out back beside the building. It had been his winter's work repairing the wear and tear of the lobster season.

He took the power cord off a hook behind spools of pot warp and dug the charger off a shelf, nearly falling over empty gasoline jugs. He tied off the end of the cord to the junction box. The cord tangled as he unwound it to the boat, but he managed to keep the end out of the mud. He slipped on the ladder and had to catch the charger before it cratered into the gunk. He got it all hooked up to the battery terminals and went back down to the garage and plugged the damned thing in.

It would take several hours for the battery to charge, and it was nearly noon. Donny made his way past his old truck, now sunk into the lawn on flat tires, and then past his new truck, the same model. He figured he could scavenge parts off the old one. He made his way up the wooden steps, paint worn off long ago, and into the old house.

He shed his boots in the mudroom, peeled off his heavy rubber rain gear, and padded in stocking feet into the warmth of the kitchen. He tossed a couple of sticks into the wood stove and ruffled Tut's head. With a Budweiser out of the ice-box, he sat down at the Formica table. Tut came up off his blanket along the wall beside the stove. The dog stretched his front legs out like paying homage then arched his backbone in a yoga pose. He yawned, leapt up on the kitchen chair, sat down, and looked Donny in the eye.

"For a nasty bastard, you sure got it good. Warm enough for ya?"

Donny turned his attention to the view beyond the dirty kitchen window to the house going up next door. He'd been watching all winter long. It was amazing what you could do with money. Even on the coldest weeks, the construction crew from out of state showed up to build and build.

The garage and house had been framed up by Christmas and roofed in by the end of January. Made sense that they wanted to finish the outside work in the freezing cold so they could start the inside work in nice weather.

They were now nailing up cedar clapboards to finish the siding. They used the long, expensive boards — why have a seam when you could afford not to?

It was a huge house, New England-style, six thousand square feet of living space, three chimneys, and a three-car garage. Could work on a mess of traps with that kind of space.

The beer was good so he got another.

He watched a Range Rover pull up next to the contractor's pickup truck. The tall man, wearing a barn coat, got out and yelled something at his passenger. The woman, in a knee-length leather coat with an animal collar, stepped gingerly into the mud, and they both made their way to the house.

Donny hadn't met them yet, which seemed rather un-neighborly. On whose part? He wasn't the kind to take them over a welcome-to-the-neighborhood cake like a credit to get on their plus side, but maybe he could have gone over to say hello.

The couple came out of the house. The Range Rover pulled out. Donny and Tut heard it rumble up their driveway. Donny watched the man park behind the F150.

Tut went to the other window and growled from deep down, sounding bigger than his 25 pounds. The UPS guy called him the nasty little bastard, and the vet said it'd be easier to vaccinate a mailbox filled with concrete.

"Shut the fuck up, Tut."

Donny watched as the mud nearly stripped his neighbor of his unlaced boots as he came to the door. The woman remained in the car.

Donny waited for the knock. When it came, it was more like a pounding. Tut went to barking and threw himself against the mudroom door.

"Excuse me, Mr. Coombs. Hello?"

It was a deep, cultured voice like you'd hear on C-Span. Donny made him wait. Another pounding.

"Hello? Anybody home?"

Donny told Tut to "go lay down and be good." Tut got to looking moody and went back to his blanket but sat there alert. Donny crossed the mudroom, opened the front door and storm door.

"Yes?"

"Hello, Mr. Coombs. My name is Delano Nelson. I'm your neighbor. May I come in for a moment?"

Donny opened the door wider.

"Sure, come on out of the weather."

Mr. Nelson came up the steps and walked directly into the kitchen, leaving muddy footprints. Nelson stepped to the stove and rubbed his hands together. Tut's gaze was piercing, and he silently bared his teeth.

Donny followed him in, careful not to dirty his socks, and shut the door to the mudroom.

Nelson stood so straight it looked like it hurt, as if he had a 12-inch spike up his ass. Early forties and gym trim, outdoor clothes pressed and sharp, his hair sculpted and on the long side, contoured over his ears like a mannequin's. The weather had done no damage. Donny went to insert several more sticks into the stove, making Nelson step back.

"Nice weather," Nelson said conversationally with a smile, trying to be especially nice.

"For a cormorant. Welcome to Maine," Donny said.

Nelson looked down at Tut.

"May I pat your dog? I don't think I've ever seen a dog that color."

Tut was mud-puddle brown, and his coat had the texture of a Brillo pad.

"I'd advise against it."

Tut was now letting a low-level grumble come through his clenched teeth.

"Don't let his sweet disposition fool you. He's got some territorial issues, and he's not much fit for affection."

"Yes, I can see that. Maybe once we get to know each other. I'm quite good with animals."

Nelson moved off the stove and away from Tut.

"Let me get right to the point, Mr. Coombs. I don't want to interrupt your day."

He looked over at the beer can on the table. Donny thought he might check his watch, but he didn't.

"You see, my wife and I are building our house, and we plan to move in shortly. We've had to build the house somewhat closer to you than we would have liked because of the hydrology. If we could have, we'd have set the house much farther away."

"That's okay, Mr. Nelson. This way we can wave to each other every morning."

Donny said it with a smile. Nelson looked distracted.

"Yes, well, my wife and I were wondering if we could come to some sort of understanding with you. We hoped that you'd consider sprucing up your property a little bit."

"You mean like with shrubs or something?"

"Yes, well, no. We hoped that you might consider removing some of the, uh, items in your yard, the ones that obviously have no further value. It wouldn't matter if your property wasn't the first impression one got when one came into our driveway. I hope you understand our point of view."

Donny rubbed his chin, the thinker. A host of smart-alec comebacks crossed his mind, but he kept his mouth shut this time. Nelson took the chance to look around the kitchen. It was cluttered and worn down, but Donny had done the breakfast dishes.

"May I offer you a beer, Mr. Nelson?"

"Well, it's a little early for me, thank you. And my wife is waiting in the car."

"Pity."

"You don't have to agree right now, Mr. Coombs."

"Feel free to call me Donny."

"Thank you, Donny."

"I'll have to think on it awhile, you know, decide which items might have outlived their use and all. You don't mind the boat, do you?"

"Oh, good heavens, no. We want to fit right in, and anyway, I imagine it'll be in the water soon for the season. In fact, I understand we may have a mooring next to yours in the harbor. We have a delightful sloop being built in Rockport."

"Glad to hear it, Mr. Nelson. We can wave from our boats too."

"Yes, well, I look forward to your answer. We are staying at the Camden Manor Inn for the next several weeks while they finish the house. You can call us there."

"I'll make sure to call as soon as I've figured it all out."

"That would be splendid. Thank you in advance. I'll be going now."

Nelson let himself out, and Tut stood on hind legs at the window to make sure the intruder kept moving.

Donny got the broom and dustpan, swept up the dirt, mopped the linoleum, and got another beer. He smiled as he sat at the kitchen table and looked out onto the Nelson house.

It was going to be a contest of who could be more neighborly.

Chapter 2

Early May

Delano Nelson slid his bone-china cup to the side. He and Eliza sat at the heirloom dining room table that had been delivered the day before. The morning sunlight poured through the picture window, swept across the table, and illuminated Eliza's auburn hair, catching the highlights. It caught the thin scar beneath her ear and accentuated her taut cheek and impressive bone structure. She stared at her organizer, pencil poised in midair.

The wind was tossing whitecaps across the bay and bending trees toward the south. But there was no sound from outside. The refrigerator hummed, and the grandfather clock clicked in the foyer.

Delano refocused on what his wife was saying.

"It is so important to manage our houseguests, honey. Otherwise, they'll consume the summer and make our life miserable."

His plans for the summer were already coming unglued. He'd have to fight for time on the boat.

She looked up.

"And that brings me to our neighbor. Sweetheart, you absolutely must get him to clean up his property, and that includes cutting down that ghastly tree. It's smack dab in the middle of our view. And his ugly little mutt is a threat to Alexandra."

At the sound of her name, Alexandra eased off her dog bed and came for a treat. She walked with caution as her paws ticked on the polished mahogany floor. Eliza fed her a bit of toast, going into her cutesy voice.

Delano's nerves crunched like the crust in Alexandra's mouth. The dog looked over. Alexandra and Delano stared at each other.

He thought she knew how ridiculous she looked, all trimmed out in poodle fashion. He almost sympathized with her, as if she understood about the finer things in life and what was owed her, paying the price for being a pet.

He said, "Honey, don't you think we should get Alex spayed?"

Delano brought his cup back and took a sip of bitter cold coffee.

"Heavens, dear, she's a champion, and she'll be bred when she reaches the right age."

Her tone ended all further discussion.

Delano tried the houseguest subject.

"If we keep the number of guests down, we can take the boat up the coast. This is vacationland, after all."

Eliza tapped the pencil on the calendar.

"We are establishing ourselves in this community. Word will leak out about the people we know. At a bare minimum, we need to fill three weekends each month. Of course, September is much more open. We can go boating then."

Delano let out a muted sigh. Alexandra returned to her bed in the sun.

He said, "I think Donny and I understand each other. No one likes pressure, so he's trying to save face. I'll offer some kind of replacement hedge if he agrees to take the tree down."

Delano slid his chair back and stood.

"I need to get to Rockport Maritime. You remember, the launching is this weekend, which reminds me. I have to check with the harbormaster about our mooring."

He brushed crumbs of toast off his brick-colored trousers, and Eliza frowned. He slipped his blazer off the back of his chair, put it on, and then took his plate, cup, and saucer into the open kitchen.

Alexandra lifted her head when the china clinked on the black-marble counter.

Eliza penciled in another group of visitors.

Without looking up, she said, "You look splendid today, sweetheart. I like the yellow shirt. But how can you even stand to get within five feet of that dreadful harbormaster? Isn't he threatening to put us out beyond the town moorings? Why do we have to be so far down on the waiting list?"

Delano stared at his dishes.

"With the amount of taxes we pay in this town, it shouldn't be a problem."

Eliza was on a roll.

"Have you thought any more about joining the harbor committee? Remember, at the last meeting of the Coastal Conservators, it wasn't said directly, but it was certainly implied that we need to save these people from themselves. They're ruining the very finest things of Maine. Who's going to come here when the docks smell like a fish sewer, and you have to walk through slime and dog droppings just to get to your boat? You can make a difference, and it will look good."

"I'll think about it."

At the very least, he could lease a mooring in close, even if he had to rent it from Donny Coombs.

Chapter 3

Donny looked out on a dark, gray morning with drizzle that he knew was borderline freezing rain. Donny was wrapped up tight in two thick wool blankets on only a sliver of bed with Tut packed right in tight and pressing him over to the edge. Donny shoved Tut back to the middle.

Tut went for a full-out front and back leg stretch while lying flat on his back.

Donny rolled out of bed and hit the kitchen in his boxers and white socks, goose bumps the size of pinheads popping up all over his upper body. He threw some sticks into the wood stove, splashed in a quarter tin can of kerosene, and tossed in a match. He set the percolator, leaned over the sink, and looked out onto the Nelson estate.

Today was Town Meeting, the time to set everything straight and see who was who. Generally, everything was pretty cut and dried. They elected the tax assessor, the town clerk, and the selectmen.

There was usually a little pull and tug over line items in the town accounts. The school budget ate up most all the money percentagewise, but someone always wanted to prop up the welfare state and put in some nanny warrants.

This year, Donny expected something special. Old Delano and face-lift Eliza had introduced their warrant to clean up the town. Watching it get shoved back down the Nelsons' throats would be a sight to see.

Donny poured some black coffee and sat in the kitchen chair closest to the stove, letting the dry heat bake his bare skin, hot on the stove side and cool on the other.

He surveyed the offending items in his yard — the assortment of spare parts which the Nelsons determined had no further value.

Those included the old truck up on blocks and the lawnmower that threw a rod last spring. The new Toro had mown around her all last summer, so she looked to Donny as if she belonged right where she sat.

Then there was that pile of traps, some relatively new and some old, each with the gummy sinking line coiled up nice and neat. Leaning against the garage was the scallop drag with all the gear that went with it: the mast and boom and blocks and tackle. All an enthusiastic statement that Donny could diversify in the winter and fish for scallops if he wanted to.

There wasn't anything he needed to be rid of, and chances were he'd need some of the parts at some point. In fact, it all looked like money in the bank to him and not the trust-fund money that did all the work for you, doubling every five years so you could come on up to Maine and tell people how to live.

Donny liked a scenic view as much as the next guy, but he had to go out every morning in the dark and earn his keep.

The wood stove was warming up the kitchen nicely, and Donny was feeling more awake with the coffee.

Tut came in and flopped down on the linoleum beside the stove, sounding as if he fell from two feet up. The dog sighed and looked up at Donny from between his paws.

"You want to come over to Town Meeting? You'll have to stay in the truck, and it's gonna be on the cold side, but you can growl at all the people from away and make a good impression."

Tut's stubby tail twitched.

Donny dressed in a flannel shirt, just about new from Reny's, a nice pair of jeans he'd picked up from the new Goodwill store down to Rockland, and pale yellow work boots from Marden's in Waterville. Just to be an asshole, he grabbed his fluorescent orange, zip-up, hooded sweatshirt from the hook, pulled it on, and zipped it up to his neck.

Donny opened the door, and Tut took the opportunity to gobble one extra mouthful of kibble, as though he might be at risk of starving to death. Donny had to hold the door open to the weather, letting in the drizzle. He yelled at Tut to get a goddamn move on.

Tut pissed on the truck tire and then leapt up into the cab, planting muddy paw prints right across Donny's seat in the F150. He looked so gung ho that Donny smiled and said, "Bastard!"

For as long as Donny could remember, Town Meeting was held in the Grange Hall down on Beach Road, halfway between the ferry terminal and Lincolnville Center. He'd been going most all his life. Even as a kid he was dragged down once a year by his parents and grandparents. They had to keep telling him to smarten up and behave himself. Now that all his close relatives were dead, he'd started to skip these meetings where nothing much happened anyway.

These last few years, though, there'd been some hot words when some of the locals clashed with a group called the Coastal Conservators, who wanted to put up some zoning rules. This meant that Dick Matheson couldn't carve off a chunk of his property for his son to put up a double-wide trailer and raise a family with that pretty girl from down Thomaston way. Franny Harper couldn't sell her sourdough bread from her house anymore, as the Harpers had done for three generations before her.

But all the fuss had nothing to do with Donny, so he hadn't paid much attention. It was different now, what with the Nelsons telling him to clean up his act, even wanting to put it in the town warrants.

The Union Harvest Grange Hall didn't have a parking lot, so the assortment of Subarus, Saabs, Volvos, and pickup trucks parked along the sides of the roads that came together at the four corners.

As testament to the level of contention, the roads were so jammed that Donny had to stash his truck close to the ditch down in the hollow where it was especially muddy. Before he slammed the door shut, he apologized to Tut for the lousy location.

"Sorry, buddy, but there ain't gonna be too many assholes to bark at. Just the same, keep a sharp eye out. You never know. Don't ever forget, this is your planet."

The big, square, two-story building went up in the mid-1800s, erected by farmers and boat builders on concrete footings. It was now sided with old, white clapboards and topped with a rusting tin roof. The wooden steps leading up to the front door were worn raw, with dead grass and winter gravel to each side.

He was only five minutes late, and the whole place was filled right up. Donny took a deep breath, feeling some of the tension and wanting to settle down his nerves.

The bustling room smelled of wood smoke, wet wool drying, and ancient memories. On this bottom floor, the whole thing was open and perfect for meetings.

Twenty years ago the town voted to pick up a bunch of cheap, high-backed wooden chairs that were being sold for practically nothing, not all being in the finest shape. Back then, Donny's father and a bunch of the town's lobster gang who still made their own wooden traps agreed to fix them all up. Those chairs had remained solid and straight. Only a few were getting wobbly now, and they were all lined up along the walls.

The floors were wide planks, fastened with square-headed iron nails, darker under the seats and worn lighter in the aisles and down the walkways.

A 55-gallon oil-drum stove dominated the middle of the room, open space around it so no one got overheated. Donny caught a glimpse of orange flame at the junction of the stove-pipe. A metal realtor sign lay flat on the floor to catch any embers falling out the door.

The ceilings were the original pressed tin, the walls tongue-and-groove wainscoting interrupted by tall casement windows with cherished antique warbled glass that let in the watery, gray light.

Upstairs was where they'd held those secret Grange meetings. Those secrets were bound to die with the last of the Grangers because they couldn't convince any young people to join and take the time out of their busy lives to learn the rituals and the secret ways. Though his father, grandfather, and great-grandfather had been Grangers, Donny himself had never been upstairs.

There were people standing against the back wall: open-hooded sweatshirts under canvas Carhart jackets, flannel shirts, long beards, and navy watch caps or diesel-engine baseball caps, brims curled almost circular. All the seats were full. Behind the stove and back behind the waist-high, court-like barrier was the desk where the moderator was now standing and talking about procedure and protocol.

Halfway up the right side, sitting amongst the Weed clan was Bert, who had turned and was waving at Donny to come over to where he'd saved a seat.

As Donny came down the aisle, he noticed the left side was taken up by a lot of well-dressed folks he didn't recognize. Their puffed-out vests and jackets from Land's End and Eddie Bauer made them look inflated. He recognized some from saying hello at the gas pump at Mill's Corner Store. Del and Eliza Nelson sat up close to the front. Donny weaved his way past knees to the seat saved by Bert.

Bert slapped him on the leg.

"I was worried you weren't gonna show up, and I'd have to say some words on your behalf."

The Nelsons turned around at the brief commotion, looking serious, and nodded.

"Reckon I'll have a few things to say for myself." Donny nodded back at the Nelsons.

The moderator was Bill Dyer, who had the backhoe and earthwork business north of town. He was a good choice, with a level head and calm demeanor. He called the meeting to order, and the crowd hushed, side conversations dwindling as the anticipation of business settled in.

"Now, I'll allow that this might turn into one of those meetings with raised voices and hard feelings, but there's no need for any of that. This is the way things get done around here, the town's people getting together and deciding how things are going to be. Oh, there'll be different opinions, but the vote'll decide on what's to be. Please try to keep things on a non-personal level, 'cause otherwise I'll have to intervene. And I hate to intervene."

The meeting commenced, and within five minutes, Donny was nodding off. Nominations came from the floor. The town clerk got voted in and then the excise-tax collector. The selectmen got elected without much fanfare.

Donny took notice of the Nelsons. Eliza was looking good as she helped Del out of his L.L. Bean field coat, too hot up close to the stove. His chocolate-colored knit sweater looked like an import too, maybe from as far away as across the ocean.

The school budget riled up some folks about how come it cost so much to teach the kids nowadays. Back then they didn't have PowerPoint presentations, computer labs, French, Spanish, and food science. If it was good enough then, it should be good enough now.

But then Edna Drinkwater stood up, a teacher herself before she retired.

"If we want to do good for our kids and have them turn out right, we'd better make sure they get three things: a kind heart, a sense of humor, and a good education. And by God, you better not scrimp on the good education part."

That woke up most of the crowd, and they started to stir. Bill had let the fire go out in the stove, but it was still plenty hot in the room. The windows were a bit fogged up.

Mark Hollingsworth, a trim man with closely cropped gray hair, had moved up in the late '80s from Massachusetts. Having some boat-design talent, he'd started the shop in Rockport that was now building Del's fancy sailboat. He wrestled a window open.

Bert's uncle Joe on the other side of the room startled everyone with four loud whacks, one on each side of his window, to get the lower sash unstuck.

Bill Dyer shepherded the meeting down each item. Abbey McLaughlin got up and made an emotional appeal for the ambulance service. Joe Weed added a plea for the Lincolnville Volunteer Fire Department.

"All the volunteers come from old-time local families, and we sure would be pleased if some of the newer residents would step up."

Then Bill said, "We now come to Articles Seventy-Three and Seventy-Four. The first would enact an ordinance to restrict certain noises, and the second would establish a set of standards for property aesthetics and upkeep. These warrants have been seen on a regular basis down south. There's no way to avoid these issues, and we will vote on them today. I believe this all started as a conflict between the Nelsons on Route One and their neighbor Donny Coombs.

"Mr. Nelson, would you like to say a few words?"

Everyone in the hall looked at Del Nelson as he stood up and surveyed the room. Donny had to admit he looked good — slim and well turned out. Del ran a hand down his front, absently straightening any wrinkles in his brown sweater. He looked down at Eliza, who smiled up at him encouragingly.

"For those of you who don't know me, my name is Del Nelson. My wife, Eliza," he touched her shoulder, "and I moved up here to live full-time, to become part of this special community. We want to fit in, to contribute. We want to add to the Maine experience, not detract.

"Toward that end, we're proposing these two articles because we think — and I think a sizable group of you will agree — that enacting these ordinances will enhance the very reason we're here: to experience the beauty and charm that the Maine coast has to offer. It's a shame that this issue has gotten blown out of proportion. I don't understand why anyone would object.

"I think these two warrants are good for this community. They deal with the sight and noise pollution problems that are beginning to plague Lincolnville. I'm willing to answer any questions anybody has."

With that, he sat down and looked back at Bill as Eliza patted his thigh.

Donny didn't think much about what he wanted to say, just stood right up and took the floor.

"This is a joke, right? If I read these warrants correctly, they say that the town is going to start regulating what I keep in my yard and how early in the morning I can get out and work on my gear and my boat."

While the right side of the room grumbled supporting sounds, Donny took a breath and tried to calm himself down.

"I don't mean to be unreasonable, but the Nelsons here, they come up to Maine to be with all the beauty, they buy their land and build their house, and all of a sudden they want us to think they're surprised that I got an old truck and dragging gear and traps piled in the yard, like they never noticed it before. I think they ain't got no business telling me this shit. The town got no business telling me nothing either."

Bill spoke up quickly.

"Now, Donny, there's no need of any foul language from you or anyone else. We got kids present, and we're going to be respectful."

Bert said in hushed tones that could be heard clearly throughout the hall, "Like the kids ain't never heard the word 'shit' before."

That got a chuckle going across the aisle. The gavel came down hard. Bill didn't want to lose control this early.

"That will be enough, Bert. When you got something constructive to say, you can add it to the conversation. I see Edna might have something to say. Edna?"

The room turned to watch Edna rise from her chair and smooth her flowered dress.

"I may not be the oldest resident here, but I'd be pretty close. I've seen all kinds of change, especially with how the schools have been run. The change has been mostly for the better, even if it was met with resistance from the local people. And as I look around this room, I'm struck by the division in the community. There seem to be a whole lot more of you new folks at this meeting. You're really good at showing up and saying your piece and voting. Mostly these town meetings have been boring affairs with nothing much to decide.

"This issue is different, and I'm disappointed that more of the old-timers, the skidder crowd and the backhoe and excavator operators, aren't here. But they are, right now, digging holes for foundations for new homes down in Matheson's field by the water.

"That fight over Dick Matheson's right to do whatever he wanted with his property points out the division we have here today.

"As most of you know, Dick owned the big field that runs all the way down to the shore from his lumber business on Route One. He employed his crew from the town, paid taxes on the property, and figured he'd be able to cash in when he retired.

"When that time came, and he wanted to sell, come to find out all the rusticators who drove down Route One had fallen in love with the view, and they didn't want to be looking at houses instead.

"Dick said fine, he'd sell it to some conservancy outfit, and they could preserve the land. But they couldn't come up with the money, even though Dick discounted it some. Finally, a compromise was reached, but only after years of being in court.

"I'm not saying the end result isn't acceptable, what with the houses being down by the water, and all the drivers still have their nice view. But, was it right to put Dick through all of that, with him being such a good citizen all those years?

"And now we've got these warrants. It's like you new people think you're living in a postcard. I think you all mean well enough, but you keep this up, then your postcard will look like some fancy marina in Florida. All the lobster boats and working wharfs will be gone. Think about it."

Edna said thank you and sat down.

The room got quiet as everyone thought about what Edna had said.

Eliza Nelson raised her hand and Bill pointed the gavel her way. She stood up, looking sharp in a canvas coat and yellow scarf.

"I really appreciate what Mrs. Drinkwater had to say. And I think there's a misunderstanding about what we at Coastal Conservators want for the community.

"We've seen what has happened down the coast where perhaps the effort came too late. The attractiveness was leached out of the area to the point that everything looked like those strips with the fast-food restaurants and megastores and gas stations. The charm was gone, and so went the tourists and their dollars.

"We just want to make sure that doesn't happen here. We pay good taxes to live in this beautiful place. Now is the time to address this issue."

Eliza sat back down with a satisfied look. Heads nodded around her.

Someone way in the back said, "You can address it right where the sun don't shine."

Billy came down hard with the gavel again.

"No matter how each of us feels, there's no need of insulting language. Any further outbursts, I will adjourn the meeting, and we will have to come back for a special session."

Mark Hollingsworth rose to speak, holding his cap in his hands at his waist, spinning it a little as he thought a moment.

"I think the ultimate reason to let things stay the same is that the tourists come up here as much to see the rustic beauty of a working fishing village as to see the schooner sails against the islands. Get too fancy, and you'll kill the very reason people come up to Maine. There is, to my way of thinking, a good reason to go slow here."

From his seat Del said, "What can be attractive about the stink and slime coming out of the bait barrels? There ought to be a harbor ordinance about the mess down at the pier."

Bert's nephew came out of his seat.

"That's the smell of money, Mr. Man. There's beauty in being able to make a living. No matter what you think, like Edna said, you ain't living in a friggin' postcard."

Wally, the newest and youngest in the town's lobster gang, had a doublewide down Beach Road and hadn't even started to get his boat ready. The shrink-wrap was still drum tight across his Young Brothers 37-footer in his yard, and none of the traps were ready either. He was fat and lazy, but he had a point here; it was probably the smartest thing he'd said in his life.

Donny rose again, wearier now.

"Mr. Nelson, you're going to like to serve lobster to your guests out on your porch, outside fireplace, view of the islands, and maybe our boats headed out to haul our traps. Where do you think those lobsters come from? They come from that stink of bait, the heavy black smoke from Bert's Caterpillar engine. That's where they come from."

Bert let out a whoop. Donny continued.

"I look around, and I know that there're a lot of people in this room who think different. On this side, you got all the people I known all my life. We fish, we dig ditches, we plow snow, we run skidders and excavators. We clear your land and dig your foundations. We wear hooded sweatshirts and cuss.

"You folk on the other side come up here with money, your college degrees, time on your hands to attend meetings and join organizations. Don't get me wrong, I like some of what you're doin', and I think other local people like it too, but this is going too far.

"Do you really think you're better than us, that you got the right to run our lives, tell us how Maine should be? I think you ain't got the right. We been here for three hundred years, and you from away think you can come up and after three weeks tell us how to live?"

The discussion went back and forth, the communitarians with Obama bumper stickers on their Subaru and Volvo station wagons and Range Rovers stressing the need for controls for the good of all. Local sentiments ran toward the right to figure for yourself what's worth keeping on your private property, and where else can you park your scallop drag if you can't afford a three-car garage. What about tradition and the Maine way of life?

Del Nelson stood up and got out a parting shot.

"I can't believe you people won't admit the damage you're doing to the coastal communities by sticking your heads in the sand. We appreciate the local-color factor, we do, but Donny, be honest, don't you think your yard is over the top with all that junk? If it's a matter of money, Eliza and I have talked it over. We'd be glad to pay to have it all hauled off."

Someone blurted out, "Fuck you and your money."

Bill banged his gavel until the room settled down and everyone on both sides of the aisle did a slow burn in silence.

"Will someone make a motion to call the question?"

"So moved!"

The votes were cast on preprinted ballots that the voters stepped to the front and slipped into a ballot box.

As Donny and Bert stood in line, Donny grew uneasy, feeling outnumbered, even though he thought his arguments had made the most sense.

He leaned over to Bert and said, "I think we're in trouble. If I'd thought it was gonna be close, Jesus H. Christ, I'd have got all of your cousins to turn out."

Bert said, "Could be the turning point, when they finally take over the town, sons of bitches."

Bill got the count and focused the crowd.

"By a vote of 112 to 97, the motion to approve both warrants has been passed. There being no further business, this 2010 Lincolnville Town Meeting is adjourned."

Both factions were stunned into silence, each group trying to assess the implications of what had just happened.

Donny stood up.

"Are you shitting me? This isn't even funny."

He stormed out of the Hall into a cold drizzle, disoriented, like coming out of a movie and it still being daylight.

Tut was thumping his little tail, and Donny gave him a thoughtless pat on the head.

"Well, Tut, they finally got it done. They now control the place."

Chapter 3

He gently pushed Tut over to the passenger side and almost got the F150 stuck in the mud, he was so angry, reckless, and careless in pulling out.

Chapter
4

Late May

Donny had *Pot Luck* wound right up, but with a full load of 40 four-foot aluminized wire traps on deck and across the transom, she was slogging across the bay toward Islesboro. Because his family had fished the west side of Islesboro for as long as anyone could remember, he had implicit territorial rights that went beyond his Lincolnville area.

The boom years of the recent past, when demand had been solid and steady, had taken a turn down. Each year had brought record catches, so that even University of Maine graduates with degrees in economics were borrowing money and buying boats and gear.

More and more lobstermen, record landings, and now slacking demand due to the Great Recession meant a lower boat price and the subsequent financial pressures. There was always tension among lobster gangs, but this year it looked to be especially bad.

Donny brought the throttle back as he came up on Gilkey Bell, spun the wheel to starboard, and steered south close to the tip of Acre Island.

Tut looked up from his nest on the chart shelf under the port windshield, but figuring the change in rpms didn't amount to much, went back to sleep.

Donny fished doubles along this side of the island. It was his custom to be the first to set his gear. Today, however, where there should have been open water, his traditional territory, he found a mess of lavender buoys.

This didn't bode well. He'd been on the periphery of lobster wars before and had heard of controlled aggression spilling over into violence, as well as the tremendous cost in boats and gear and lost opportunity.

The waters of Maine were crisscrossed with invisible lines marking fishing territories: from this ledge to the tip of that island and out to the shipping lane, from this sightline to that deep water, from this rock down to that motel. From Kittery to the Canadian coast, it was the same, the lines based on history and backed by nearly unanimous acceptance of how things were.

Intruders were punished with increasing degrees of persuasiveness until they moved off. Some took more persuasion than others. It was incumbent on the lobstermen to protect their spots, or the whole system would unravel.

Killings were rare as lobster wars ran their course. Lobstermen were smart enough to do the calculation. The punishment of confinement in prison far outweighed the satisfaction of eliminating the competition. However, that didn't stop them from threatening, destroying, and doing all sorts of illegal acts to protect their territory.

Donny untied the first tier of traps and took the first double off the top. He laid the two traps on the rail, annoyed at having to set in so close to the lavender buoys. He removed the coiled pot warp and buoy from inside the traps and placed them on the deck by his feet so they spooled out as the traps sank to the bottom.

He speared a bait bag from the tray with his spudger, a stout bait needle with a wooden handle at one end of a bronze shaft and an eye at the other. He threaded the bait line through the eye, slipped the dripping ball of chopped herring and redfish into the trap and tied it off. He repeated the procedure for the tailer trap.

The depth sounder showed good ground on the edge of hard bottom just outside the ledges. He figured the lobsters were in deeper water waiting for the warming summer waters to signal the migration into shallow ledges to molt and shed their shells.

He brought the boat into a slow clockwise circle and pushed the tailer trap, his first, off the rail. It sank into the dark water, came up tight on the joining rope, and pulled the main trap down the rail and off the stern. The coiled rope paid out until the buoy hit the transom and popped overboard.

A myriad of responses swirled in Donny's head as he went about the routine task of setting his traps, with *Pot Luck* working her way south along the western side of Acre Island, down around the Ensign Islands to Lime then south again to just north of Lasell.

Once, way back, Donny had tried to put some pressure on the caretaker of Lasell, a lobsterman, only to have his gear cut the next foggy day. At $80 a pop, all things considered, $160 for a double, such indiscretion was expensive. That was the message, which Donny got loud and clear.

Lavender had been busy and foolish. Either he was making a direct point by setting along Donny's line, or he was stupid. One way or the other, it meant a whole set of complications.

The Coombs clan had always fished fewer traps and caught more lobsters, all highliners, because fathers passed down their knowledge of lobster migrations to sons — catching them as they moved across the bottom, from cold and deep to shallow and warm. Once shed, they then went out again to feed and harden up.

The problem with being successful was that no matter how secretive you were, word leaked out, and others figured all they had to do was set along your route.

Donny shoved the last baited traps overboard and headed back across the bay to the harbor. He fished alone, which was more dangerous, but also more lucrative. Though he could handle only half the legal limit by himself, he didn't have to split his take with a stern man. Fishing by himself had the added benefit that you didn't need to make idle conversation.

As *Pot Luck* steamed back, bow high into the northerly chop spewing geysers of spray and leaving a carpet of white foamy wake on the blue sea, he took the saltwater washdown hose and flushed the deck.

True to the Coombs style, Donny brought her in fast, tossed orange fender balls over the side, turned her sharp, gunned her in reverse, and nestled in beside the pilings under the crane.

Bert Weed was scrubbing down his boat at the dock. Donny brought along a good wake that tossed both boats.

"Ever think of landing like a normal person?"

Chapter 4

Bert was a short, gristly man with a small boat and not so many traps. The time he didn't spend as a lobsterman, he was a caretaker for summer people.

Tut came off the shelf, popped up on the transom, and growled at Bert. Bert shook his head.

"Tut, you asshole. I've known you from a puppy, and you're still as ornery as ever."

Donny came to the stern.

"Bert, who fishes lavender buoys?"

Bert grinned.

"You found some crap out in the bay? Spot me a cold one when I get done here, and I might tell you."

"I'll be down with another load. Then we can talk."

Donny left Tut onboard and carefully climbed the ladder in his rubber boots and foul-weather bibs. It took him ten minutes to get his truck and trailer from the lot and back it down to the crane. He had to maneuver around Bert's pickup.

Bert was leaning on the back of his truck with a can of Michelob in his hand.

Hearing the familiar truck, Tut leapt from stern to float, then came up the incline and pissed on the light pole.

"Hope you fish better than you park, Bert. Some of us have to work for a living."

"Figured if you couldn't back that thing in here, I'd collect some insurance money."

"Your truck is worth what? Five dollars?"

Donny leaned on the other side of the truck and took one of Bert's beers from his cooler.

"So what do you know about lavender?"

"It's supposed to be the other way around. You buy the beer, and I tell the story. What the fuck you drinking my beer for?"

"Figured you'd tell me quick, so I wouldn't drink the rest."

"Well, it's working."

Bert crushed his can, threw it in the bed of the truck, and reached for another.

"We all got together and decided you catch too many lobsters. Every single one of us here and on Islesboro is gonna set right on top of you, so you can share. It's time to end the Coombs reign. One hundred years is too much."

Donny drank half his beer, placed a foot on the tire, and laughed hard.

"Now you got me to thinking. I'm going to find me a girl, have lots of little fishermen children, and push every one of you out. Nothing but Coombs boats in the harbor. Then we rename the town. But first I need to make an example of lavender. So who do I got to fight?"

Bert rubbed the two-day stubble on his cheek. He cleaned up nicely when the summer got going, and he had to present himself to his rich caretakees. This early, with only the lobsters to impress, he let himself go.

He looked as if he'd been stuffing rotten, chopped herring into bait bags all week long. His orange, rubber-bib overall was caked with bits of fish. Donny wondered if he'd wiped the gurry on his face on purpose and then let it dry.

They both turned to watch the ferry come in. She belched dark diesel smoke into the cloudless sky as she shifted into reverse and backed into the pen.

The line of cars and trucks waiting to board started their engines. They were all basic island folk hauling necessary supplies. In a couple of months, Donny and Bert would be local color for the tourists and worthy of a photo op.

Donny turned back to Bert.

"This is a hell of a way to start the season, Bert. Talk to me."

Bert said, "You know him and his family — Stanley Maven. He borrowed a ton of money for his boat and gear, and he's aiming to pay it off sooner than later. I guess he figures he ought to set where the lobsters are."

Bert shrugged his shoulders and said, "I don't need to tell you about his old man. Ornery cuss. I'd bet ol' Henry is egging on little Stan to make a point, take back some area for Islesboro. Obviously the kid needs some schooling. He don't understand the way it works — yet."

"He numb like his father? I got to tell him nice to move his gear off mine?"

"He'll say he got there first."

"We got there a hundred years ago."

Donny raised his eyebrows and added, "You got time to give me a hand with these traps?"

"Yeah, sure. Betty would rather I dick around here, prefers me out of the house. She thinks I'm a bad influence on the dogs."

As Donny climbed down to *Pot Luck*, and Bert fastened the first of the traps to the crane's hook, the ferry pulled out. At five o'clock, this was the last run.

Bert swung the traps over and lowered them down to Donny, who slid them into position. They repeated the procedure until the trailer was empty, and *Pot Luck* was loaded with another 40 traps.

They put their boats on their moorings, hung up their foul-weather gear, and rowed their punts back to the dinghy dock.

Walking up the incline, Donny asked, "Any advice for the little Stan situation?"

"Use your charm, Donny. I gotta get home, no matter what the dogs think."

Bert racked open the driver door. It squealed in protest. He climbed in, slammed the door shut, and fired up the engine. The corroded exhaust system made the truck sound like some racecar.

"Glass packs?" Donny asked.

Bert spoke over his elbow, hanging out the window.

"Right. It's really a Monster Truck."

He looked Donny in the eye.

"Be careful with the Mavens. They have a history of being easily offended and taking things a bit too far."

Bert drove off the pier.

Donny let Tut into the cab and headed the half-mile south to home. As he stacked up the trailer with another load of traps, he pondered his next move. There were easy solutions to hard problems, and hard solutions to easy problems.

And then there were the Mavens.

Chapter 5

Being May, the summer people had yet to wrap up enough business in the big cities to take two solid months off to play tennis, sail, picnic, and have cocktails in the evenings on the veranda. Their children were just about getting done with boarding school.

The lobsters hadn't come in yet, but the subtle rush for territory was under way, and most of the fishermen had put in their boats and were setting traps.

The boatyards were splashing boat after boat to get their customers out on the water. A majority of floats had been hung and inclines set.

Some of the caretakers had even started flying American flags at the end of their docks.

As for boat traffic, the big parade was still some weeks out. The kayakers, like speed bumps, who tended to head out in the fog but never showed up on radar, were still out of harm's way on land. Young, stupid, rich kids in fast outboard runabouts weren't due until around solstice.

Large fleets belonging to established summer families were on moorings in front of their 12,000-square-foot summer cottages. The captains and caretakers wanted everything ready to go as soon as the first deck shoe hit the light-gray weathered boards of the long dock that extended out past the low-tide mark.

It was seven in the morning, middle of the week, low tide. The dull, gray, cold might burn off but probably wouldn't.

Donny parked his truck and gathered his toolbox, cooler, and two oars. He and Tut walked along the ferry line, past vehicles waiting for the eight o'clock boat, the first run, dump trucks and loaded flatbeds from local building-supply companies that fed the construction frenzy on Islesboro, and headed down past the rank bait boxes on the pier to greet little Bert Weed, who was smoking a butt, sipping from a Styrofoam cup, and smiling.

"She sounds like your type, Donny."

"Who sounds like what?"

"Wait and listen."

Bert cupped his hand and held it to his ear, his eye and smile not leaving Donny for a second. He leaned towards the edge of the pier. They heard the cranking of a big outboard. The cranking stopped. It cranked again but with that run-down sound of a dying battery. Silence.

Then, from down below out of sight came a torrent of cussing.

"You stupid, good-for-nothing, Goddamned piece of shit!"

Then they heard a sharp crack, almost loud enough to be a gunshot.

Bert chuckled, and they both edged over to the side of the pier and looked down to the float.

She held the oar over her head and swung it down as hard as she could over the cover of a 250-horsepower Evinrude. This crack was even louder as the housing split, and the oar broke in two. She jumped up and came down on the boat deck with both bare feet.

"Goddamn it all to hell!"

The young woman stood in a 25-foot, bright-white, center-console Mako speedboat with twin 250 outboards. Her hair was ponytailed back and blonde. A summer girl on a summer boat with flushed cheeks, orange foul-weather slicker, loose khaki shorts, and wicked strong, tanned legs, held half an oar in her hand.

"Trouble?"

Donny set down his cooler and rested his hands on his knees. She whipped her head up.

"What's it to you?"

Bert glanced over at Donny, winked, and said, "This guy's a miracle worker with outboards."

"I'll pay you."

She looked and pointed at the port engine. Bert nodded to Donny.

"Reckon I can take a look."

Donny got his stuff and eased himself down the steep incline to the girl. He set his things on the float and wiped his rubber boots as best he could before stepping aboard.

Her face was pink, flushed from anger, but she smiled. It left little dimples on her cheeks. Donny offered his hand, and she shook it firmly and looked him in the eye.

"I'm Shelly Payson. I didn't mean to be rude, and I'd appreciate your help."

"Donny Coombs. Let's see what's up."

He sat on the waterway and looked directly into her pale green eyes and smiled back.

"How are you going to fix it sitting there?" she asked.

"I need a history. What's the story?"

"What, you writing a book? It doesn't start."

"But it ran fine over here?"

"I actually keep it there as a spare, in case the other one needs parts. I never start it if I don't have to. Daddy says it saves gas."

She tilted her head and blinked.

"Actually, it sputtered and died when I came in."

"Good to have spare parts. Daddy must be a smart guy."

"You'll meet him soon as you get this thing running. I'm here to pick him up."

Donny looked at the cracked cover and the bottom half of the oar floating away. He swept his gaze down to the fuel line snaking up from an aft plate. There was too much space in the coupling. The line had vibrated free and explained the whole deal.

But Donny didn't want the girl feeling foolish or inadequate. And for some reason, he wanted to make a good impression. Plus, he wasn't above some showy chivalry.

He leaned over the engine and unhooked the clasp on the back of the housing. With care, he placed the two sections on the sole and surveyed the motor. The complexity made him chuckle.

"What's so funny? You see the problem right off?"

Shelly was leaning over his shoulder, smelling clean and flowery.

"I was thinking how simple they used to be. Now, look at all those ignition wires and springs and coils and computerized fuel injectors."

Donny leaned over again and wiggled some of the wires. He didn't know what they went to, but he wanted to look busy.

"Could be the martingale, or maybe the turbo encabulator."

He tapped on the starter, reached down and pumped the bulb on the fuel line and snapped the coupling together. Then he sat back down on the waterway.

"Want a beer?"

She said, "So much more than a breakfast drink! You think it'll help?"

"Beer always helps."

Donny reached into his cooler and took out two cans of Bud. He cracked hers and handed it over. He opened his and drank it half down.

She sipped, though he suspected she was a gulper at heart.

"Since the battery is low, we start the good engine and let it charge. When we start the spare engine, I'd suggest you run them both. That way you're sure it's fixed. And you go faster."

"What about the gas?"

She leaned back on the seat. Donny shrugged his shoulders.

"To hell with the gas. Go for speed."

"What will Daddy say?"

"Who's Daddy?"

"You always this impossible?"

Donny made a display of twiddling the shifters and looking back on the engines. He turned the key and the starboard engine came to life.

He waited a spell and looked up to Bert, who gave him a thumbs-up and rolled his eyes.

Donny clicked the port control into the neutral slot.

"OK, God willing, here we go."

He turned the key to the port engine. The fuel pump spent some time sucking; then she caught and roared, blue smoke pouring out the exhaust port on the lower unit.

Shelly raised her can in a toast. Donny clinked it with his empty one.

He replaced the two pieces of housing, took duct tape from his toolbox, taped them together, locked the rear clamp, and shook the case.

"It should hold unless you go for air off the ferry wake. Call the boatyard, and have them order you a new case and another oar."

Donny got another beer. Shelly shook her head.

She said, "I owe you."

"And so you do."

He reached to his breast pocket and dug out a pack of smokes and offered her one.

She shook her head.

"I don't smoke. How much can I pay you?"

"How old are you?"

"Old enough to smoke," she smiled.

"You owe me an answer."

"I'll be twenty-one this July."

He smiled back.

"Then you can pay me with a date."

"What if my fiancé and my father don't want me to go out with you?"

"Your father again. Who's going to tell them?"

A horn sounded above, and a gray-haired man with a tanned faced and good teeth peered over the edge.

"Hey, sweetheart."

He glanced over at Donny and stopped smiling.

"Hey, Daddy. Welcome to vacationland."

Shelly scampered up the incline and hugged her father. He paid the cabbie. Bert offered to carry one of the large duffle bags down to the float so he could be closer to the action. All three came down the incline.

"Daddy, this is Donny. He just saved me. The left engine wouldn't start, but he got it going."

Daddy took in the beer cans. Out of politeness, he shook Donny's hand and said, "Thank you."

He was tennis fit, fiftyish, L.L. Bean clad, layers of fleece and Gore-Tex, and cunning rubber booties.

Bert untied the bowline. Donny stowed his cigarettes in his shirt pocket and got the stern. Shelly gave a nod to cast off, and they tossed the lines into the boat. Daddy brought in the fenders.

Shelly expertly eased the boat off the dock. She turned to Donny and ran two fingers across her lips, zipper-like.

Then she called to him, "So it wouldn't go without fuel?"

Chapter 5

She winked and goosed her boat out into west Penobscot Bay.

Chapter
6

I hate this fog."

Eliza pulled the brush through Alex's coat, concentrating on the bristles raking her fine hair. Eyes closed as she reveled in the attention, Alex rocked with each stroke.

"All this dampness raises hell with sweetie's coat."

She ended the statement with the lilting baby talk that made Del want to slap her.

"And when do you think Mr. Coombs is going to clean up his yard?"

The plate-glass window was full of fog. It had rolled in from the south and consumed the islands. Del removed the breakfast plates and cups from the table and loaded them in the dishwasher.

"We have to be prepared for him to delay, just to make a stupid point."

He sprayed hot water onto the remains of egg yolk on Eliza's plate, lingering until there was no trace left.

"I don't understand why it's so hard. You'd think that these people would want a clean property, especially as they're right on the coast. It wouldn't be so bad if they were hidden inland."

Eliza looked up from her dog.

"They're just backward. It's like they don't know what they have. And I'll bet they dig in their heels just to irritate us. You'll see. Maybe I should call the junk guys and get it over with.

"Speaking of which, what about that tree?"

The offending oak was coming in full of leaves and further obstructing their view.

"How are we going to get Donny to take it down? Can we offer him money? Tell him we'll pay to have it cut down and removed. You could suggest he can have the wood for his fireplace."

"I don't think he has a fireplace." Del looked out through the window at the tree in the fog, barely visible. "I know he has a wood stove, and we could have a forester cut it all up into stove-length pieces. Even have it stacked up, as long as it's neat, beside his kitchen door."

Eliza gently removed Alex from her lap and set her on the floor. The dog went to her bed, curled up, and closed her eyes.

"He'll never agree. I think that tree has some sentimental value. This may sound cruel, but what about poison? I'm sure there's a way to make it look like the tree just died. Then he'd have to take it down."

She smiled at the thought.

Del sighed. He poured a splash of black coffee into his mug and sat at the table beside Eliza.

"I don't think we should do anything drastic. We ruffled a lot of feathers at the Town Meeting. Did you notice, at the end, the stunned silence? It'll take them some time to get used to things. There's so much to do, but we might want to go slow."

"I swear, Del, sometimes you are such a wuss. How do you poison a tree? I'm going to call our lawn people in Cambridge and ask how they'd do it."

Del didn't want to look his wife in the eye, knowing that at this stage there was no holding her back. He took the last sip of his lukewarm coffee and set the cup on the polished tabletop.

Alex stirred in her bed, alert, and looked toward the window. The bottom edge of the plate glass looked out at the flowerbed and mulch. Eliza and Del followed her gaze. Tut sniffed his way into view, looked in, saw Alex, and wagged his stub.

"Damn that dog!" Eliza shot out of her chair and lunged at the glass, waving her hands. "Go away! Get out of here!"

Tut looked up at her, seemed to smile, and then started to wag his tail again. Del, knowing it would send Eliza over the edge if she weren't there already, stifled a laugh.

"How the hell can that asshole let his mangy dog wander all over the county? Del, shoot it! Do something!"

Alex was over at the window with her nose smudged against the glass. Tut had lost interest in Eliza and was making eyes at the poodle.

Eliza spun on her husband.

"If that fucking dog comes anywhere near Alex, especially when she's in heat, I'm going to string it up by its ugly little neck and hang it on the fucking neighbor's door! Maybe I'll poison the little fucker alongside that precious oak tree."

She swooped her poodle off the floor and stormed out of the room, cooing baby talk while Alex strained to get a last glimpse of Tut.

"Now don't you let that nasty dog do anything to you, sweetie," her voice fading as she moved deeper into the house.

Del sat there in the aftermath as the quiet came back. Tut was still looking in, his head tilted just a bit. He really was an ugly little dog, bristly fur the color of dirt, with a lot of scar tissue, built like a cinder block, one ear bent back. But he sure could smile as though he knew what was funny. Tut lifted his leg, pissed on the glass, and then moved off and out of sight, maybe angling along the house to another room where Alex might be hiding out.

Eliza came back with a pad in her hand and a pencil in her hair.

"I want you to address the dock issue and all that horrid mess. And then later we should bring up the comprehensive plan and make sure that any new building comports with the aesthetics of the community. It's all such a no-brainer, but I think there will be resistance to change, no matter how much sense it makes. All we ask is that they don't distract from the natural beauty. They must realize that attractiveness brings in new residents like us and summer people and tourists."

Eliza put her hand on Del's arm.

"Sweetheart, you were marvelous at the meeting. If anyone can convince them, you can. When your boat is launched and sitting on the mooring making the harbor look so pretty, I'm sure you'll get elected to the harbor committee. Then you can push through the improvements.

"You have allies in town. All the restaurant owners want to attract business from visiting boaters. After all, the town set out those guest moorings. But who wants to wade through bait slime and dodge dog shit on the dock?"

Chapter

7

T he alarm went off at 4:30 a.m. Donny grunted, and Tut
leapt onto the bed and snuggled in.

"Nice try, but it's fishing time again."

Donny rolled out of bed and made it to the kitchen to put
the coffee on. It was still pitch black out.

Donny tuned in channel 2 on the kitchen-table VHF and
listened to the synthetic female voice run through the area
weather: patchy fog this morning, calm water from Stonington
to Cape Elizabeth. Offshore winds becoming 15 to 20 in the
afternoon, seas 1 to 3 and building to 3 to 5 feet by late afternoon. Low tide at 9 a.m. and high at 3 p.m. Sunrise at 5:03
a.m.

He took the cooler from the mudroom and tipped out
yesterday's melted ice into the sink. In went a six-pack of Diet
Coke and some cubes frozen solid in the freezer. He poured
coffee into his mug and the remaining into his dull-green
thermos. He made up two bologna and cheddar sandwiches
on white bread, wrapped them in aluminum foil, and set them
on top of the soda.

Tut gobbled a charge of kibble from his bowl.

They got down to the pier before the rest of the gang. A
glow coming up over the northern tip of Islesboro cast a pink
sheen across the water.

It was hot already, and Donny started to sweat as he
pitchforked great heaps of dripping herring bait from his Xactic; a square, double-sided, insulated, gray, plastic hot tub
with dried fish guts coating the side and filled with salted herring soup, the fish just beginning to come apart, chunks of
flesh clinging to exposed bone. It was set with the other fish
boxes along the inside rail on the pier.

The Xactic got swapped three days before and was three-quarters full, so he didn't have to bend over and sift out the fish from the slurry at the bottom. Easy pickings today. He filled three trays, enough to bait up the 100 traps he planned to haul today. He put the top back on the Xactic and bungeed it down tight. He popped on the tray tops, stacked them, and slid them over to the edge and under the dockside crane.

His lower back was beginning to act up already, and it was barely light out.

Donny and Tut rowed out to *Pot Luck* and brought her in under the crane, the top of the pilothouse just about level with the surface of the pier.

Billy backed his truck and trailer down, piled high with 20 brand new traps.

Donny said, "You look so damned optimistic, we all might get the idea you know what you're doing."

Billy laughed. "That'll be the day."

"You don't suppose you'd work this crane and drop down my bait?"

"What's in it for me?"

"Michelob Ultra and a pat on the back when we get in tonight."

"Best deal I'll get today."

Billy looped the slings under the bottom tray and hoisted the stack; then he swung it out and lowered it down to Donny, who unhooked them when they hit the deck.

Donny pushed the trays over by the pilothouse and brought them in close. He set the box of pliers, bands, and lobster measure on top.

"Much obliged. You know I'd do the same for you any time."

"Cold day in hell that'll be."

But Billy winked down as he secured the crane. Then he fetched his punt, stood in the bow, and worked the oar side-to-side, sculling himself out to the *Little Rocker*. He was the only fisherman who still rowed out the old way, by standing up in his small, tippy boat.

Donny watched him. It was quiet this early. A crow cawed. There was the hum of the Lobster Pound refrigeration, a cackle of seabirds, and a lone call from a loon. A bunch of pier pigeons flapped by overhead.

Lincolnville was a small, friendly harbor. Not all that protected outside and shallow inside, it held minimum space for boats, just enough for two crew boats for each of the two boatyards, five lobster boats, two center consoles, and an island runabout. One sailboat bobbed out there at the limit.

It was a working harbor, and the folks from away sat on the shore in the sand after eating a lobster dinner from the Lobster Pound and admired the working boats. Donny thought it'd be real different and not nearly so attractive to see a bunch of pleasure boats out there on the moorings. Take the shine off the coin.

He slid *Pot Luck* back to the float, slipped out of his sneakers and into his boots, and pulled on his orange, bib Grundens overalls. He got rubber gloves off the hook and started to fill bait bags. Billy came in under the crane.

Then Wally Weed, Bert's young nephew, drove down, tipped himself out of his truck, and got to grumbling about the boat price.

"Fella can't make a living, and that's a fact."

"Word is you got a job on the road crew, working that two-sided sign. What is it again? Stop and Slow?" Billy teased.

Wally took the bait.

"Yeah, well, it ain't too hard a job, what with only two options, but you also got to work the radio and get the sign turned right, and it only pays just above minimum wage, but it's enough to support the fishin' and keep me in beer."

"Sounds kinda like the Social Security. Keeping me on the water, if only there were any lobsters out there to catch."

Wally stopped untying his punt and turned to Billy.

"They ain't going to be much of that left, let me tell you."

"Much of what?" Billy asked. "The Social Security or the lobsters?"

"The government money. The nigger's going to have it all spent by next Friday, you ask me, if it ain't already gone."

Donny looked up as he dropped another bait bag into the tray.

"What? You can't say that, Wally, calling the president a nigger."

"Well, that's just what he is, for Christ's sake."

"Listen to me, boy, you can't use that word. Black, African-American, you can use them."

41

"I thought he was from Indianesia or some fucking place."

Billy piped in, "Yeah, he's from somewheres like that. I'll also give you that the lobsters are scarcer than hen's teeth. Makes you wonder what the hell we're doing this for."

Donny looked them both over.

"Wally, I think I'm going to put you in for some sensitivity training, maybe the both of you, what with your piss-poor attitudes."

Wally struggled his fat frame into his little boat and said, "Hey, now. At least that's somethin' we got. Attitude. And it ain't costing us nothin'."

Landings were the highest they'd ever been for this time of year, but the price paid off the boat was way down, the recession killing the lobster-tail market in Vegas and on the cruise ships. Plus, it now cost $370 to fill the Xactic, which would only bait up some thirty trays and fish about thirty-five traps each.

Donny didn't have to do the math. Any way you cut it, it was expensive to fish, and you never ever wanted to skimp on bait. Add in $3.00 a gallon for fuel, and the younger guys had big problems making payments on the new truck, new boat, new house, and new wife. Especially if they'd let the macho bullshit take hold and bought a fast boat that burned 200 gallons a day to haul 250 traps. They would soon join the ranks of bankrupt businesses.

Pot Luck, on the other hand, was all paid for, and she sipped fuel. Donny didn't owe anything on his house, and he'd bought his F150 with down and dirty cash.

He went back to stuffing his bags and topped off the first tray, enough to get started this morning.

"I've had enough of your bellyaching. They's lobsters out there, and I'm going to get them."

Billy said, "Nice work, if you can get it."

He shook a last pitchfork of bait out of his Xactic into his second tray and then clicked the tops on tight. He grabbed the handle of the tray with the hook end of his two-foot gaff while holding onto the wooden T end. He pulled the tray over to the incline and slid it down to the float on the smooth side.

"I named this hook thing yesterday. I call it Captain."

Donny chuckled.

"Clever, real clever."

Tut was comfy up on the dash as Donny slipped his lines and idled out, already relishing the peace and quiet. Once out beyond the boats, he turned north and left the helm to straighten out the deck.

The hot tank was just beginning to steam. The saltwater was heated by a coil that took the hot water from the engine, circulated it around, and in the process heated the tank. This homemade heat exchanger made it easy to scrub down fish guts and crab pieces at the end of the day.

He made sure the cold-water line was pumping into the lobster barrel. It was empty now, but with any luck, there'd be crustaceans in it on the trip home. Maybe not full this early in the summer, with the lobsters not all the way into the shallow rocks.

Later, after they'd shed and were hungry as all get-out, the traps could yield six, even seven, pounds each, working up to close to ten pounds when things were cranking toward the end of the season. Even the guys who fished all 800 traps with a stern man, when things got screaming, they'd have to hire a third guy — the third nerd — to help out for $100 a day.

He stuck the other cold-water hose through the scupper. He wouldn't need it until he had to flush the tray of keeper crabs to be bought up by the Lobster Pound up to Belfast.

These were the critters that would be boiled, their legs yanked off, and the meat picked out of the first joint. Mixed with mayo and put on a little bed of lettuce for crunch and secured in a hot dog bun, it would be sold as a crab roll.

With the deck all ship-shape and ready to go, Donny hefted the Davy, a stainless block, and hooked it onto the stanchion hanging out over the starboard side.

Pot Luck idled over to the shore at the mouth of Ducktrap River, and Donny worked the shallows in close, the tide being high enough for him to maneuver.

He brought the boat in alongside his first buoy, leaned over, and hooked the warp just under the float with the gaff he kept handy on the rail. Donny settled into the routine to be repeated 50 times as he fished nothing but doubles.

The buoy went forward along the rail, out of the way. Line into the Davy up high, down into the wedge space between the two back-to-back plates on the hydro-slave hauler, which pinched the line, rotated counter-clockwise, hauled in one end, and spooled out the other.

Donny eased off the control handle when the main trap broke the surface and came up under the block. He tugged her onto the rail and spun her so she lay in tight. A bunch of juvenile lobsters, maybe a keeper or two, about four crabs, and some urchins.

He set the hauler to pull slow on the tailer trap line as he opened the door and took out the half-empty bait bag, opened it up, and dumped the old bait into the trap. Still good enough to add to the plume and entice the lobsters over for dinner.

The bigger crabs went into the bushel basket off to his left. The smaller crabs went into the bait pail to be smashed up with the shingle spade and added to the herring. Then he took out a lobster, measured it, and tossed it overboard. Too small.

The obvious little ones he left alone, still in the trap. Maybe they'd eat some more and get bigger before they escaped out the head. If they got used to coming into the trap, they'd be easier to catch when they were big enough to be legal. And it kept them safe from the seals — no seal candy today. He didn't bother with the urchins; no sushi market this time of year. He tossed them overboard.

The tailer trap came up, and he shoved the main trap ahead to make room on the rail. This trap had a keeper, just over three-and-a-quarter inches long from the eye to the end of the carapace. He banded it and tossed it into the lobster barrel, emptied the tailer's old bait bag, tied a fresh bag into each trap, closed the doors, and tied them up tight.

Donny looked over at the shore and up at his chart plotter and then brought *Pot Luck* around to starboard. Waiting until it was just right, he tipped the tailer over the side, holding tight onto the line till she straightened out so she'd sink right.

She sank and took the line, and when it came taut, she pulled the main trap along the rail and over the stern, the line spooling out, toggle hitting the transom in the same place at the bare spot, and the line kept paying out along the side until Donny rolled the buoy off the rail, and he moved on to the next trap.

In close, setting in the rocks, the traps could get hung up and the line tangled. So you had to let the hauler strain to yank the trap off the bottom. It was hard on the gear, but that was where the lobsters were. That was how you fished.

With all the controversy about right whales and the like getting tangled up in gear, the environmentalists forced the lobstermen to get rid of their floating line from the main to the tailer trap. Now they had to fish with sinking line that could get caught in the rocks, tip the boat over, and dump the fisherman overboard. Or, at least, break the line and make him lose a trap. And when it was gone, it was worse than useless; it was a ghost trap, a killing box until the heads disintegrated.

Well, all that didn't apply this far up the bay, so Donny didn't have to worry like the guys farther south.

He worked the string along the shore up the western side of Penobscot Bay. Good, bold water in close to the land and deep enough not to worry about running aground, even at low tide.

He was averaging about a half pound a trap. Not great, but good enough to cover expenses. The water was warmer for this time of year and about three to four weeks ahead of schedule. Sixty degrees on the surface and six degrees warmer than normal thanks to the good spring weather. That meant the lobsters were moving in early.

It was starting already, and his deeper gear was coming up empty. The other guys, perhaps paying less attention or working on past timing, were not adjusting to the early nature of things this year. Most of their gear was still out farther.

Donny had been fishing these waters for 20 years, starting out in his flat-bottomed skiff and hauling 50 traps by hand when he was just 15. He figured if he didn't know his shit by now, he might just as well haul the boat and flip burgers up to McDonalds.

Some giant hooded seals had come up from the south. These guys were huge, weighing in at seven hundred or eight hundred pounds, but they were rare enough not to be a problem. Not like the harbor seals, the sea slugs. In shallow, you used to secure the bait bag on a string. It could move up and down. But the seals got so plentiful that they reached in through the head and stole the bait. They tore the heads, flipped the trap over on its side, and devoured the herring.

Now Donny cinched the bag down, rafted up the string, and tied her in tight. He'd even wired in sharp, rusted-out, 16-penny nails with the pinched end down. It would scrape and stab the ever-loving shit out of any seal.

Even so, Donny got suckered in by the cunning little baby seals, and he wasn't the only lobsterman who gave in to a soft heart and saved one of the little ones.

The wind was coming up from the south. It promised to blow this afternoon. Nothing serious, but still uncomfortable out here working alone.

He'd have to figure if the small catch balanced out the need to re-bait, most of this string having gone untended for five long days. When the fishing got real good, and the traps were brimming with legal bugs, he'd let the gear soak a day or two at the most, coming out in God-awful weather and rough seas to tend those traps.

But it only got sloppy this far up the bay, not subject in this close to the giant storm swells and the tight and high waves, whipped up by long, strong, and steady winds. He could remember only a handful of times in all his fishing years when he'd been shore-bound by the weather.

Donny worked his way across the bay toward Islesboro and came up on one of his buoys married up to one of Stanley Maven's lavenders. Donny fished enough traps alone to keep him busy, and that left precious little time to spend sorting out someone else's gear. All the fishermen shared the bottom, of which there was plenty to go around. There was no need of this.

Donny threaded his line through the hauler and pulled a ball of tangled warp to the surface. He took the sharp knife out of the sheath screwed to the bulkhead right beside the hauler control, set in handy in case he got wound up in the line spooling out over the side and was dragged overboard and pulled under. With the knife along for the ride, at least he had a fighting chance to cut himself loose down a couple of fathoms deep.

There wasn't any danger now, just aggravation, and Donny got to cutting and slicing at the purple and yellow poly line that belonged to Stanley. It meant that Stanley would lose his trap, but it was time to get serious with the messaging. Donny piled the pieces at his feet, and when he got all done untangling the warp, he gathered up the evidence and stuffed them all in the trashcan down below.

Evidence was onboard, but he liked Jack, the marine-patrol officer up here. Besides, Jack had a lot of water to cover and was stretched awfully thin. Years ago, the patrol guys thought it was their job to put the slam-down on the fishermen, hassle them about lobsters that came in right at the legal length. They strutted their stuff, probably kids who got picked on in school, now out to even the score.

But these days, the relationship was really good, as if they were partners on the water, everyone wanting to do the right thing, innocent until proven guilty, the way it should be.

Jack tried to get aboard each of the fishing boats once a year, a random check for shorts and such, so if anything came of those pieces of line down below, Donny felt pretty confident he could explain the situation and maybe even get Jack to have a word with Stanley, whatever good that would do.

Donny knew full well why Stanley was camping all over him. Stan was new to the game and didn't have the smarts to figure how the bugs moved. He watched where the other guys set and followed their lead.

Donny knew his reputation, well deserved, for having a special feeling for lobsters and how to catch them. He didn't think about his skills and talents much. Maybe he'd just been doing it for so long.

Either way, Stanley was an instant fisherman. With a fresh boat and a new chart plotter, he was good to go. He'd set his gear right alongside Donny and make a fortune. Well, if Donny didn't nip this situation in the bud, it would get old fast.

Over time, Donny had assumed a leadership role for the small Lincolnville lobster gang. He arranged for the bait truck to come up from O'Hara's in Rockland with a box truck full of Xactics, each brimming with fresh salted herring, sometimes fresher than the lobster that got sold around town. The truck would back down the pier, and they'd swap out the empties for the full ones.

Donny also bought up the catch from the guys and some of the other fishermen up toward Belfast, paying the going boat price, up a quarter to $2 today, $2.50 for the weightier selects.

He'd also established good relations with the owners of Lincolnville's four restaurants over the years, all down by the beach. The two Lobster Pounds were natural customers for the harbor's catch. The French place did fancy things with the lobster meat, while the pub served mostly steaks and prime rib and also an occasional lobster.

This early in the season, the Lincolnville guys sold all the lobster they caught right in town. Later on, when the catch bumped up, they'd follow the statewide pattern of selling 20% locally and shipping the rest up to Canada for processing. It wasn't much to arrange the bait buying and the lobster selling, not with at most ten fishermen to deal with. It was well worth the fifty cents a pound difference in what he gave for the lobster and what he got from the restaurants.

It was nothing like the harbors farther south out on North Haven, and especially Vinalhaven, where they landed the most lobster in the state. It was a full-time job to arrange those deals. They had to form up a cooperative and hire a special guy or gal to do all the phoning and ball rolling.

They were always in bait and never had any down time. They bought their fuel cooperatively and sold their catch to big wholesalers who shipped all over the world. It was bigtime fishing with lots more pressure — with the potential for hurt feelings and fights and sunken boats.

But it didn't matter what part of the coast you fished these days. The simple laws of economics applied equally across the board. Too much supply with too little demand meant the boat price would be down for a long time to come. Donny fully expected the fights to get rougher as payments were delayed, and the banks started looking to take back a truck or a boat or a house.

He'd fished through lean times before and seen it happen. It wasn't pretty. But his grandfather had drummed it into his father's head, and both had hammered it into his own numb skull that you didn't need to go in whole hog. You could work up slowly and not borrow a pile of money. Keep expenses down, fish only the traps you could handle alone, and put away cash in the good years so you could carry through the bad ones.

Of course, his father and grandfather would have tanned his hide if they'd been alive and gotten wind of his activities years back. Picking up bales of marijuana and bricks of cocaine out between Monhegan and Matinicus, ferrying them into small coves, and exchanging them for cash money from lowlifes, hard cases, and even some dark-skinned characters — though not many of those, as they stood out so perfectly in one of the whitest states in the nation.

He'd been talking recently to one of the boatyard guys, and they'd been trying to figure who was making money on the water. The boatyard got by on a two-to-three percent margin on gross sales, leaving precious little to plow back into the business. The demand for the Maine hull, the lobster boat for the fisherman, and the lobster yacht for the rusticator, were so far down that the boat-manufacturing outfits were laying people off, and their profit margins weren't any better than a boatyard's.

The fishermen were barely making a go of it. The average age of the Maine fisherman was over fifty. Some young blood came in when times were flush, but Donny and the yard guy foresaw a great washing-out of anyone overextended and married to the bank. Maybe the Somali pirates had it right.

As for any new blood doing it the old-fashioned way, slow and steady, those days were long gone. That meant working through the licensing requirements, spending years acquiring experience as a stern man, and then ponying up what it cost to enter the business. Who could afford, or have the patience, to do all that in this day and age?

The whole lobstering business was changing, and by the look of it, the greater fishing industry to boot. How do you save the resource without sacrificing the fisherman? And if fuel went much higher, say to four dollars a gallon, everything would come to a screeching halt on the water.

It took some planning just to function, let alone profit, with all the obstacles out there. Donny had fuel delivered to his 500-gallon tank up to his yard. He put in for reimbursement on the road tax, bringing his fuel price down to about $2.40 a gallon. He didn't figure in his time to transfer it to the fuel tank in the bed of his truck, cart it down to the pier, and pump it aboard *Pot Luck*.

And he had a reasonable boat, not like the showboats that went streaking across the water, bow right up high and stern dug, gulping fuel all the while. That was a ticket to the poorhouse for sure.

The fog was thickening, but the forecast called for it to burn off and come in hot and sticky, dew point way up there, with a chance of thunderstorms. A low-pressure system racing in from the west and filling the sky with cloud debris and patchy sunshine.

Donny circled in close to the shore. The tide was out now to reveal a band of dark-green seaweed clinging to the ragged rock with a line of barnacle field skirting the water's edge.

Here he fished eighteen fathoms of line to the main trap and an extra dozen for the tailer. It was legal to fish up to three traps this far up the bay, but then he'd be hard-pressed to fill the bait bags before coming up on the next haul. Down east and farther south, they could fish a ten-trap trawl, but then they needed a third nerd full-time.

On this point of land, some rusticator had built a huge glass-and-cedar-shingled cottage in amongst the spruce trees and clumps of bayberry bushes.

Donny eyed it as he cleared the waterway of a stubborn junk of stray herring bait, a little hose spraying a constant stream of water to wash the gunk overboard and keep the rail clean. He stuffed another couple of bags for the next haul, mindlessly working as *Pot Luck* idled over to the next buoy in close to the rocks.

It was Saturday, so he'd have to break off at four o'clock, the time all lobstering was cut off along the coast until a half-hour before dawn on Monday morning.

There weren't many complaints from the fishermen, who took this forced day off, as they all agreed with the main pur-pose of the law — to discourage the recreationalist wannabes, guys with five traps, maybe ten if the wife took out a permit, who gummed up the works on the weekends. They were apt to sneak the shorts home to feed the houseguests, screw up the resource, take the bread out of the real lobstermen's mouths, and be a general pain in the ass.

Donny's gear was a mix of yellow and green vinyl-covered three-foot wire traps. He'd experimented with differ-ent colors, and those fished good, while the red ones didn't fish worth a damn.

His crab basket was getting full, so he rinsed out an emp-ty bait tray, topped her off with saltwater, and left the hose in there to run. He dumped the crabs in to keep them fresh in the circulating water, ripe for the lobster-pound guy, who bought all Donny could catch. The little crabs were ready for their pounding, and Donny obliged by crushing them into chunks with the shingle spade and tossing them in with the herring.

A lonely little rock bass from the last trap went whole and alive into the next bait bag; maybe entice a couple of legal bugs on the next go-around.

When things got hot later on in the summer and early fall, he'd land close to two thousand pounds on the days he hauled two hundred traps, a real long day from baiting up on the dock, pushing off before dawn, and working hard till the sun went down.

Fish long while the fishing's strong, his grandfather used to say.

Wally hailed Donny on the VHF.

"Yeah, what do you want?"

"Got a joke for you. Tell it to you, then I quit. I'm over by Ducktrap in ten feet of water and getting blown into the rocks, risking my boat, and for what? They ain't no lobster in the fucking bay. But listen up good, this ain't no bullshit. Life is like a roll of toilet paper — the closer you get to the end, the quicker it goes."

Wally let out a peal of laughter.

"And you can go to hell for all I care. Signing off."

Donny shook out the old bait into the trap and sniffed at the new bag. The fish smelled sweet, not tangy or fishy like when it had gone by, getting all mushy and soft and spoiled. The lobsters knew the difference, so you needed the prime plume, a good scent from good bait to get them in through the heads and into the kitchen part of the trap.

He tipped the tailer trap over, watched her sink, circled to starboard, and flipped the line across the top of the main trap, watching it slide aft along the rail, as if pulled by an invisible force off the stern, the sight never losing its magic.

Gentle swells rolled the boat from port to starboard, and Donny opened the next trap's door. He divided out the keeper crabs from the bait crabs. The lobsters might like these crushed little critters, craving the calcium as they filled out and hardened up their new soft shells.

He turned to port, and the boat listed to starboard. The lobster tank spilled water that flowed across the deck and washed out the scuppers, taking with it a single lucky crab escapee. Fate was a wonderful thing.

Pot Luck idled out to deeper water as Donny took the time to wolf down a sandwich and wash it down with some Diet Coke.

Donny started to work south, back toward the harbor, the routine the same but the pace different. The bottom was a hundred fifty feet down, and the line was fifty-eight fathoms long, so it took more time for the traps to come up.

Donny was the only one hereabouts who fished bigger traps out deep, four-footers, with more floor space for the lobsters when they came in thick. Until the fishing picked up, though, they were a pain in the ass.

More tension on the line meant additional strain on the hydro-slave plates, making the whole operation noisier. More pressure on the gear, more line on the deck, more danger from getting hung up in and possibly pulled overboard, the next to last experience of many a lobsterman.

Donny wore a sharp little knife in a plastic scabbard on the front of his bibs. He'd heard from one lucky son-of-a-bitch that you could reach up and cut your foot free as you got pulled down to the depths. He hoped never to find out if it was bullshit or not.

A single seagull floated in the air beside the boat, wings out straight as she swept in and plucked a junk morsel of old bait off the stern. Donny was feeling right neighborly to provide lunch. When the bait was too spoiled to dump back in the trap, he emptied the bag over the side. A whole flock of the bastard birds circled and swooped, screamed, and fought for the scraps.

The fog was burning off. The ferry was making its way across the bay toward Islesboro. The Coast Guard's *Abbey Burgess*, a buoy tender, was making its way up the bay. He noted a couple of full schooner sails on the horizon toward Rockland and a speedboat coming down from Belfast.

Not much traffic out here. A good day to be on the water, working or playing: hot, humid, and hazy. The swells were gentle and smooth, but farther south he could see the waves beginning to ripple up. The onshore afternoon breeze promised to come up and blow hard.

There was a nice rhythm to this work: roll, rock, haul, harvest; then measure and band and toss into the barrel; then bait, tip the traps back, and move on. The lobster barrel was half-full, and a feisty bug was swimming around tail first, flipping itself up and around.

Donny liked the sound of water sloshing over the deck and spilling out the scuppers. The hot tank was steaming in the corner with its immersion coil sticking up from the surface.

Now a few more gulls were flying overhead, not interested in the bits of bait still sitting on the transom, then settling down in the water to float alongside the boat, waiting with a keen eye for the bigger chunks.

On the next trap, a crab was half out the crab vent, on the opposite side from the lobster vent, two small circular holes through which the babies could find their way out, allowing them to get used to the routine: in to feed, out to play, in to feed — and then the whole thing crashing to a halt when they reached legal size.

He tugged at the crab and scaled it into the water. Donny wasn't much interested in crabs, but he was willing to go along and gather up the biggest. The real money was in the lobster, which wouldn't come into a trap that was full of crab, as if they didn't like to coexist. Picky little bastards.

As he baited up, he wondered again if the lobster population would still thrive if all these lobstermen didn't cycle the herring back into the bay in the bait bags. He figured there wasn't that much free-range natural food on the bottom to support a population to lead to record landings and swamp a limited demand.

One of his tricks was to sneak in some different bait, maybe some alewives or poggies or redfish, on the assumption that the lobsters liked a little strange, got bored eating the same old herring day after day. Why should they be any different than he was? Besides, it seemed to work, and he could catch almost the same numbers as two guys fishing twice as much gear.

He wondered about Stanley and how this camping thing was going to end. A couple years ago, a fisherman in Lincolnville drank too much, beat his wife, and abused his daughters. The guys could barely live with that, but they would definitely not abide him hauling other guys' traps. They had suspicions, but nobody'd seen him doing it.

One night around ten, Bert called Donny and woke him up to tell him this guy Aaron was headed out of the harbor.

Donny called the other guys and the Marine Patrol down to Rockland and told Jack that he'd best head out and be on the alert for word to come over the VHF about something fishy going on in the dark.

Donny led the fleet out, all running lights off. They found him off the Ensign Islands, at first just a blip on the radar screen. Making sure their firearms were loaded and handy, they confronted Aaron, sitting there in his boat surrounded by buoys that weren't his.

Donny idled back and yelled over, "What the hell do you think you're doing?"

"That ain't no business of yours."

"If it ain't, whose damned business do you suppose it is, you sitting out here in the dark in the middle of another guy's gear?"

It got real tense after that, five boats bobbing in the water, four tempers about to flair, and one guy scared shitless.

About then the Marine Patrol boat came up on the flotilla, which was very good timing. An hour and a half had elapsed since Bert's call.

That ended Aaron's fishing career. Though the evidence was skimpy, everyone knew that he'd tossed all the lobsters overboard, well aware that four angry guys were coming for him through the darkness, and his rail was covered with mud. That was enough. He pulled his gear, trailered his boat, moved inland, and never showed his face in the harbor again.

Donny hoped it wouldn't get that far with Stanley. It was already taking up too much of his energy.

The wind was coming on and chopping up the sea. *Pot Luck*'s bow plowed into the waves as it made for the next buoy. The rough water didn't bother him. It was a beautiful place to make a living, and he was good at it. It wasn't easy money, like pot and coke. But he was his own boss, and he had a nice little vacation in the winter.

Donny pulled a small crab from the next trap, stabbed it with a temperature probe and went about his business. After the two traps went back over the side, he checked the temperature. It would be the same at the bottom, the only temperature that mattered.

The surface was 60 degrees, quite warm for this early in the season. If it was warming up where the lobsters lived down below, that would be the trigger to shed their shells, squirm out like they were in Cirque du Soleil or something, and end up soft and vulnerable until their new hard shells gave them more protection.

According to the crab, the bottom was still colder than the surface, but as the season moved along into the late fall, the bottom temperature would slowly edge up. When it equaled the surface temperature, the lobsters migrated down the bay and out into deeper water offshore, and the season was over.

Pot Luck rolled in the troughs and pitched on the crests.

Tut yawned and leapt off his perch, stretched on the deck, and pissed on the lobster tank.

Donny plucked a smoke from the crumpled pack beside the compass and lit up.

Tut jumped up on the port waterway, walked up the narrow passage on steady sea legs to the bow, and growled at a sailboat.

The fancy sloop on a reach across the wind presented a broadside triangle off *Pot Luck*'s bow and then became a sliver of sail and smidgen of stern as she made for Warren Island, the state park.

Two black porpoise fins cut the water in close. Six gulls floated off the starboard side.

The barrel was half-full with a hundred fifty pounds of lobster living in the cold, circulating saltwater.

Donny pulled the palmed-size transmitter from the ceiling-mounted VHF radio and hailed Bubba Smith at the Lobster Pound to give him a heads-up on the catch, hoping to get a full crate by the end of the day.

It made him think about the quiet interplay between the classes of people on the bay and shore. The summer people saw the bay as their playground and complained about the number of annoying lobster buoys that could get all caught up in their sailboat rudders and power-boat props, as if it was the lobstermen's fault.

The lobstermen complained about all the pleasure craft getting in the way of their season, cutting off the gear to be lost on the bottom, as if they'd done it on purpose.

Then there were the vacationers who knew how to buy his catch directly from his float. He and they were like the crabs and the lobsters in the traps, a grudging acceptance of the way it was up here in Maine, in a sense feeding off each other.

Donny provided the fresh-caught bugs plus an opportunity for the tourists to feel like they had some skin in the game. And they provided him with a ready market of under-the-table cash a little above the boat price.

All in all, it was as good a system as could be expected under the circumstances, and it was small bother for the short vacation season. Come Labor Day, the bay and the towns emptied out, and he'd sell his catch up in Canada.

Donny made for his next buoy. It was 2 p.m., and the traps were yielding too little for all the effort. The rest of the traps needed bait, but it was uncomfortably rough out here. Ten hours after rolling out of bed, he called it a day.

He headed back toward Lincolnville with the helm capable of holding a steady course at a slow speed. He went aft to begin the cleanup routine. It was a slow plod back to the harbor, but it gave him time to straighten up the boat.

The tide was coming in again, and it was sheltered in the harbor. Donny brought *Pot Luck* into the floats and hefted the crab crate onto the dock. He set the empty bait trays beside the crabs. Then he pulled in along his bait shack nestled in amongst the outside pilings of the ferry pen. He tied her loose so she lay off because of the choppy swell that surged through the pier and washed around the pilings.

He unlocked the door of the house on his float. It was big enough inside to store his extra crates and his scale off in the corner. He went back aboard and tipped his day's catch onto the deck, separating the light-banded shedders into one crate and the hard-shells with the tighter green bands into another. He weighed up the crates and made a note on the clipboard hanging from a nail on a two-by-six wall stud. He unlocked and opened the trap door in the floor, pushed the crates into the dark green water, and tied them off good and tight, safe from anyone who might want to steal his lobsters.

Next he tossed onto the dock the boat's floor mats, which cushioned his feet and gave him purchase through the day.

An empty, white, plastic pail got a shot of Dawn dish soap, a slop of bleach, and a charge of water from the hot tank. He dipped a long-handled brush in the fluid, swirled it around, and started at the helm, scrubbing off the accumulated grime that had dried along the working surface of the dash and controls and down the inside of the rail.

He scrubbed the foaming soap into the crannies, Dawn being the only cleaning agent that could make a dent in the herring oil. Other soap didn't hold up, Palmolive and Dove clumping up like sperm in the pail.

He worked his way aft along the rail, soaping up the sides and the waterway, scrubbing harder where the bait was stubborn. The gaff got special attention, brushed along the length, rolled a quarter-turn, and brushed some more.

He rinsed the boat down and watched the bubbles disperse and flush off the deck. The floor mats got dunked in the harbor water off the side and rinsed off.

This was work the stern man would do, but he was wicked cheap that way, liking the solitude of fishing alone, and liking it more that he didn't have to share the value of his harvest. A stern man could add up to between twenty thousand and forty thousand for the summer and a part of the fall, with some winter work thrown in to check and repair the broken gear.

Pot Luck went back to the mooring to dry off, all clean for tomorrow's haul. He and Tut rowed back to the docks.

After getting his first beer out of the cooler in his truck, he drove the crabs over to the Lobster Pound.

A good day.

Chapter 8

T he Payson cottage had once been the Islesboro Inn. It was one of the many cottages that lined the southwestern shore of Islesboro, a section of understated opulence once referred to as the most exclusive resort in the world — Dark Harbor. The description "cottage" was at best a misnomer, at worst a mocking fabrication. These massive houses, imposing, shingle-covered, gabled, were built in the early 1900s by magnates from Boston, New York, and Philadelphia.

When Richard Nixon visited Key Island, the President said, with atypical innocence, "I have never in my life seen so many hotels all in a row."

Shelly heard her father's footfalls coming down the long second-floor hall. He knocked on her door.

"Time to wake up, Sunshine. Summer's a-wasting."

"You call this summer? I'll be down in a minute."

"Carla has breakfast in the sunroom. Then I thought you might like to go to the Yard with me. *Bellwether* is ready. I'll tow, you steer. Wear your boat shoes."

One of the first improvements her mother made after buying the Inn was to have the porch glassed in. Then she filled the cottage with family furniture and threadbare Persian rugs passed down through the generations. She organized cozy seating arrangements of antique, re-upholstered, wing-backed chairs intimately facing each other in front of the four fireplaces.

The sunroom faced west, so it received no morning sunlight, but the view was startling in its expanse of coastal Maine, though gray and heavy with moisture today. It looked over the trimmed and tiered lawn that stepped down to the water and their dock, south to Dark Harbor Boat Yard on

Chapter 8

Seven Hundred Acre Island, north to Gilkey Harbor and the ferry terminal.

It was raw outside, but the room was welcoming, warmth coming off the propane heater in the corner.

Shelly appeared in shorts and a polo shirt. Chase and Cornelia Payson sat with their backs to the inside door. Carla, sharp in her black uniform and white apron, poured coffee. Shelly tossed her Aran Island sweater on the wicker sofa and pulled out a chair at her table setting.

"Good morning, Mummy, Daddy. I think I'll just have coffee this morning, please, Carla."

"Yes, Miss."

She turned over a sturdy mug, poured thick black coffee, then departed silently.

Cornelia looked up from the local paper, tipped her head so she could see her daughter over the half-glasses, and said, "You really must have the soft-boiled eggs. They're divine."

Shelly looked down at the remains of her mother's breakfast — twin empty eggshells in porcelain cups, scooped clean, only a little yolk still on the adjacent spoon. The sight made her stomach turn. She still tasted the acidic wine she'd consumed with her parents the night before. On the alcohol front, she realized she'd never be able to keep up with either of them.

As if reading her mind, her father said, "Perhaps coffee is just the ticket. Anyway, we need to pick up the sailboat."

He leaned over to see Shelly's feet and nodded approval at her footwear. Shelly spooned raw sugar into her cup, poured in some cream from the small pitcher, and stirred.

"What's on the agenda after the boat?"

She took a sip. Her parent's plans for her were usually a bone of contention, but she could be flexible with the little things.

"Your mother is headed for the mainland to do some shopping."

Her father laid his napkin beside his plate of half-eaten scrambled eggs.

"After the boat, I thought you and I might go to the golf club. It isn't open yet officially, but we can still play a little. It'll do us good."

He ran his fingers through thick hair, going really gray now after his early retirement from the investment firm he'd founded. At fifty, too early to be put out to pasture, he devoted exaggerated energy to his leisure time.

With a forced smile, Shelly said, "As long as we don't keep score, Daddy. Can't we just this once keep competition out of it?"

"But if we don't keep score, what's the point?"

"Let's play intuitive golf, for the fun of it. Golf doesn't always have to be tragic. You might like it."

"I don't think it'll catch on, but I'll give it a try. Now let's get moving."

He stood. Shelly slurped the last of her coffee. Cornelia looked up from her paper in time to receive an air kiss from Chase. Shelly came over and kissed her mother on the other cheek.

"You two be careful on the water," Cornelia said. "Do you need anything special from the mainland? I'm catching the four o'clock ferry back, so make sure you're here for cocktails."

Chase turned back and reminded his wife about the cases of wine on order from the Market Basket. Shelly followed her father to the front hall where their slickers hung on hooks.

They walked down across the damp lawn to the dock. When her father took Shelly's hand, it reminded her of the times they'd spent together when she was young. She liked the warmth and affection of his hand and it felt good to touch him. But this time she felt the urge to assert her independence and take her hand away. It bothered that he still saw her as a little girl and needed to direct her life, just as he directed everything else.

Instead, she took a deep breath of heavy air. She didn't take her hand away because she couldn't do it without hurting his feelings. Soon enough they were at the boat, and he let go.

The Mako was tied to the dock. As she boarded, he said, "You take her over. When we get there, I want you to explain the outboard cover. No time like the present to take responsibility."

He said it with no malice and with a friendly smile. She started the motors, and Chase untied the lines.

The ride across to the Yard was invigorating. The waves were out of the south, and the water was choppy. Fog was rolling in and had already consumed the Ensign Islands. Shelly skimmed the water as fast as she could go, and the wind beat at them. Chase stood beside her and held on tight to the stainless-steel tubing wrapped around the windshield.

At the Yard, they found both floats full of boats and people working on them. Shelly brought the Mako into the only available spot, a slip on the inside left. There was a time when an audience would have made her nervous, but now she prided herself on her boat handling, and she nestled in gently against the dock.

Chase leapt out and tied the bow. Shelly tossed the stern line around the cleat to hold her fast. She watched her father step over coiled fuel lines and around buckets full of foamy water and brushes on handles to approach a couple washing down a blue-hulled cabin cruiser on the opposite side of the float. Chase greeted both by name, Jim and Melissa, a part of his annoying habit of knowing everybody's name.

🐚🐚🐚

Chase walked to the outer float where their sailboat was getting sprayed down.

"Good morning, Barry. She looks ready to go."

Barry twisted the hose nozzle shut and turned to shake Chase's offered hand.

"Yes, sir, Mr. Payson. Got the mast stepped yesterday. As per your instructions, we didn't tune the rigging, leaving that for you. I put the sails down below. She should win some races this summer, that's for sure."

"You putting pressure on the skipper?" Chase chuckled. "Is John up at the office?"

"He should be coming right down, ran after an impeller for the Bertram there."

Barry nodded across the dock to a 31-foot sport-fisherman powerboat with both engine covers tilted up, exposing two massive inboards. Embedded in the port engine, ostrich-like, was a mechanic — probably Joseph, given the ass crack and splayed legs.

Chase turned back toward the incline and saw Shelly in conversation with John. "Thanks, Barry. Will she be ready to tow any time soon?"

"All I've got to do is wipe her down; then she's good to go."

John looked over to Shelly, who was admiring the cruiser and talking to the cleaning crew. He turned to Chase.

"She said she tried to fix the outboard and broke an oar and the housing doing it. Told her she could have a job here any time. She'd fit right in. We've got an oar up to the office, and the new housing should come in day after tomorrow."

Chase smiled and shrugged.

"She's a bit impulsive, my daughter."

They both watched for a moment more. Then Chase said, "She and I'll be towing *Bellwether* back shortly. I take it all went well with the repairs."

Both men looked at the sleek sailboat, and John spoke.

"She's right up to snuff, as good as she was when she was launched here in the thirties. We did it all — stiffened up the mast step, replaced 23 oak frames and 14 planks, new paint. Next fall we strip the bright work, and she'll be better than new. I just hope you'll be an inspiration to the others."

Chase didn't have to confirm his love for the boat and the whole class of these graceful racing machines. He was on the yacht club committee dedicated to their preservation, an endeavor that was oftentimes more costly than buying a bigger, modern sailboat with accessories.

The boat was designed in the early thirties by Boston-based Sparkman and Stevens. A good number of them were built at Dark Harbor Boat Yard. They were known as the Dark Harbor 20s, a number that referred to the length at the waterline. They measured 31 feet overall, arrow-like, with a small cockpit comfortable for four and a sparse cabin with two single berths on either side that supported sail bags and spinnaker poles. No motor, no lights, no head, no electronics, and no comforts. Just sleekness for day-races across the bay.

"I can count three owners who are going to pony up. The others should come along once they see that the reconstruction translates into winning."

They both looked out to the water and the fog, now thicker than ever. The boats on the far moorings had disappeared. Chase motioned at the fog.

"It going to be like this all summer? I'll be needing your recommendations on a radar unit for the Mako."

"We've been installing a nice piece by Raymarine that's got the radar, GPS, and chart plotter all rolled onto one screen. Priced real good too, around four grand installed. I can get it in with the outboard housing and hooked up some-time next week."

"Go ahead and order that too, while I'm spending mon-ey."

"Good as done. And we can deliver *Bellwether* if you don't want to deal with this fog today. Looks like the inside of my head on Sunday morning."

They both became aware of the approaching boat at the same time. The sound came first; then the bow appeared. *Pot Luck* was painted on both port and starboard sides.

"Coming in a bit fast. Barry," John called, "Make sure *Bellwether* doesn't get knocked around."

Pot Luck throttled down, but came in hot to the inside of the floats, swung to port, and curled around to nestle up against the cruiser. Just before they came together, Donny tossed two round mooring balls over the side to cushion the touch. Wake followed and tossed the boats against the dock.

Joseph swore. *Bellwether's* halyards slapped against the mast. Barry held the sailboat off the dock.

John said, "Jesus H. Christ, Donny!"

Donny smiled over and said, "Sorry about that. Lost my head, but no harm done."

The docks and boats stopped thrashing, and calm re-turned. Chase watched as Donny turned his attention to Shel-ly.

"Well, hello again."

Donny looked the clean cruiser over, then down to his boots.

"No sense to make more mess. Suppose you guys could pass me over that gasoline line?"

To Chase's satisfaction, John said, "No more fuel if you do that again."

But he also knew that a customer's a customer, so he wasn't surprised when John added, "Jim, will you pass the line over?"

Melissa handed the nozzle to Jim, who held it out to Donny. Melissa walked up the incline and turned the pump on. Donny made himself comfortable on the waterway as he refueled his lobster boat. Jim and Melissa went back to clean-ing. Barry got out a rag and wiped on *Bellwether*.

John and Chase came across the bridge to the inside float, Chase glaring at Donny. He turned to Shelly.

"John and I are going up to the office and order those parts. Why don't you come along?"

"You don't need me for that. Go on ahead. I'll stay down here and keep Donny out of trouble."

John shook his head and said, "Good luck with that."

He turned to leave. Chase looked hard at his daughter, frowned, and then, against his better judgment, turned his back on her to follow John.

Joseph left the Bertram and said to Barry, "Coffee time."

Worked like magic; they picked up Melissa and Jim as they walked by and all four trooped up and away.

🐚🐚🐚

Over the sound of rushing gasoline, Donny said to Shelly, "You getting all squared away here?"

"I 'fessed up to everything, and John wants to hire me as a mechanic."

"Sounds about right for this outfit. There's a good career in oar-to-outboard repairs, at least in the sale of oars."

Shelly shed her boat shoes, stepped aboard the cruiser, and sat on the stern, her bare legs stretched out.

"Fog's thick." She tipped her head to the water.

"Yeah, it is."

"And damp."

"That too. Your father don't like me much."

Shelly was close enough to notice the blue-gray shards in Donny's pupils. They seemed to dance with mischief and delight. He had long lashes for a guy and smile wrinkles.

"Sorry. What did you say?"

"How come your legs are so muscular?"

"I row."

"So do I, but my legs don't look like that."

"I row crew, in college."

"You row with your legs?"

"You push with your legs, row with your shoulders. It's hard work."

"Sounds like it."

Donny paused. It seemed to Shelly he was making a show of concentrating on the fuel flowing into his boat.

He turned his strange eyes back on her and said, "Seems your father don't like me much."

"I wouldn't take it personally. He doesn't like any of my boyfriends."

"Since when am I your boyfriend?"

"What I mean is, to him I'm still a little girl, and he doesn't like any boys, you know, in relation to me."

"So that's what we are? In relation?"

"You've got a pretty quick wit for a fisherman."

"People say that."

The sound of fueling pitched up. Shelly watched as Donny backed off the handle, trickled in a bit more, and then let the handle go. She sprang up and went to turn off the pump. When she turned back, she saw him fumble the fuel cap; he'd set it on the waterway and when he grabbed for it, it slid off and plopped overboard.

There was sound enough for Shelly to say, "Did what I think happened, happen?"

"I was aiming to replace that cap anyway. Got a better one down below."

He disappeared down in the cabin and came out with another cap, which he screwed on carefully.

Shelly watched her father come down the incline. He cleared his throat and then asked, "Are we ready to go?"

She turned and said, loud enough for Donny to hear, "Since the fog is so thick, and all we have is a compass, Donny volunteered to tow *Bellwether* across to our mooring. He said he was headed that way anyway. I can steer the sailboat, and you can follow in the Mako."

"I don't think that will be necessary, honey. Let's leave Donny to his own devices."

"It really is no trouble, sir. I'm going right past your place."

"All settled then." Shelly bounded down the incline and practically skipped to *Bellwether*.

When she looked back, she had to stifle a laugh. Her father seemed almost transfixed by how quickly his control of the situation had been overruled.

Donny untied *Pot Luck*, brought her around to the other side, and backed her down, stern to. Shelly untied the sailboat and pushed the bow out. She caught the line that he threw, threaded it through the chalk, and tied it to the bow cleat.

When he went back to the throttle and eased forward, she scampered back to the tiller and pushed it hard over. She waited for the line to tighten and her boat's bow to swing over to be directly behind the towing bit. They got under way, threading through the moored boats. Finally, Shelly turned to wave at her father.

"C'mon, Daddy!" she called.

Donny towed Shelly directly to the mooring in front of the Payson cottage. Shelly felt a tingle of thrill that she and Donny communicated so effectively without words. She cast off Donny's line and fastened the pennant to the bow cleat. Donny hauled in the towline and then took the wheel and maneuvered over. As if on cue, her dad brought the Mako up alongside *Bellwether*.

"Almost like we practiced!" Shelly beamed with delight.

"Good job all around," her father said quickly. "Thank you, Donny, for your help."

"My pleasure, sir. Off to my traps now. Be seeing you."

Shelly got another little chill as he winked at her. Smiling, he put *Pot Luck* into gear, gave her too much throttle, and blasted off into the fog and disappeared.

Chapter 9

Each trap coming out of the water oozed with possibilities. If it came up full of keepers, you'd done it right. An empty trap was a slap in the face and a call to think it through harder.

Over the past week, he'd finished setting his gear along the western shores of Acre Island and southward. Each double had its destination and just the right amount of line for the depth. It was a ritual to take up positions and establish territory.

The lavender buoys were clustered around Donny's. Stanley was an admirer, watching where Donny set, moving his traps in close, nearly right on top. It was anything but flattering; it was, in fact, in violation of all protocol. Donny knew that if he let this thing go any further, it would get out of hand.

The fog had rolled in again this morning, which made it five days out of seven. Donny liked the fog. It created a personal world. It was like life itself, with you in the middle of your perceptions, a circle of recognition that was private and solitary.

The radar screen swept the immediate world, with him at the center, painting the line of coast, the cut of coves, and the navigational buoys.

He worked this string, going south along the shore hidden by the fog. He loved this work, alone with the country music and his thoughts. In the early morning as he'd tossed and turned, he'd figured out how to deal with Stanley Maven.

On the stern, away from the action, was a pile of cinder blocks, each with a line and a buoy. After he'd hauled the day's worth, he'd set these overboard in a line out in deeper water, to draw Stan off his real gear. It was a good next step.

The half-hitch knots he'd tie just below Stan's buoys would send a clear message: the Mavens would move off, and there'd be no more trouble. If that didn't work, the whole thing would escalate in a hurry.

The black boat came out of nowhere. Donny was busy baiting a trap, and the drone of his idling gas engine masked the sounds from the other boat until it was right in close. Donny looked up at Stanley drifting ten yards off his starboard side, his foot up on the gunnel, his elbow resting on his thigh.

Tut came off his perch, walked the rail, and growled. The gong sounded off the Ensign Bell, lonely in the fog.

Stanley took off his cap. His eyes were bloodshot, and his dirty hair was plastered to the side of his head. Food and debris flecked his beard.

"You're getting in my way here, Donny. I can't have you fishing all over me."

"That's real funny, Stan, 'cause I was about to say the same thing to you. I shouldn't have to explain to you the way it is out here, but there's gonna be real trouble if you don't get your fucking gear out of my space. I'll tell you friendlylike right now, but I won't be friendly if you don't adjust your attitude. Two days to move off; then you may never see your gear again."

"You think you're so high and mighty, fishing over here all these years. Well, you ain't got the right. It's about time someone taught you a lesson, and I'm just the man to do it."

Donny took a long breath.

"Stanley, you don't want trouble, and trouble is what you'll get if this goes too far. There ain't no need of it. There's plenty of space here. All I ask is that you respect that I been fishing here all my life, and you just got to go somewheres else. It ain't rocket science."

"I ain't respecting nothing, asshole. I'm setting my traps wherever I want to, and if you so much as touch my gear, there's gonna be hell to pay, and you'll be the one paying it."

"I'll allow that you don't know no better. You got a lot of money tied up in your new gear, and it'd be a shame to come out and find it all gone."

"Two can play that game, Donny. But I got a better game."

He reached into the pilothouse and came out with a rifle, which he laid across his knee.

Donny stood up straight.

"C'mon, Stan. You can't be that stupid."

Donny touched the throttle, pulled away to the south, and they watched each other getting eaten up by the fog.

All fishermen had to deal with trouble from time to time, but it generally got settled, no one willing to risk an all-out war. He knew there was jealousy in the bay. He'd had guys try to follow him before and set where he'd set, so they didn't have to think for themselves. This would settle out, but Stanley didn't seem to realize he'd come out a loser. Or maybe he didn't care. Maybe he knew they'd both come out losers, and for him, that would be a win.

Chapter 10

Tut sat on the chair at the kitchen table and looked out the window at the Nelson's house. His dull-brown highlights spiked up punklike. He had scar tissue on his nose where flaps of skin had been sewn back. His mouth was capable of a ferocious growl with bared teeth or a carney smile. You might dismiss him, but that would be a mistake. His eyes were keen to complexities, and his brain was busy scheming his next move. It was as if he knew he was smarter than all dogs and most humans.

Donny took a sip of coffee and admired his dog as it focused on the house next door, waiting for a sighting of Alex, his new love. He'd been out roaming this morning.

The phone rang. "Hello?"

"Your ugly dog was over here and molested Alexandra."

It took Donny a moment to put the voice to his neighbor Eliza.

"Well, it don't seem he'd do her no harm. I'd say he's sweet on her."

"That's precisely what I'm talking about. I think your mongrel has mated with her. Mr. Coombs, you will rectify this situation. If your dog has impregnated my Alexandra, you will pay for the abortion. Whatever the situation, your dog is not to come on our property. If he comes over here again, I will call animal control and have him taken to the pound. Am I making myself clear?"

"Let me get this straight. Tut humped Alexandra, and you want to call my cousin?"

Tut turned his head and looked at Donny. Was he smiling?

"I will not abide your use of foul language."

Mrs. Nelson's shrill voice had gone up a notch. She was shouting.

"I'm no sniveling debutante. I'm a lady. I'll whack your fucking dog with a two by four if he ever comes over here again."

Donny liked her a little better now.

"I hear what you're saying Mrs. Nelson," he said, trying to keep the smile out of his voice.

"I'll try to keep Tut here, but he doesn't take well to confinement. I'll cover any expenses, and I'm sorry for your inconvenience."

"Your dog has ruined Alex's life and has made mine a living hell. Just keep him off my property!"

She slammed down the receiver.

Donny set the phone down easy and put both hands on the table.

"Tut, you little bastard. What were you thinking?"

The phone rang again, and Donny braced himself.

"Hello?"

"Donny? This is Dory. I just got a call from your new neighbor. Has Tut run afoul of those Nelson people? Mrs. Nelson wants to know if Tut is registered. I checked the records and was shocked to find out that we have no license for Tut. He's what? Seven years old?"

"Dory, you know I ain't never registered a dog in this town. I doubt any of my ancestors did either. You want me to start now?"

"If she presses the issue, then it's a matter of law, and there's nothing I can do. But let's wait and see. Can't you make peace with these folks?"

"Sure, Dory. As soon as I clean up my yard, shoot my dog, and cut down the oak tree, we'll be great friends. Short of that, they probably won't be too fond of me. I'll just have to continue charming them, I guess. It might take some time."

"You do just that, bub, and give Tut a pat for me."

She laughed and hung up.

"Well, someone likes you."

Donny put his coffee cup in the sink.

"Come on, you rutting bastard, let's go fishing."

Tut leapt off the chair and headed for the mudroom.

🐚🐚🐚

Around noon, a flatbed car hauler pulled into Donny's yard. It backed up to the old truck, set on blocks in the grass. Two guys got out, tilted the bed, hooked a chain onto the rear axle, and winched it up. The guys threw the derelict lawnmower on the side and drove off.

❦ ❦ ❦

Donny slowed as he came up the road to his driveway, set his beer can between his legs, and turned in. He pulled to a stop, shut down the engine, and looked at the vacant space. Tut had his front paws on the dashboard and looked ahead, then back at Donny.

"What the hell?"

The blocks had been dragged along the ground and left gouges. The grass was all yellowed and stunted under where his truck had been, and longer tufts ringed the perimeter. Even the lawnmower was gone, the one he kept for parts.

Donny sat there and then drained his beer and threw the empty can to the floor mat.

Chapter 11

It was pea soup again, pearly and silent, a blanket obscuring everything beyond a hundred yards. The fog matched Donny's mood. He could touch his anger at the removal of his truck, but beyond that it was a blur. He didn't know which way to turn.

He'd almost marched over to the Nelson's to throw a fit. He'd fumed over a couple of beers in his kitchen, trying to sort things out. They owed him the value of the truck for sure, and it would be top dollar. He could maybe bring charges, but the clean-up-your-yard warrant had passed, so he wasn't even sure he was on the right side of the law. He fought back his dark thoughts and tried to see a better way, a cleaner way, to deal with his neighbors.

In the end he went to bed. He woke once in the night, alarmed by a feeling of darkness shrouded by a dream that made him afraid. When he got up, he was drained. He went through his early-morning motions blankly, waiting for some solution to occur to him.

At least he had a plan for Stanley. He was down at the dock ahead of everyone else and off into the bay as the sun rose and lightened up the fog. This was quiet stuff; no need to spread it all over town. He got out to the islands by five-thirty and started to set his cinder blocks in close to the shore. That should make sense to Stan, if anything made sense to him. The full moon was two days away. The old-timers generally moved into shallower water then out deeper when the moon got new.

Weather was coming in at the end of the week, and if Stanley got taken by this ruse, the waves might stave up his gear. Of course, many lobsters were still out deeper, waiting for warmer water. Donny would keep his real gear right where it was.

He set twenty blocks along the western shore of Acre Island and all the way south to Lasell. Tut kept to his nest on the dashboard, tucked up under the port windshield.

Donny hauled coming back up with little to show for it — a handful of keepers was all. It took extra time because his gear kept getting tangled up in Stanley's. Wherever it did, Donny took Stanley's warp and tied a couple of half hitches around the buoy's spindle, a gentleman's knot that said get off my traps.

Donny set a course for home and wondered what the hell he'd done to deserve all this grief. Winding the engine up gave Tut the signal that they were headed back. He leapt off the dash with a thump, lifted his leg on the lobster barrel, took the port rail up to the bow, and leaned into the wind.

Donny got back to the docks at noon, time enough to wash down the boat. He sprayed the deck with the saltwater hose, scrubbed the gurry, and rinsed out the scuppers. Some fishermen let the mess build up so their boats looked like floating pieces of shit.

Donny had been taught right, and he kept *Pot Luck* nice and clean. She was an old boat with a good engine. Not many guys fished with a wooden boat any more, thinking that fiberglass reduced maintenance costs, but Donny had never liked the Clorox-bottle boats and how they rode out in the bay, popping up and down and not cutting through the waves as *Pot Luck* did.

He put her on the mooring and rowed in backwards, stern to, so he could see the rest of the gang coming down the pier to wait for the bait truck.

Tut stood on the aft seat and growled. Bert was telling some kind of joke, waving his beer can around in the air. Billy and Wally stood there drinking and listening.

Donny took a Michelob Light out of Bert's cooler over by the incline, shook off the ice, tapped the top, and popped the tab.

"Help yourself to my beer, why don't you, you highliner parasite."

Bert laughed and gave Donny a little shove.

Wally chucked his empty can and stole a fresh one, Bert's turn to buy the round.

Donny reached into his sweater through the neck, came out with a Camel, and fired it up.

Wally looked through his grimy glasses, shifted his weight onto his left boot, straightened his beard with his free hand, and asked, "Making money today, Donny?"

"No one makes money in this business. It's just an excuse to go boating. You know that."

"Hear you got trouble with Islesboro. Stanley Maven decided to put you into retirement!"

"We'll see about that. The way I figure it, he'll last about till next week. I left a note in his trap that you want company over around Flat Island. Plenty of lobsters on that side, free for the taking."

"He comes over and fucks with me," Wally said, "I'll give him a sex change, and he'll start wearing a dress."

That set them all to laughing. Though Wally was mostly hot wind, he was a third or fourth cousin to Bert, part of the scrappy little Weed clan. Not many wanted to take on the Weeds. Together, they were like a pack of dogs around a prized bone.

Bert kicked his empty can over to the cooler.

"I hear you're going to take after Tut and mate with that Nelson lady, make it one big happy family. After they told you how it was at town meeting, I guess they might add your house to their property and adopt you as a pet."

Donny pitched his butt over the side of the pier.

"You wait," he said, getting serious. "These people are trouble. They get the mainland cleaned up, then they'll be looking down here wanting to get rid of this bait. We'll be like Camden Harbor before long, all yachted up."

"You can't eat quaint. I think you should tell both of them to move back to where they came from. We'll stand behind you."

"How far back? About a mile and a half?"

"I'm serious, Donny. It ain't right what's going on."

The O'Hara ten-wheeler beeped as it backed down onto the pier. They all gathered around. The driver climbed out of the cab and slid the back door up out of the way.

The guys got to sliding their empty Xactic tubs off to the side, making room for the full ones coming off the truck. The driver scooted a nifty hydraulic hand truck under a full tub, lifted it up, and backed it onto the tailgate. He lowered himself down, drove it over along the railing, and lined it up.

The guys that fished eight hundred traps spent up to two hundred dollars a day on bait. Add to that the cost of fuel, new traps, rope, and buoys, and you had to catch a mess of lobster just to break even. With the boat price so low in the spring, most guys didn't earn a profit until late summer or early fall.

Guys like Billy, with his new forty-two-foot Duffy and thousand-horsepower Caterpillar engine, new truck, and house, Donny didn't figure he'd ever come out even, owing all that money to the bank till the day he died and beyond.

The bait truck drove off, and Donny said he had to go make up with the neighbor lady. Thing was, he still didn't know how to do it.

Chapter 12

E liza straightened the edges of all the No Trespassing signs and set them on the piano bench in the great room that looked out on the bay. She peered into the foggy murk. The lone oak was beginning to look sick, and she smiled. She fingered the pile of signs and turned her attention to Del.

"You should have time to post these along our property line. I bought enough for you to put them all the way down to the beach. I bought some placard thingies so all you have to do is staple the signs onto the boards and drive them into the ground."

"Is this really such a good idea, darling?"

Del sat on the overstuffed love seat with Laura Ashley fabric and rubbed his chin.

"We're putting so much pressure on them. I thought we were going to come up here and make an effort to fit in. What happened to that plan?"

"That plan went out the window when I saw how backward it is up here. Underneath all this beauty is a primitive culture that cannot see into tomorrow. All this Yankee individualism is an excuse for idiocy. If the locals had their way, Maine would look like everywhere else in the USA. We have to stem this development pressure, clean up their mess, and preserve the natural beauty."

"Are we really going to close off the right-of-way to the beach?"

"It's our beach. We paid for it."

"Doesn't it matter that the townspeople have used it for generations?"

Eliza looked over at her husband and thought how silly and sentimental he'd become. A man who looked strong and purposeful but was turning soft underneath. Well, she didn't need his help in this fight. It was true, they'd come in peace, but it had become hand-to-hand combat with the insults and vulgarity at the town meeting and that disgusting dog and horrid tree and spitting tobacco juice out pickup truck windows and … it made her feel alive.

"If you don't have the backbone to post these signs, I'll do it."

"Where is all this hate coming from, Eliza? It's unbalanced. Is it so important to make this point? It will only make everything worse."

"It doesn't matter. The last thing we want is to fit in with these people, for God's sake. What are you thinking? You need to concentrate on how to get introduced to the people in Dark Harbor. We simply must get on the list and then have someone sponsor us. It's not easy to break into the club. Now, will you post these signs, or do I have to do everything around here?"

Chapter 13

S helly came down late for breakfast. The day's agenda was simple and open, and she planned to get her conditioning out of the way first thing. She often marveled at the strangeness of her sport. She trained for hours and days and then rowed backwards in a race that lasted six or seven minutes. With eight to ten races in a season, she trained for months for a single hour of competition.

There was no time off. Any slippage in conditioning meant diminished prospects of retaining her seat in the girl's Harvard varsity eight boat. She'd been a star in the girl's eight at Exeter and a standout on the rowing machine at the annual Crash Bs. Her prowess in crew had been a factor in getting into Harvard, and she'd rowed her way onto the top boat her junior year. The athletics also helped keep her head clear for the rigorous academics of Harvard.

Carla was in the kitchen in her black uniform cleaning up the breakfast dishes.

"Good morning, Shelly. Can I get you something to eat?"

"No thanks, Carla."

Shelly took a mug from the glass-fronted cabinet and poured coffee.

"I've got to do my run. I'll wait to put on the calories at lunch. Speaking of which, what have the masters planned for the day?"

"Turtle soup for lunch and roast lamb for supper, just the three of you."

Carla put a fry pan in the drying rack, wiped her hands on the dish towel, hesitated, then said, "Your parents mean well. I don't think you should refer to them as 'the masters'."

"Oh, Carla, I really don't mean anything by it. I just get frustrated sometimes. When I'm in Cambridge, I only have to answer to myself."

"And not your professors, coaches, resident advisors, roommates, and, uh, boyfriends?"

Shelly reached back, grabbed the top of her sneaker, and stretched her quad, looking like a one-legged stork.

"So you're telling me that I'll always have to answer to someone?"

"Yes. The trick is to pick the right someone."

The kitchen door swung open, and Cornelia strolled in, followed by the two Corgis, River and Mary.

"Good morning, sweetheart. I see you're dressed for your run. Afterwards, I'd like to have a word. You received a call this morning while you were still asleep from someone named Donny. He was very polite. His number is there on the pad."

She motioned with her hand.

"Is he the lobsterman that your father mentioned to me?"

"He's the one who fixed the outboard and towed *Bellwether* back from the yard."

Shelly shifted her weight to the other foot and grabbed her other ankle. She set the mug on the marble island counter. It made a sharp sound.

"Well, I'll be off, Mummy. We can talk after my shower, about an hour and a half."

She went out the back door. The fog had yet to burn off, which made the hour run more comfortable. She turned at the end of the crushed-stone driveway and slowly jogged along the shore road to warm up.

Soon the rhythm increased, and she set a strong pace that would take her through the hour. Running became automatic, and her mind turned to Donny. She liked his attitude and the suggestion of trouble in his gaze. How much trouble was the question.

Her parents would go apeshit if she went out with him. That thought made her smile. Coming to where the shore road dead-ended at the main road, she turned north. Traffic on the island was sporadic and slow, and everyone waved. Still, it was stupid to get killed. She kept to the left, running toward any oncoming cars.

Chapter 13

With damp, shampooed hair combed straight back, Shelly found her mother reading in front of a smoldering fire in the sitting room. She looked up from her book and set it down on the side table. She motioned her daughter to a chair beside the fire.

"Darling, tell me about this Donny fellow," she said, settling into her wing-backed chair as if preparing for a long and serious talk.

Shelly leaned over the fireplace screen and rearranged the logs so that the flames took hold. She took off her cable-knit sweater.

"I told you about the boat and the towing. There's nothing much more to tell. He's a little older than me. He has nice eyes."

"Your father says he is a lot older than you, and he thinks there's something going on between you two."

"Good heavens, Mummy, how can there be anything between us? We've only met twice!"

"He said there's an attraction. Is that right?"

Shelly moved away from the fire to a chair next to her mother. Her relationship with her mother was warm and without the overbearing burden of the protectionism from her father. Still, she sometimes suspected that her father served as the front man, while her mother set the agenda and pulled the strings.

"I like him, what I've seen, anyway. What did he say on the phone?"

"He asked if he could speak to you. I lied and told him you were on your run. He asked if I would give you the message to call him when you got back. He called me Mrs. Payson. I said I would. All very cordial and proper."

"Yes, he's very polite."

"So, you're planning to call him back?"

"Sure. Why not?"

"Shelly, I don't want you to do anything you'll regret. You need to be very clear, before talking to him, of your boundaries."

Shelly's face reddened and she twisted her sweater in her lap.

"Are you talking about my boundaries or yours?"

Cornelia leaned forward to accentuate her point.

"Sweetheart, I'm talking about universal boundaries. Some things are just not done. One of those things is for someone of your status to have a relationship with someone of, uh, his status, no matter how innocent that relationship might be. I just don't want you to lead him along, and I'm not talking about sex, which is, of course, completely out of the question.

"None of this will come to any good. I want you to call him and thank him for all his help and say that you're unavailable for the rest of the summer, that you have to train for the upcoming crew season.

"If you give him any encouragement, you'll be leading him down the wrong path, and you'll both get hurt. Mixing our world with his can only lead to bad things."

Her mother sat back and looked intently into Shelly's eyes.

It was Shelly's turn to lean forward. She remembered her conversation with Carla and wondered, briefly, at which master's feet fate would put her. Several responses crossed her mind, all of them disrespectful. She held her tongue.

Cornelia put a gentle hand on her daughter's arm.

"Shelly, honey, I am only telling you this for your own good. I've seen relationships between classes end in agony for both parties."

Her mother turned and retrieved her book from the table and put on her glasses. She looked over them and scrutinized her daughter. Shelly knew it was over and got up to go.

"What are you going to do?"

"Mummy, I'm going to try very hard to do the right thing."

Shelly hurried out of the room. She calmed down over a glass of orange juice in the empty kitchen. Then, without a thought or a plan, she called Donny's number.

"Hello?"

"Donny?"

"The same. That you, Shelly?"

"Donny, don't you have caller ID?"

"What's that?"

"Oh, forget it. What the hell do you want?"

"You twist your ankle on your jog or something?"

"I don't jog. I run. And no, I didn't twist my ankle. What do you want, Donny?"

Chapter 13

"That's a loaded question, but I just called 'cause it's Sunday, and I ain't allowed to fish, so I thought I'd collect on that debt you owe me and have you take me to lunch."

"Lunch? Where on earth would we go to lunch, assuming I have any intention of taking you? The only lunch place is the yacht club, and it would be way too cold out on the porch. It's thick fog out here."

"Out where? It's a little misty here is all."

"I'm telling you, there's no place to get lunch."

"Ever hear of the mainland, Shelly? You know, that big piece of land out your window."

"You want to pick me up in the fog and take me to the mainland for lunch?"

"Actually, I'll pick you up, but you're taking me to lunch. Say, in about a half an hour? I'll swing by your dock, and we'll head to Camden, eat at the Waterfront Restaurant, and I'll have you home by three. How about it?"

Shelly looked at her watch.

"You get to the dock in thirty minutes, eleven on the dot, and I'll be waiting in my foul-weather gear."

"You bet, see you at eleven, on the dot."

The line went dead.

Shelly raced up the stairs to her room and checked herself in the mirror. She thought her khakis were too formal, so she threw them into the corner and pulled on a pair of blue jeans. The polo shirt was too preppy, so she switched to a plain, white-pocket tee. She exchanged the sweater for a red-fleece vest that would look nice against her yellow slicker. Cold and damp meant white wool socks and her high-top Keds. Finally, she brushed her hair and held it back with a tortoiseshell barrette.

The note she left in the kitchen said she'd gone for a long walk up island to think things over and that she'd miss lunch. That brought a smile. Shelly was careful to sneak out of the house, flank the lawn, and stay just enough in the mist as to be invisible.

Pot Luck came out of the fog and swung into the dock. Shelly leapt aboard, and Donny maneuvered out past *Bellwether*.

She made her way forward into the pilothouse. Donny offered his hand, and they gave each other a firm shake and a clear look in the eye.

"Y'ever been on a lobster boat?"

She took in her surroundings. The surfaces were rough but freshly washed down and organized.

"First time."

"I could explain the whole setup, but it would be easier to show you. I'll take you out fishing sometime."

Warmth from the engine made it cozy in the house. They both stood close to the wheel as Donny explained the finer points of radar and GPS navigation.

Down past the Ensign Islands they turned west toward Camden. Donny appeared to have dressed up in new jeans, a plaid, button-down shirt with the collar askew, and a Carhart canvas jacket. He'd shaved and smelled of cheap cologne. Shelly straightened the collar.

Halfway across, Donny said, "Here, you take her."

She brushed against him as they switched places.

"Hold her steady on two hundred forty degrees. They ain't no boats on the radar, but keep your head swiveling, just the same."

Donny went aft, unlatched the engine box, and pulled it up. The roar filled the pilothouse. He put his hand on something, looked up, considering, then nodded and shut the box back down. He came forward, but showed no inclination to take the wheel.

"She's been running hot, and I wanted to check the manifolds. They seem okay. Time will tell."

He punched some button on the radar, and the sweep on the monitor outlined what she assumed was the mainland.

"See this notch here? That's Camden harbor. Now you can steer right for it. I'll tell you if we hit anything."

Chapter 14

Donny was getting tired of the straight and narrow, toeing the line and taking it, especially with all the shoving and pushing going on. He hadn't mentioned a thing to the Nelsons, not wanting to give them any satisfaction. Then he'd found a check in the mailbox from the hauling company for more than he thought the junk truck and lawnmower were worth. That pissed him off even more.

He parked his truck down on the pier next to the Xactics. Everything was lit up by the mercury vapor lights this early in the dark morning, another cool and foggy one at that. The eastern sky over the islands was getting a hint of life, a dull freshening in the fog bank.

Tut leapt out and went about marking his territory, stopping to piss on each boulder set on the side of the pavement to keep the flatlanders from driving their cars into the water on their way to the ferry. Tut was just about as territorial around his town as the fishermen were with their traps.

Donny's bait box was filled with herring and redfish, fresh and pungent. He set to stuffing his bait bags, two hundred of them, tossing each one into a tray, which he slid down the incline to muscle onboard *Pot Luck*.

Any normal person would hate this part, trying to keep the stink from getting all over him, mushing fish heads into the string bags, cinching the little rope tight, then tying it off, but Donny liked being all geared up with his orange Grundens bib overalls and matching rubber gloves.

Although it was monotonous work, it allowed him to sort through his feelings, plan his approach to the Stanley problem, or maybe get the Nelsons off his back. All this aggravation was making him feel off balance, which was costing him energy he'd need to battle it all out.

The storm was a day off, and he'd have just enough time to move half his gear out into deeper water, protect it from the rolling seas that could stove it up on the ledges. Hopefully, Stanley would be drawn in by the cinderblock fake-outs. Serve him right.

This lobster season was going to be such a pisser that it would probably break some of the guys. The federal right whale regulations created all kinds of trapping hassles and could get someone killed. Now, the feds were also regulating the herring catch, making the cost of bait skyrocket, up to $20 a bushel and climbing. Fuel was close to four dollars a gallon, OPEC and oil companies getting rich, with the common guy trying to make a living and getting shafted again.

Ignore the Nelsons; that's what he'd do. He could mind his own business, even if they couldn't mind theirs.

He smooshed the last fish into the last bag and kicked the last tray over to the top of the incline. It slid down on the smooth side, gravity pulling it along, till it clunked on the float, knocking into the other trays.

The morning was lightening up. He parked the truck up in the lot, rowed Tut out to the boat, warmed her up, and brought her into the dock. They headed back out with eight trays of fresh bait.

Donny checked his heading on the compass and squared it with the GPS and the radar. They got swallowed up by the fog, their own world, with Tut curled up in his spot, the VHF silent, and country music just loud enough to come over the sounds of eight cylinders pounding out under the insulated engine box, the exhaust jetting out the stern and mixing up with the fog, a skim-milk veil over creamy water.

Donny never tired of being out on the water by himself. He trusted what he'd learned from his father about being safe, keeping up a good boat that would treat you right and bring you back.

The fog kept the yahoos back on land, off the bay and all lost and confused and tired of watching out and listening for invisible dangers, so he didn't have to worry about getting rammed. Every day, he loved to come out here for the peace, the steady work of hauling his traps, each one of the four hundred breaking the surface like a box of treasure and a testimony to how he was making his gear count.

He couldn't do anything about the boat price, the Canadian buyers dried up of money from the failed Icelandic banks, the demand for lobster down with the Great Recession. But he could drag these suckers off the bottom and bring in more lobster than the guys with twice the traps, and he could damn sure outfish and outfox all the Stanley Mavens who might challenge his right to it all.

And there he was, just where Donny expected him. As he came in close to the island he could see Stanley camped out on top of his cinderblocks. His chuckle made Tut raise his head and look out the windshield to see what was funny. All those lavender buoys set in shallow and the traps at risk of smashing up when the waves crashed in. Donny pulled off from shore to his lead traps and started his day's work.

This early in the season, when he was lucky to get a single keeper in each trap, was character building. But he was spot-on this morning, and he'd set right. His thirty traps this side of the island were averaging two pounds per haul. He scaled the small young ones and the big breeders back into the bay and tossed the keepers onto the tray to be banded on the way to the next buoy.

He pried out a lobster and turned it over, a big-ass female, her belly covered with clumps of orange berries, thousands of eggs. He looked for a notch and then grabbed for his knife and cut out a V in the second flipper to the right at the end of the tail. When she'd spent all her eggs, the notch would tell anyone who caught her again that she was brood stock, and they'd leave her alone, set her back to replenish the fishery. He treated her right: eased her back into the water and watched her sink down freefall, then her tail working.

Stanley still had a lot of lavender gear beside Donny's day-glow orange buoys. Donny checked the radar, making sure he was alone. He hooked on to one of Stanley's buoys and hauled the trap — mostly crab and urchin and one short. Must be using shit bait. Donny reached for his hammer and gave the door a couple of good smacks, caving it in some, a stronger message to back off. Tut sighed.

The rest of the morning, he gave Stanley's traps the same treatment, hoping this would be the last of it. The next step was to cut line, and that just left ghost traps on the bottom to snare and waste good lobsters. If it went that far, he'd be causing some serious damage to Stanley's checkbook and probably his own. A war could ruin everyone involved, so he hoped to hell Stanley was brighter than he looked.

It was a good haul. They made it back by mid-afternoon, socked in by thick fog the whole time.

The other guys were still out. He rinsed the empty bags off the side and threw them into the tub to be filled in the morning. He hosed down his boat and scrubbed her shiny, hung up his foul-weather gear, stomped over to the punt, and whistled for Tut. They rowed in as the ferry blew her horn for three seconds, spewing exhaust out the stacks as the props churned the water, and left the pen. Donny waved to Captain Hinckley, who touched his cap and headed off to Islesboro.

Chapter 15

Through the kitchen window, Donny watched Tut sniff around the Nelson shrubs along the garage. He hadn't slept well. With the storm, everything was put off to later this morning. He sat at the table with his second cup of coffee, reflecting on the good and the bad, mostly bad. Shelly was a high point, something special going on there, a spark.

It'd been a long while since he'd been sweet on anyone. Most of his girlfriends had been dead ends, harbor trash, barely able to finish high school and anxious to settle down with someone who brought home steady money. They all seemed to want more from him than he was ready or willing to give. They all became like moorings or boat anchors, keeping him in one spot — not that he had any place to go really. But he didn't want to wind up with child support and an angry ex-wife who thought that because they'd shared a bed, it gave her the right to his house, his boat, and a chunk of his lobstering money.

Tut pissed on another bush as though he owned the place. Good dog. The rain had let up, and the wind had died down, but it still had enough gumption to sway his oak, which didn't look so good; the leaves weren't coming in as they were supposed to. He didn't think the Nelsons would go so far as to mess with his tree, but then again, they'd cleaned up his yard for him, the pushy bastards.

His father always asked, "If you put wishes in one hand and a pile of shit in the other, which one do you think weighs more?"

He and his grandfather had disappeared off their boat during a winter storm. Donny was seventeen with his own boat, but he was fishing the east side in the lee. They found the boat on the shore, all busted up and no one onboard.

The Coast Guard and Marine Patrol searched for days with boats and a helicopter looking for them, plotting the tides and currents to figure where they might have ended up. But no one ever came up with a body or even an idea about what had happened. All the Lincolnville and the Islesboro fishermen had helped with the search. They were all in this together, scared deep down that it could have been them but thankful it wasn't — this time.

His father had been crusty as a hard shell. He smoked and drank enough for two men, but he'd taught Donny to fish and stay safe on the water. How he'd made a fatal mistake had all of them scratching their heads while raising their beers in a silent toast.

His mother, who came from inland, the little town of Millinocket, had never liked the coast or commercial fishing. She just got up and left when Donny was fourteen. A few years back, he'd heard she died, lung cancer having eaten her up in a couple of months. They said it was from smoking, a family tradition that Donny was upholding, dancing with those little cylindrical devils.

He reached over and flicked on the NOAA weather radio. Winds diminishing from the southeast, then turning north to light and variable. Patchy fog later in the day, with visibility one to three miles. That was how he felt today, diminished and foggy, with little desire to do anything at all. Seemed he'd been right-out straight for a long time now.

Donny opened the screen door, which was beat to shit and needed paint. Just another reminder of all the work he needed to put into the house he'd grown up in. Once he got to scraping the old paint off, he knew he'd find all the soft wood that needed digging out and replacing. Maybe the Nelsons would spring for the repairs, being so gung ho on things looking pretty and all.

Donny placed curled fingers on the tip of his tongue, blasted a whistle, and Tut came back at a run, excited to get out on the water, his second favorite thing next to flirting with that pretty little dog Alex.

They loaded the cooler into the truck and waited for a gap in the traffic, already getting thicker with out-of-state cars, early for this time of year. Maybe they were a good sign because they'd be wanting to eat lobster down at the Pound, paying with the almighty tourist dollar.

Life was picking up down at the beach too. The town was waking up from its winter hibernation, half the businesses still shuttered, waiting for warmer weather and the grand influx.

He came down the hill to the small strip of stores and restaurants lined up along this stretch of Route One. The Beach Store was still shut, but the Lobster Pound parking lot had some local cars clustered around the entrance, some early workers sweeping the restaurant out and getting ready for the season.

Now that was the way to make a living! He'd heard that the owner cleared a million dollars a year, and he was only open from May to Halloween. Sweet. But he might get hurt this year if the damned fog stayed clinging to the coast. After all, who wants to pay lobster prices to get tied up in a bib, fight through the shell, dip lobster meat into congealing butter, and drip permanent stains on your skirt, all while looking at fog?

The ferry was between runs, so commotion was at a minimum, only a few cars and trucks in line waiting for the boat.

Tom, the ferry's traffic coordinator, was looking up and talking to a driver in a big rig — from the building-supply place up the road where Amy Daniels worked — stacked high with lumber and cinderblocks and foam insulation.

Tut sniffed his leg, and Tom leaned down to rub him behind the ears. Tom was one of the few townspeople who could do that without getting bit.

"Keeping everybody behaving there, Tom? Want a beer?"

"Wish I could. Wish the state paid me to drink. Wouldn't that be something? If you got any left when you get back, I'll take a spare."

"You know there's is no such thing as a spare beer, Tom, but I'll keep one with your name on it so long as I don't think Tut looks dry and give it to him first."

"Tut drunk? Now that's not a pretty thought. He's mean enough as it is."

"Mellows him out, just like me. We both turn into pussycats."

"Pigs fly, and you and your neighbors are having a block party this weekend. I'm coming over for the show. You know, he's down at the float right now. Maybe you can plan the festivities. I like those scallops wrapped in bacon and some fish eggs on toast and some Wild Turkey."

Donny took a look down to the docks and sure enough, Del was on the float, holding the bowline to a gussied-up double-ender.

Donny grinned and said, "Guess the show's about to start, Fourth of July coming early this year. Get out your lawn chair."

He patted Tom on the arm, and he and Tut headed down, wondering how this encounter was going to turn out.

Del looked up as Donny came along the incline, flat because the tide was high. Tut kept his distance but was watching carefully, maybe fixing to snap at a leg going by. Del eased a long oar onto the seats; the oar had leather patches so the oarlocks didn't mar the varnish. He slowly set the other one in and then turned his attention to Donny.

"Well, hi, Donny. I guess we're neighbors all around, even down here. I got my boat coming up in a day or two, and Clayton has rented me the mooring in close to *Pot Luck*."

They both looked out at the mooring field. Donny didn't have anything to say, so Del filled in the silence.

"You know, I don't want any hard feelings, and I don't want you taking things personally. Eliza and I really do want to be good neighbors."

Donny put both hands in his rear pockets and said, "I got that check for my truck and lawnmower the other day. You got strange ways of making friends, thinking that's the right way to do things."

"Eliza can act impulsively sometimes, and between you and me, she goes off the handle, know what I mean? Well, I'd have done it differently, but it is what it is."

"If this is what it is, then I'd say we got trouble coming up. I see you posted the path down to the beach. That ain't gonna set well with the town folk, seeing as we've all used that path to the beach for decades. My family used to own that land, and we never had any problem with folks going down for a picnic and a swim. You cutting it off like that appears to be right unfriendly, just when you say you want to be good neighbors. Don't seem like you got such a hot plan."

"Why don't we start over fresh from now on?"

Donny looked over Del's shoulder and saw Tom, up at the ferry line, making a gesture that said, "Punch him one, man," with a smile on his face.

"You pull those signs up. That would be a start, good faith and all. You trespassing to take the truck away, we can let that slide, I guess. Now you and your friends got the town tied up, what with your success at the town meeting and all. I guess that's the law, but you might want to give it a little rest."

"That sounds very reasonable, Donny. I'll relay your thoughts to Eliza, and we'll see what we can do. I'm glad we have come to an accommodation. This is real progress, and I'm glad we had this talk."

Donny looked down at the Nelsons' new rowboat: freshly painted white topsides; beautiful sheer, white, canvas gunnel guards; inside oak ribs and cedar planks varnished without drips or sags or even a holiday.

Donny went to untie his punt with the plywood gone bare and an inch of water sloshing on the bottom. The two boats side by side looked like Jekyll and Hyde.

Del cleared his throat, looking down at the toe rails of Donny's punt, screws sticking out where the gunnel guard used to be fastened.

"Do you think you might put some padding on your rowboat? If these two are going to be knocking against each other down here in the chop, I can just imagine the damage."

"That's a thought, yes sir. I can just see that damage too, to your little varnish farm."

Chapter 16

The mooring was a five-ton block of granite with an inch-and-a-half staple. Settled into the mud with enough suction so the Yard's workboat couldn't budge it, not even hauling hard with the hydraulic winch and boom, its stern pulled down with the effort until they just gave up.

The three-quarter-inch galvanized bottom chain, all twenty-five feet, was fastened to the staple with a seven-eighths-inch shackle, the pin screwed in tight with a massive crescent wrench and then fastened in with copper seizing wire like all the other shackles so it couldn't work loose.

The top chain was half inch and measured out another twenty-five feet. That came up to an eye-to-eye three-quarter-inch swivel attached with a five-eighths shackle and ending with an A3 poly mooring ball, enough buoyancy to lift all that chain at high tide.

Just below the ball, shackled into the top chain, was the twenty-foot, poly-nylon, double-braided, yellow pennant with floats tied in every three feet and ending with the eye that went over the top of *Pot Luck*'s bow cleat. The fiberglass stem of the eight-foot mast buoy was attached with small spliced line.

The whole rig was two years old and cherry, at least according to the diver who went down to check it out late last fall. It had held the boat right there, even during the blows that came up stronger than expected or when Donny was willing to gamble on his mooring gear and decided not to motor *Pot Luck* over to the more protected moorings in Cradle Cove at the Boat Yard.

So there was no need of it with the storm that wasn't much even by Maine standards. But somehow, somewhere, something let go, and *Pot Luck* had drifted into the beach, at least according to what Bert just said on the phone. It was nine-thirty, and Donny, four beers into the evening, was getting set to bed down.

He and Tut dashed out, peeled off, and got down to the beach quickly. He parked next to Bert's truck in the Lobster Pound parking lot and took a flashlight from the glove box. He stalked down the sand beach where his boat was lying on her side. The tide was out, so she was high and dry, pointed straight up the beach as if she were headed to San Francisco.

Donny looked left to the rocks and right to the pilings at the ferry terminal.

"Could have been worse, I guess."

Bert circled around to the stern, and Tut followed, turning in to sniff at the scummy bottom, grass just starting to skim over the green bottom paint.

"Something or someone sure is shining on you. Look at how she came in and settled soft in the sand, instead of what would've happened to my boat, come in on the rocks and get all stove up."

Donny went to the bow. He took hold of the pennant hanging off the chock and shone the light along to the end that had the ball. The last link of the chain looked scuffed and gnawed at by a hacksaw blade — nothing natural about it.

Bert came around the port side and scoped it out.

"You getting messed with for sure. And not real subtle neither. Which one of your enemies likes to swim with a hacksaw?"

Donny looked over at the water.

"More'n likely the bastard hauled up the chain and sawed her down from a punt." He scratched his head. "Tide won't be back in till early morning. You give me a hand? I'll run up to the house and get the hydraulic jack, and we can pump her up straight."

"I'll stay right here with Tut so we can both piss on your boat. Bring some beer."

Donny made it back in ten minutes with the jack and a five-foot-long eight-by-eight, and they went to work. They put the wood under the starboard toe rail, then ratcheted the lever and tilted the boat back up straight until she was balanced on her keel. Donny got some four-by-fours from his pickup and wedged two on each side to stabilize her. They each cracked beers, lit up smokes, and looked the situation over.

Bert took a long pull on the cold one.

"She's down far enough so you'll have plenty of water to back her off when the tide gets up. You won't need me."

"Wind is supposed to come around to the north, so that's another stroke of luck. Guess now I have to ask around and see if anyone saw anything fishy."

"My guess is no one did, or you'd've heard something already."

Donny packed up his tools and his dog and took a last look at his boat on the beach. He was getting damned tired of this shit. Someone had to pay. Who and how were the only questions.

Chapter 17

Donny tossed and turned, mostly awake, until he was aware of a disjointed dream. Stanley's head came out of the deep, wedged in one of his traps, half-eaten, which meant his head tasted good to crabs. So he knew he slept at least a little.

He had some time to glance through the *Bangor Daily News* as he finished his fried-egg sandwich and second cup of coffee at the kitchen table. The Great Recession was still coming on strong, but the analysts and journalists were all enthusiastic, claiming the worst to be in the past. What's the big deal if one out of ten Americans can't find work?

The article in the local section about lobstering allowed that even though last year's catch was a record, almost 76 million pounds, revenues were down ten percent. With competing lobster boats scuttled out at Owl's Head and the shooting over a fishing dispute on Matinicus, the Marine Patrol was expecting heightened territorial tensions as incomes got squeezed even further.

Tut tilted his head to the right. Donny set the last of his breakfast in Tut's mouth, uncharacteristically gentle when taking food.

It was almost 3 a.m. and the night still pitch black as the tide was starting to come in. They both made for the truck, picking up the moist dirt in the driveway and tracking it onto the floor mats and seats. That didn't bother Donny; he'd be plenty dirty long before the day was done.

The wind was light as Donny and Tut rowed from the dock to *Pot Luck* on the beach, the tide washing in to cover the prop but not yet high enough to float the boat. Donny tossed his dog up over the rail and climbed onto his boat. He figured another half-hour before he could back her off, so he checked the oil and transmission fluid, smoked a Camel, and watched Bert wave from the pier.

Bert was a good distant cousin but not much of a fisherman, not that he needed to be, given his good-paying caretaking job for the indestructibly rich people from Texas. Bert rowed over, diverting in to shore on his way to his mooring.

"I heard that your friend on Islesboro might be facing the repo man, gonna take his boat back and then his house. You hear about the foreclosure?"

"I ain't in the loop, but even if I was, I wouldn't pay it no mind. The song says I got enough trouble minding my own business. Why would I want to mind somebody else's?"

"Might give you some insight on your enemy."

Tut stood on the stern, leaned his head low, and growled at Bert as he kept his punt even, dipping a port oar then a starboard. Bert laughed.

"For Christ sake, Tut, how many years do we go back? Since you was a pup, you little bastard."

Tut growled deeper, but his stump was wagging something fierce.

"You think that's why Stanley's all over me? He needs every last dollar?"

"Makes sense to me, but someone ought to tell him that ain't the solution, coming up against you."

"You tell him."

"I thought you were telling him, in your way."

"You'd think he'd of gotten the message by now. I made it perfectly clear last time I was out. Gonna see if he heard the news when I get off the beach. You find anything out about who might have parted my chain?"

"It's been what? Six hours? You think I got my ear on the railroad track? Maybe Stanley's talking back, you both in a conversation without any words. Or maybe your neighbor lady came out to see you on the boat, but you wasn't there to saw *her* chain, so she got pissed off and sawed yours."

Bert laughed at his own joke. "You're stacking up enemies like cord wood. Ever think about making peace?"

"The only thing that would satisfy them is for me to disappear into thin air."

"If it's any consolation, when you do, I'll set all over Stanley in your spots."

Chapter 17

Bert lowered both oars into the water and pulled the handles to his chest.

"Time to fire up. Your stern is floating wicked good, should slide right off, finest kind."

Donny jumped up and down, and sure enough, the keel had floated off the sand. The engine caught nice, and he threw her into reverse. The prop churned water along the rounded bilge, the skeg slid sweet, and she was afloat. He backed down, but the bowline from his punt got wound around the propeller, and the engine stalled.

"Jesus H. Christ!"

The light northerly breeze gently pushed *Pot Luck* off the shore. The bowline to the cleat was snug right up, and the punt's bow was digging into the water. Donny started the engine, eased her into forward, and the line slackened some.

"If it ain't one fuckin' thing…"

He went aft to manhandle the twisted line off the shaft knowing if she didn't break loose, he'd have to go swimming.

He reached down, muckled onto the bowline, pulled hard, and the line came slack. He pulled some more, and the whole mess broke free.

"I'll be go to hell," he said to Tut. "That's another thing going our way."

He tied the punt in close and leaned over to retrieve the lumber he'd used to prop up his boat.

The fog started burning off as they headed out. *Pot Luck* held her heading while Donny filled bait bags, and Tut snuggled down on his bed on the dashboard. They came up on his Acre Island string, and Stanley was still camping all over him. Donny figured it was time to ratchet things up a bit, so he cut off the five buoys close to the northern tip of the island.

As he worked his gear south, his catch dwindled down to almost nothing, and he wondered if Stanley was stealing his lobsters. Most of his trap doors looked natural, but as he came around the Ensign Islands and brought his gear to the surface, the bungee cords holding the doors closed were hooked down lower than was his custom, proof Stanley had been fucking with them.

They hauled two hundred traps that morning and early afternoon. Most of the fishermen had their gear in, but there was still plenty of room for all the gangs. He worked the borderline north of Lasell Island and met up with Bobby Wentworth, who was setting his gear later than most.

Bobby came over, idled down, and floated just off Donny's starboard side. Donny worked his hauler as Tut raised his head and then came off his perch to protest the intrusion by running up along the waterway to the bow and barking.

"Shut up, Tut!"

Donny waved back at Bobby. As was his tradition, Bobby was already half-shitfaced and looked like he'd been scraped along the bottom in a scallop drag. His five-year-old Holland 38 looked even worse, especially for this early in the season. The topsides were all stained, and the waterline had an inch of grass swaying in the current. For all the poor presentation, Bobby was east bay's highliner. The Wentworths and the Coombs had fished the edges of these territories for generations.

"How you hittin' 'em, Bobby?"

"Right out straight, but ain't no lobsters nowhere."

Bobby smiled a sloppy grin, a hole where a front tooth should have been. He reached down and came up with a Narragansett tall boy and took a pull, wiping his chin with his sleeve.

"Never are for us. Those bastard rookies must be catching them all."

Bobby nodded to that, the usual poor-boy banter from the same guys who were the envy of them all. He chucked the empty can off the side, something even Donny had given up a decade ago, conscious of keeping the bay clean. Bobby propped a foot on the rail and got serious.

"Hear anything about gear getting cut over to North Haven?"

Donny pulled his trap up to the rail and leaned on it, not paying attention to his haul.

"Can't say as I have. Don't talk to them guys much. What's going on?"

The seagulls swooped in and screamed, circling closer to be first to score the old bait dumped out of the bags. Donny reached into the trap, brought out the herring, ragged and spoiled, and turned the bag inside out so the mess fell away from the rail. He put her in forward, and the boat inched ahead, away from the coming feeding frenzy. They both watched the gulls go for the scraps.

Bobby said, "Francis Dyer lost some gear last week, and his little brother Dean said there was some talk."

"Jesus Christ, Bobby, you're tighter than a hen clam. What are you getting at?"

Bobby chuckled.

"There's a new guy from Islesboro, fishes your side and up the east bay along Pendleton Point. I heard he hated to say anything, but he volunteered that he'd seen your boat coming from that direction in the fog the other morning."

"You wouldn't be meaning Stanley Maven?"

"He might be the one, can't say for sure, this all being third- and fourth-hand."

"How long we been out here, you and me? Just about since we were out of diapers — then before that our fathers and their fathers. You ever known me to set anywhere other than what we done for generations? So what the hell would I be doing way over there?"

"You'd have no business over there, and that's a fact. Is there something going on between you and that boy? I don't fish up to the northerd, and nobody tells me nothin' nohow."

"Ain't nothing I can't handle, but he's been all over me, and he ain't getting the messages I been sending. Maybe he ain't as numb as I been thinking — that's if he's making trouble for me with the Dyers. I'll tell you, though, I've had just about had enough."

"Well, Donny Coombs, I'll sure set the record straight if I see any of them. I'll tell them I think they're getting lied to by this Maven fella, but they don't like losing gear, and they ain't the peaceable kind. They'll come down hard on whoever, no matter what. I was you, I'd give them a call direct. Maybe they can settle this thing with Maven for you, fisherman's justice and all."

Bobby reached down for another beer and said, "Off now to live the dream. You ever thought of baiting up a trap with that ugly dog of yours, little King Tut? He might fish real good."

Tut had lain down on the bow but now came up with mention of his name. His lips curled up, the hair on his back bristled. He let down a long, low growl that made Bobby laugh.

"Fucking dog. Reminds me of the old lady."

Bobby put his boat, *Legalized*, in gear and gave it to her, roaring off with a cloud of diesel fumes lingering in the vacated space.

Chapter 18

Shelly stood at the kitchen phone covered in sweat from her run, receiver to her ear. She listened to the fifth ring, the sixth ring, and swore.

Carla looked up from cutting crust off the cucumber sandwiches and turned to the stove to stir the chowder.

Shelly slammed down the receiver.

"No answer. Can you believe he doesn't have voice mail or an answering machine? He doesn't even have a cell phone! How the hell am I supposed to get in touch with him?"

"This gentleman sounds refreshing, if you ask me."

"The definition of hard to get and damned annoying. Keep referring to Donny as a gentleman around my parents, will you, Carla? They don't like him."

"What's not to like?" Carla smiled. "A local boy with no college education, and he works for a living. Sounds solid to me. What does he look like, now that you're so interested?"

"I like his eyes. They smile a lot, and he has laugh lines. He's playing up the naughty-boy image with Dad, which is a bad idea. Other than that, he's wiry and strong and doesn't smell like bait all the time."

"You're not playing him along just to get your father mad?"

"Who, me?"

Carla turned to Shelly, giving her the look she'd known all her life. Carla had been with the family for fifteen years, as long as she could remember. And she'd been a good confidante and sounding board without any of the parenting baggage.

"No, I'm not playing him. Sometimes it feels like he's playing me. But he's the most fun I've had in years of summers. It's not like we're hooking up. He was the perfect gen-

103

tleman in Camden. He wasn't even going to kiss me when he dropped me at the dock. Actually, he seems shy. I had to make the first move."

"Well, maybe he's just not used to Harvard girls showing any interest in him. Ever think of that?"

Shelly didn't want to think about it. She went to the sink, filled a water glass, and gulped the entire thing down.

"Do I have time to shower before lunch?"

"You're really pushing yourself, honey. You don't have to run so hard. This is summer, time to relax."

"If I'm out of shape when I get back to Harvard, I won't keep my seat. You know that, Carla."

"Sure I do. Family tradition. Golden Oar this year. After graduation, the National Team. Then the Olympic boat and a future in finance or law. So where's this lobsterman fit in?"

"You know I like to run — it clears my head."

An hour later, she bounded up the back stairs as Carla organized the silver place settings for lunch.

Shelly came down to the dining room fifteen minutes later. Her parents were discussing the finer points of a letter to support the elevation of Watty and Maisie Perkins from associate to full membership in the Club.

An urn of chowder sat in the middle of the polished table. A plate of quarter sandwiches nestled between the candlesticks. The placemats from Peru were adorned with the family silver, the cloth napkins folded into triangles.

Cornelia was in mid-sentence. "...if there's any fuss. They seem to be perfectly proper. Maybe too few memberships, but they're a marvelous couple and have those two darling children. For heaven's sake, they've been coming up all their lives."

Chase ladled chowder into each of their three bowls.

"Then why haven't they joined the Philadelphia Racquet Club? Do you think they couldn't get in?"

"Don't be silly. They probably don't have the time. You know what it's like raising young children. And it's just not that important to the younger generation."

"I suppose. But according to the *Social Register Observer*, they've jumped through all the social hoops. She was a debutante and came out at the Ritz, and Watson is on the Board of Governors for the Porcellian Club, terribly young for that too. So maybe this is important to them."

"Either way, the Club would be foolish to reject them. We need young blood, with all us grownups about to keel over and die."

Chase helped himself to a sandwich. "Any thoughts on this, Shelly?"

He smiled as he slid the mini-sandwich inside his mouth and bit down, the cucumber popping.

Shelly arranged four little sandwiches into a square on her plate and helped herself to more chowder. She weighed her words, not wanting to arouse her father, given the sensitive subject she wanted to address, but at the same time needing to express her opinion.

"I think they shouldn't even apply. Let the Club come begging to have them. What could they possibly have in common with all the old members and bizarre traditions? You don't even like half these people. So what if you've known them all your life?"

The top of the white wine bottle sweated beads of moisture in the ice bucket. Chase wiped the bottle with his napkin and divided wine among their three glasses.

"In life, you need to weigh the pros and cons. The Club maintains the cohesiveness of the summer community. We are the doers, and we need to pay attention, keep these traditions alive. Lord knows, it's obscenely expensive to keep this house going, the boats in tiptop shape, the memberships up to date, but it's the price you pay for continuity. And the benefits far outweigh the costs."

"Benefits? What benefits?"

Cornelia said, "When the time comes, dear, you'll appreciate the connections and the reassurance of familiarity."

Shelly softened and said, "Well, you might be right. Now can I ask you a question?"

"Certainly, darling," Cornelia said.

"What is it this time?" Chase feigned exasperation.

"Would it be all right if I asked Donny to come over for drinks this evening? Not supper, just cocktails."

She looked into her mother's eyes. Cornelia eased her spoon down beside her chowder bowl and examined it in silence. Shelly watched her face.

Chase broke the silence.

"I think it's a splendid idea. It'll give us a chance to meet him, get to know him a little better. Don't you think so, darling?"

He pushed his plate toward the center of the table and leaned back in his chair. He looked at Cornelia and then turned his attention to Shelly.

"Don't take this as an endorsement, but I think the more we know about this man, the better. I'll agree to have him come over."

"Can't you give him a chance, Daddy? You don't even know him, and you've already made up your mind."

"This is different. Your mother and I agree on this. It's not done. These relationships don't work. You each look at the world so differently that after the initial infatuation, you won't have anything to talk about. You won't agree on a single thing."

"Jesus, Daddy, what do you think is going on here? I go on one date to Camden, and you think we're practically eloping. He's a nice man. He's funny and polite, and I like him. So what?"

"Camden? What date to Camden?"

"Chase, I think this is a bad idea, but I'll go along with it." Cornelia put her palm on Chase's forearm. "Let's see what happens."

She looked at Shelly.

"Obviously, there's only one way to convince you, and that's to let you find out for yourself how hopeless it is."

Chase said, "This should be interesting at the very least."

"Daddy, I expect you to be polite. No sword fighting. And I don't even know if he'll come. He doesn't have any way to leave a message, but I'll try again this afternoon. Thank you, Mummy. I know you'll like him."

Chase slid his chair out and set his napkin beside his empty plate.

"He can't even afford an answering machine. This is a great start!"

Shelly tried again at 3 p.m. The phone rang five times. She was about ready to hang up when Donny picked up.

"Hello?"

"Hi, Donny, this is Shelly."

"You haven't run down south for some sunlight?"

"You aren't the only one who likes the fog. Speaking of which, do you think you can find your way across the bay this evening?"

"Why would I want to do that? I've been out hauling in the soup all day. It's time to crack a few and teach Tut how to talk."

"I thought you might like to come over here for cocktails around five thirty."

"Cocktails? What are cocktails? It sounds wicked fancy. I don't got those kind of clothes."

"Don't be such an asshole. Just take a shower and put on some clean jeans and get your ass over here. My mother and father want to meet you."

"Meet me? Don't you mean your father wants to slap me silly, and your mother wants to watch?"

"Boy, you're a laugh a minute. Will you come or not?"

"Is this a party? How worried do I have to be? They want me to parade around, talk real downeast, eat the shell off the shrimp tail, that kind of thing?"

"You know what? Forget I even asked. I didn't confront both my parents and create a scene at lunch just now to call you and get insulted nonstop. Maybe they're right about different worlds."

Donny laughed.

"What time would you like me to drop by?"

"Your part of the parade is at five thirty."

"Hmm. That doesn't give me much time. Got to pick out an outfit, think of some funny things to say, shower bait out of my teeth, brush my hair."

"That's your way of saying yes?"

"Could be. What about my dog?"

"Mutt and Jeff. Bring Tut along. When we've had our way with you, then we can turn on him."

"I wouldn't advise that. Don't matter none to me, but Tut understands English, and he's wicked sensitive and takes offense real easy."

"Maybe you could just drop him off for drinks. You could pick him up a couple of hours later, be his chauffeur. He and my dad might hit it off."

"I may have to leave him here. I'm not good with competition."

"Just get your ass over here."

"Yes, ma'am."

Chapter 19

Donny went over to the sink and poured out his beer. "Hey, Tut, I've got a date with a college girl and her folks. What the hell am I doing?"

He threw his gummed-up clothes in the hamper and headed to the shower, thinking of the clean things he had to wear. He toweled off, set the alarm for 4:30, lay down naked on the bed, and fell fast asleep.

It took some time to wake up and look good. On the hunt for clean but casual, Donny went through three shirts and two jeans before settling on faded black trousers and a checkered cotton shirt he'd worn twice since Christmas. He brushed dirt off the soles of his newer work boots, the blonde ones, then sprayed them with weatherproof from an aerosol can. He liked the look of his white athletic socks showing above the ankles when he sat down and crossed a leg over a knee. The contrast looked sharp.

Wanting a view of the whole package, he remembered the full-length mirror in the closet, last used by Amy Daniels of the Coastal Builder's Supply on the morning she left and never came back.

He dug it out, rested it against the hall wall, stood back, and took a hard look at himself. He needed a haircut, tuffs of rebellious locks sprouting here and there. He patted them down with the help of spit. Slipping a comb into his back pocket, he lifted the truck keys from the peg.

Tut got off the kitchen chair and started to dance around.

"Not this time, Tut. One of us might piss on the old man's leg. Guard the house."

Tut hung his head low and looked at Donny sideways, like maybe he'd reconsider. Donny scooped some kibble into the empty bowl.

"If I'm not back by tomorrow, the house, boat, and truck are yours."

Donny and *Pot Luck* came out of the fog at 5:30 on the dot. Shelly reached over and got the bowline and cleated her up. Donny looped the stern line over the corner bit, made her fast, then went forward and shut off the engine.

"Hi there, Shelly. Thanks for the invite."

"You look good, in a relaxed Mainer kinda way."

"You won't believe this, but it took me a good fifteen minutes to come up with this outfit."

"That long?"

Donny climbed out of the boat, and Shelly took his hand.

"Just remember, my parents mean well."

"That sounds ominous. You really think this is a good idea?"

Donny stood on the dock, and Shelly had to drag him toward the incline.

"Well, we'll see if it's good, but the idea is to have a drink and a little conversation so they're not worried I'm seeing a monster. No problem."

"For you."

"Just be yourself. After all, I like you, and I'm a really good judge of character."

"I don't think I know how to be anyone else."

They walked up the sweeping lawn to the wraparound porch and into the house through the French doors. Chase and Cornelia, seated in wing-backed chairs in front of the fire, rose as Donny came into the parlor.

Chase took a step toward him with his hand out. He looked Donny over as they converged, took his hand, and stared deeply into Donny's eyes. The handshake was firm and dry. Donny held the gaze.

"Hello, Mr. Payson."

"Donny, allow me to introduce my wife, Cornelia."

"Pleased to meet you, Donny. Welcome to our home."

Cornelia shook his hand. They stood on the hooked rug. Donny waited and then filled the silence with the only thing he could think to say.

"It's a pleasure, Mrs. Payson."

Chase clapped Donny on the shoulder and said, "Let's all go to the kitchen. I've got a marvelous concoction in mind."

Chapter 19

He looked over his shoulder to confirm he was being followed down the waxed wood hallway to the kitchen at the
north end of the house. The destination was a riot of stainless
steel and marble counters.

"Sit, sit."

Chase waved them to the tall stools at the island, and
they sat in a row, Donny flanked by the women.

"Painkillers, straight from Sir Francis Drake Passage in
the British Virgin Islands. They say it's a drinking island with
a sailing problem, and I'd say it's because of these Painkillers.
I do have beer if you'd rather."

"I'll have what you're having, sir."

"Please, call me Chase."

Cornelia lay a soft hand on Donny's arm and said, "And
you can call me Cornelia."

"All right."

Shelly took her palm and ran it up and down Donny's
back. It felt good, but his heart was threatening to pound out
of his chest, and his right knee was bouncing uncontrollably
underneath the counter.

Chase removed four tall glasses from the freezer and set
them on the marble. Then he swung around to retrieve a bottle of Pusser's Rum, some coconut milk, pineapple juice, and
a canister of nutmeg. He stood on the other side of the island,
hands splayed on the marble.

"In the islands, they serve these drinks in various
strengths. The girls will be having number twos. You and I
can handle fives, I'm sure."

He filled the glasses with ice and poured a modest por-
tion of dark rum into the first two, humming as he half-filled
the remaining two glasses.

"Hundred proof, and time-tested by the British Navy.
Good enough for them, good enough for us."

He went to mixing the other ingredients.

Cornelia turned to Donny and said, "Why don't you tell
us about yourself, Donny?"

What's to tell? he thought.

"I guess you know I'm a lobsterman. Been doing it all my
life. My father and grandfather too, but they're both gone
now. I live across the way on Route One. You've been going
by the family homestead for as long as you've been coming
up, on the right as you come down to the beach."

Chase slid drinks around and made himself comfortable on a stool on his side of the counter. Donny took an exploratory sip and wondered why he couldn't taste any alcohol in the drink. He took a bigger sip and resisted the urge to gulp at the thing.

"And you make a good living, as seasonal as the fishery is up here?"

Chase put on a penetrating stare.

"I do okay, considering. This is the tight time, but come fall, I catch my share, enough to carry me through the year."

The thought of his past sideline as a smuggler came unbidden, and he smiled. Shelly squeezed his leg as if to say, nice smile.

Donny had just about finished his drink. Chase, watching, took a fresh glass from the freezer and made another.

"I hear the total landings have been record numbers these last few years, but the boat price is way down."

"You're well-informed, Mr. Payson. Uh, Chase. We're not getting paid much now, and when the lobsters come in strong later in the season, I expect we'll get paid even less. It's an almighty squeeze, and it's hurting some of the new guys."

Shelly squirmed in her seat.

"Let's not talk about lobstering. How about we go back to the sitting room and play a game of hearts?"

Cornelia gathered up her untouched drink and stood.

"Splendid idea. I haven't played in a coon's age." She took Donny's hand and moved down the hall. "But I have to warn you, Donny, I can be a witch when I capture the queen and aim to shoot the moon. You'll have to watch out for me."

Donny wondered what was it with the Payson women and handholding, but he said, "You'll have to remind me how to play. It's been awhile."

Shelly and Chase followed them to the sitting room where they all took seats at the heavy, felt-covered card table in the corner, a dedicated light hanging from the ceiling.

Donny put his drink in the table's built-in glass holder as Shelly leaned over and said, "Watch out for Daddy, too. He can be ruthless."

"Great."

The drink didn't taste like much, but he was feeling a little wobbly.

Chapter 19

Chase took up the cards and shuffled like a pro, set the deck to his right, and Cornelia cut.

Chase dealt out 13 cards to each and said, "Just to refresh, the object is to get the fewest points. You can't lead a heart until one's been played, and any you take in a trick will count against you. There's got to be a metaphor in there someplace."

Cornelia picked up her cards, fanned them out, and began to arrange her hand.

"You don't want to take the queen of spades. She's thirteen points against. Shelly, why don't you describe shooting the moon?"

Shelly explained and Donny recalled. He was feeling good, remembering how he used to play this game with his cousins, being wicked sneaky, shooting the moon more than once and winning big. But they were all younger than him, and this would obviously be harder. He took another sip of his drink and marveled that it was almost gone.

"It's been a long time since I've played any kind of cards. Might take some getting used to."

Shelly set down the two of clubs, and the game began.

Donny took the trick with his only club, the ten. Starting slowly and using the dump strategy, he played his jack of hearts, set them to thinking he didn't get the game.

Chase jumped right on it.

"Can't do that just yet, bub; hearts have got to be played first."

He winked over at Donny, who took it back and set down the three of diamonds.

They played and talked, Cornelia asking about his family.

"I'm about the last in a long line of Coombs. We came over early, being dirt poor in England. Went from farming there to fishing here, did well, and ended up with a good chunk of land along the bay. It's mostly gone now, sold off in pieces over the years. I guess you could say we never hit it big, but we always had food on the table and never wanted for nothing, though we never did want much. I'm the last of the name but got some cousins scattered around New England."

Donny waited for Chase to lead a big club. He took the chance Donny wasn't out and lost the gamble when Donny got rid of the queen of spades. He flashed Chase with a grin;

Chase returned it with a tight, flat smile of his own. Donny got rid of most all his hearts, but had to take a trick of four toward the end.

The queen set Chase back to last place after the first round. The deal passed over to Shelly, and Chase left to refresh their drinks. While he was gone, Shelly's left foot found Donny's shin. He smiled and felt a shiver run down his arm.

Shelly played tight and hardly ever took a trick. She kept quiet and was content to watch Donny interact with her parents, which was going good, so far.

Cornelia asked, "What about your mother?"

"I didn't know her real well. She was from inland, up Millinocket way, and she didn't take to coastal living. She left when I was little and never came back. I heard she went south and died. I was raised by my father and grandfather. I guess her leaving really took it out of Dad. He never remarried, which is why I'm the last of the Coombs line.

"They taught me to fish, and then they both drowned when I was a teenager. They went out together in a winter storm to get the last of their gear and never came back. The boat got found up on the rocks over to North Haven, a total loss. It was a loss all around. I've been on my own ever since. Finished high school in Camden and just kept on fishing. It's all I've ever known. I got no complaints. I don't owe nobody nothing, and until recently the money's been good."

Cornelia penciled in the score and said, "That's such a sad story, Donny."

He was feeling good, at ease with the banter, talking more about his family than he ever had, far more comfortable with these people than he'd anticipated.

"It's all I've ever known, so I got no way to judge. I figure I got it better than most, and I'm thankful for that."

He looked over his hand. The drinks were taking their toll, and he was having a hard time keeping his focus.

When Chase set another fresh one down in front of Donny, Shelly reached for it and poured half into her glass. She shot a warning glance at her father.

"You never wanted to go to college, get a degree?" Chase asked.

"Never seemed that important. I had taxes to pay, and I was making a good living. Had friends that went off to UMO, studied economics, and got jobs. They still didn't make as much as I did fishing. And then I'd have to move away because they ain't many good jobs around here. Never saw the point."

"The point would be to make something of yourself, get ahead in the world."

Chase seemed absorbed in his new hand.

"It's always good to look at what you're doing with your life, see what you've accomplished."

He carefully arranged his cards. Donny watched.

"Daddy, don't get started."

"I never had nothing to prove. I liked my life then, and I like it now."

Donny passed some low cards to Shelly. He felt good. They played another round.

Cornelia laughed as she tallied the final scores.

"Shelly, you won, then me, then Donny. Chase, you take the honors for last place. That was fun."

They all pushed back from the table, and Donny realized he had to concentrate on his movements.

Shelly and Cornelia headed to the kitchen, and Chase motioned for Donny to follow him out to the porch. Donny focused on his steps through the parlor, careful not to bump into any furniture.

Chase shut the French doors and turned on Donny.

"That was fun, huh, Donny?" He sounded like he was mocking his wife. "Fun and games. What I've got to say next has nothing to do with the fact you beat me in there. I want you to end this thing, whatever it is, with Shelly. I forbid you to see her. She's back to college in the fall. I want her to have fun this summer, but she still has to focus on her training for crew. She can't afford to have a fling that derails her plans for the future.

"You seem like a nice guy, reasonably smart, so I'm confident you'll see that this situation has nowhere to go but down. Let her off easy. Tell her it just won't work. Can I count on you to do that?"

Donny wasn't surprised that this was why the Paysons went along with Shelly's grand plan for the evening. Still, he had to sit down on the wicker sofa, rub his chin and gather his wits. He wanted a smoke. He fished a cigarette out of his shirt pocket and lit up. The first drag zapped him good. The tips of his fingers began to tingle, and he felt so swoony that he was glad he was sitting.

"Not having a mother and all, you were obviously never taught that it's polite to ask a homeowner if it's all right to smoke on his porch."

Chase loomed over Donny, but he was way past caring.

"I don't give a shit what you say or think. You and Shelly are over. Consider yourself warned. I assume you're man enough to keep this between us. This is the end of the conversation and your relationship with my daughter."

Chase moved to the door and pulled it shut as he disappeared into the house.

The fog was thick, and Donny could barely see his boat at the float at the end of the lawn. The evening chill was setting in, and he just wanted to be home. What the hell was he doing here anyway, sitting on this big porch, making nice with summer people? The Paysons were no different from the Nelsons. Eliza and Chase made a fine pair of stiff-neck highbrows. With Stanley Maven as shit icing on the cake.

He unsteadily studied the porch furniture and got to planning the steps he'd need to get down across the lawn and into his boat. But he couldn't just split, leaving Shelly to wonder what the hell happened. That got him to thinking about her. Even if her father was an asshole, she seemed okay, headstrong but pretty true blue. Probably more trouble than she was worth, especially at his age.

He was having trouble putting two and two together, so he gave up thinking, time enough for that later. The problem was a smooth exit and getting back to the mainland.

The door opened.

"I was wondering where you went. You and Daddy have a heart to heart?"

"In a manner of speaking. I need to be thinking of getting back, feed Tut, and get up early."

Shelly sat down on the sofa, naked legs folded up, and looped her arm over Donny's shoulder.

"Thanks for coming over. I know it wasn't easy, but it meant a lot to me. And I think Mummy likes you."

Donny lay his arm in her lap. Shelly held his hand.

"Daddy, I'm not so sure. He's really protective, and he has these wild ideas. Don't pay any attention to him. He means well, but he can be a real pain sometimes."

She kissed his cheek.

"Let's go say goodnight to Mummy."

He was steadier on his feet as they went into the kitchen. Chase was gone, and Cornelia was loading the glasses into the dishwasher.

"Mrs. Payson, I'd like to thank you for the cocktails and the game of cards."

Donny was careful with his enunciation.

"You're welcome, Donny. It was a pleasure to meet you. You're a fine young man, and you're welcome here anytime. Do come again."

Her handshake was tight, and he read in her gaze that she meant what she said. For a flash, he thought good cop, bad cop then realized he was in no condition to make any judgments.

"Well, goodbye then."

Shelly threaded her arm into Donny's and led him through the house and down to the dock. She kissed him hard; he in the boat, she on the dock leaning down. She waved as he disappeared into the fog and the darkening night.

Chapter 20

C hase was hefting the spinnaker bag, looking forward to a day of sailing when Shelly popped up and said, "I can't crew for you today, Daddy. I've got plans."

He set down the bag and turned to her.

"I hope you don't make this a habit. I was counting on the two of us taking the June series. You'll be back at Harvard this fall, and I thought we'd take advantage of time alone together. I was really looking forward to it."

"I haven't planned out the summer yet, Daddy, but today I've made a commitment. I'm sure you can get someone to fill in."

"It won't be the same."

🐚🐚🐚

Chase met the two Biddle boys at the float in the early afternoon. They'd come over in an old but pristine 13-foot Boston Whaler with a brand new Evinrude 35-horsepower E-Tec outboard skimming the crests of the waves. Chase smiled, knowing that their kidneys were taking a pounding, but they were oblivious to the discomfort, being so young. He watched Jason at the wheel come in fast, cut her hard, and nestle into the dock, riding up on his own wake and bumping into the side fenders.

His younger brother Winthrop said, "Good afternoon, Mr. Payson. Good of you to invite us sailing."

"Don't thank me yet. My daughter says I turn into Captain Bly when I get hold of the tiller. And I'm expecting a lot out of you boys. Remember, there's no substitute for winning."

Chase helped them put the whaler on the pulley line. They loaded a cooler and the spinnaker bag into the Paysons' runabout, and Chase maneuvered out to *Bellwether*, coming in alongside with exaggerated care even though the tender had fenders all around. Winthrop leapt aboard and took the gear from Chase. Jason let the tender tail off the stern of the sailboat.

Even though it was the first race of the season, the Biddle boys, 16 and 18 years old, had been racing all their lives, first with lessons from the yacht club in turnabouts, then the Herreshoff 12-footers. The Biddles owned a Dark Harbor 20, but money was tight this spring of the Great Recession, and they'd opted to leave her on the hard.

The cooler and sail bag got stowed down below. Jason took the hand pump from Chase, cracked the floorboards, slung the tube off the starboard side, and started to pump out the bilge sections. Winthrop went to unfurl the mainsail. Chase unwrapped the jib. All this was done with little talk, which pleased Chase, who was dead serious about winning this first race.

He looked around to make sure all was shipshape. He stepped up onto the cabin roof, uncleated the main halyard, and began hauling up the sail. The wind was light, and the sail flapped gently as it ran up the track. Chase wound the halyard around the winch and cranked it up to the top. The boom came free.

Jason eased the crutch to the deck, and the boom swung lazily side to side. As Winthrop raised the jib, Jason pulled the tender forward and tied it off to the mooring pennant. Chase took the tiller and back-winded the boom, and the sailboat heeled over. The rudder became effective as the water slid under the hull. Jason tossed the mooring lines off the port side and fended off the tender. They were under way.

They were early for the race. Chase wanted to get the team together and practice coming about until it was smooth, sail downwind, set the spinnaker, and jibe a few times.

Once the mechanics of sailing were taken care of, he'd concentrate on their starting strategy. This early in the summer, the fleet was small and the competition light. He expected six boats at the most. He expected to place first.

The wind was from the south, and they heeled over as they headed westward on a port tack toward Dark Harbor

Boat Yard and Cradle Cove. First out, the bay was clean of sails. A lobster boat was coming up the channel from the Ensign Islands. The ferry was halfway to Lincolnville.

Then Chase noticed another lobster boat coming from the mainland pushing up a bold bow spray. As he put his sailboat and new crew through the paces, he kept his head on swivel and noticed, with a pit in his stomach, the other lobster boat pulling up to his dock.

He and Shelly had always been close, and he prided himself in the relationship. But she'd developed a hard head, forging her own way in the world, defining herself away from the family. He regretted her independence, but at the same time he admired the qualities that would carry her into adulthood. He was scared now that her actions might be ruled by a rebellious streak in which she'd act directly opposite to his expressed wishes. And Donny was obviously not paying attention.

He shook off his negativity and concentrated on his little world of wind and sail and other skippers, bent on coming across the starting line upwind on starboard tack ahead of the fleet.

🐚🐚🐚

Pot Luck came across the bay, turned into the ferry's wake. The day was perfectly clear, a nice change from the weeks of drizzle and fog. He'd put off the morning haul due to his fishing date with Shelly, and he felt good. The bait bags were full and all Shelly had to do was watch and learn, not quite a stern nerd, but good company who didn't expect a share of the catch.

He came through Gilkey Harbor and noticed *Bellwether* off to the south. He hadn't mentioned to Shelly his run-in with her father. Maybe she sensed the tension coming off either or both men. Perhaps that was why she'd arranged for them not to meet at the dock.

Shelly hopped aboard *Pot Luck* as she swung by the float.

"Hi there!" she sang as she raised herself on tiptoes and kissed Donny's cheek. She took his hand and traced an "H" and an "i" on his palm that sent a shiver across the back of his scalp.

Donny slipped his arm around her waist and pulled her close and kissed her on the lips.

Tut growled.

"No hanky panky, big guy," Shelly said to both of them.

"All serious business," Donny said. "I am the Captain, and that makes me the law on the boat."

"Do I have to abandon ship already?"

"Walk the plank, you mean?"

"How about we catch some lobster, and I take home an offering to Mummy and Daddy?"

"For some reason, I think it'll take more than that."

Donny retraced his way through Gilkey Harbor and came up on his gear just north of Acre Island. He dressed Shelly in his clean Grundens and taught her how to pry the crabs off the wire mesh, toss them in the crab pails, remove the lobsters, and band the claws before they muckled on and crushed her finger.

They worked the string going south down the line to Lasell Island. The catch was good, over four pounds a trap, mostly keepers. She got the hang of size and how to measure the questionable ones.

"You think it's weird that I love the smell of bait?"

Shelly stabbed a bulging bait bag with the spudger, slipped the tie-off line through the eye, slid the bag into the trap, and tied it off. She was a quick study.

Donny turned the boat to starboard, and she pushed the trap off the rail. Then she let the warp pay out and come taut on the main trap. It was dragged off the stern as if it had a life of its own. Magic.

"You say there's money in this? Maybe I should give up college and buy a boat. Seems a pretty easy way to make a living, outside all day and working in nature."

Donny watched her tuck a strand of hair behind her ear and get some bait juice on her cheek. He removed his right glove to reach over and wipe the gurry off her face.

"Easy today. Good company, gentle breeze, and plenty of lobster. You come out when it's blowing a gale, you just wrote a big check for the bait delivery, and all the lobsters have moved off to Spain. Then you might be thinking an office job and a steady paycheck are the way to go."

He worked the throttle forward. They came up on plane and were off to the next string.

He shouted over the sound of the engine, "And then you get a little older, and your hearing's all shot to hell!"

Shelly raised her voice, "Sounds like whining to me!"

"What's that? What you say?"

Shelly slapped Donny's shoulder.

The last of the day's gear was east of the Ensign Islands, and they had them all hauled by 4:30. The 20 fleet was coming at them from the north, beating into the wind, four racing boats to the west of the channel and two lonely ones coming up the east — behind, bucking the trend and hoping for a fresh breeze to even the score, maybe a little tide action going out now and stronger along the shoreline.

Shelly had the wash-down hose working aft, carrying pieces of shell and chunks of bait out the scuppers. Donny took the boat in close to the shore, out of the way of the sailboats, and he wondered how he could get small enough to be invisible to Chase Payson in *Bellwether* just off the bow, ready to come about in the shallower water and head back out into the channel. *Bellwether* was in the lead.

Shelly didn't seem to notice or care. Donny put *Pot Luck* in neutral to drift with the wind and waves until *Bellwether* came about with a flapping of sails, mast upright for the split second that the boat headed directly into the wind. Then the momentum swung her off, and she heeled over, sails in tight, heading high and clean without a luff in either the main or the jib.

Shelly sat on the stern and watched her father's boat cross in front of *Pot Luck*. All she could see was the starboard topside, a good piece of green bottom paint, and the mast canting away from her. She joined Donny in the pilothouse.

"My father's head should be sticking up just over the toe rail. He likes to sit to the high windward side and watch the main, brace his feet on the lower combing, tiller light in his left hand, right arm along the edge of the waterway. But he's not there. He's chosen to sit on the leeward side, down by the water rushing along the port toe rail with a good view of the jib with an eye on the competition. He's avoiding us."

Donny put his boat in gear and motored up the bay.

He said, "Avoiding us and putting off the next fight."

Chapter
21

The Western Jetty was the Tarratine Yacht Club, nestled in the hollow of Ames Cove, the hub of Dark Harbor boating activity. To the north was Pendleton Yacht Yard, set deep in a shallow, muddy nook. Farther out along the curving land were summer cottages on water's edge, each with sweeping lawns spilling to pier and dock and American flags flying on stout, white, wooden masts.

The Yacht Club, with its luncheon facilities, was the favored gathering spot for the members, some straight from the tennis courts collecting their little children fresh from sailing lessons. A few of the hardier kids, now wrapped in big bath towels, had been swimming in the abominably cold water and left footprints on the sunbaked brown paint on the deck of the floats.

Five floats hung out from the long wooden pier, their southern sides open for club members to dock and the northerly leeward sides jammed with outboard runabouts up to 13 feet long. The dinghy dock, immediately to the right down the incline, was packed with little tenders rowed out to the thirty boats on moorings clogging the entrance to this protected enclave.

And protected it was. Nonmembers were prohibited from trespassing on the property. Members tying up to the floats faced time constraints. These rules and others made some sense for the Islesboro members, but they put members that lived on the smaller islands at a severe disadvantage.

It was once said that the son of a longtime Acre Island member was singled out by name in the annual report as a flagrant violator of the tie-up rule. The governing committee was dead serious, and the rules were enforced to keep transient nonmember riffraff from coming ashore onto these hallowed facilities.

Even members without servants could handle a light breakfast, but a home-cooked lunch could be downright inconvenient, interrupting the natural flow of a summer day, especially with the preparation and cleanup. Many members made a midday trip to the Western Jetty a routine ritual. The cost, though high, was invisible until the monthly tally came in the mail. Everything was ordered on a slip of paper and paid for with a chit: hamburgers, chowder, salads, chocolate pie for dessert, with maybe two beers, all in preparation for an afternoon nap.

And who didn't need a nap after a big, boozy lunch? The kids were well fed and safe with the nanny, and tennis with old friends was brutal. After all, it was summer.

The crowd, flush from the tennis courts, was tanned and dressed in whites. The less adventurous or enthusiastically energetic wore brick-colored trousers, polo shirts, and sockless boat shoes, a cable-knit sweater draped around the neck, arms tied loosely against the chill on the wrap-around porch in the shade, with a freshening breeze from the south.

The mood was informal and family friendly to a point. The round tables sat groups of grownups, with the children segregated at their own tables, perhaps with a mother's helper or Central American nanny. The early hour was assigned to members with children in order not to disturb the peace and serenity of the late diners. Anyone who violated this unspoken tradition with children making a fuss later in the lunch hour received a stern look from the matriarchs and patriarchs, and they might even be reminded later of proper etiquette.

Old friends up for the season met here. Grown children visited their parents for a week or two on vacation from insurance underwriting in Boston, teaching law and business at Cambridge and New Haven, or investment banking in Manhattan. But many of their wives came up for the whole summer, and the children roamed the island and the bays in overpowered Boston Whalers and Edgewater center consoles.

Because this was the maritime center of the Club, picnics were often planned and launched from here, perhaps a flotilla of power craft packed with coolers and sunblock and swim trunks and children in neversinks, all set to venture into the east bay, perhaps to Compass Island to rendezvous with an enthusiastic sailor or two who had left an hour earlier.

Shelly kicked off her boots and wiggled out of her borrowed bibs and hung them on the peg, her liberated legs bare and tempting.

They'd hauled all morning, and she convinced him to get a quick bite at the club. What was he thinking? He was starting to suspect that he couldn't think at all with this girl around.

They'd hosed down the boat, and *Pot Luck* was as clean as she got on short notice, as presentable as he was, if not more.

They came into the Western Jetty idling underneath the summer cottages that dominated the shoreline. He didn't want his wake to upset the little fleet of darling turnabout sailboats off his starboard bow. It was a concession he seldom gave to the summer folk, but seeing as he would be lunching with them, he thought it only prudent. And he was clearly within view of the yacht club lunch crowd. Fear also held him back. He toed out of his boots and hung up his bibs and changed shirts.

His father had been involved with mainland summer people as a caretaker. He'd once been invited to the dinner table of an employer but had declined. His father didn't believe that it was his place to accept such an invitation. Privately, he allowed that the rich folk "used me good." And good could mean good or bad depending on the situation.

For his part, Donny wasn't as concerned about his station in life as was his father, and he didn't see anything to be gained with Shelly by pressing the issue. In all her innocence, he knew that she saw nothing confrontational about him dining at the Yacht Club.

Donny came in smartly with a manly display of boatmanship, turned a sharp 180 degrees in close to the shore, tide half-high and coming, and skirted the rocks under the overhanging porch filled with summer people dressed in seersucker and khaki shorts staring at the old, wooden fishing boat approaching the Club. He flung her in reverse, goosed the engine, and nestled *Pot Luck* up against the side of the dock. Shelly fastened the bowline to the cleats, Donny the stern.

Tut wanted to come off the boat, probably figuring he had as much right as Donny. He was standing on his taut hind end, front feet up on the combing, head canting to the side as if asking for permission to disembark and terrorize all these intruders. A group of towel-clad teenage girls walked by, and when he growled at them, they giggled.

"Shut up, Tut! Get down and stay on the damned boat!"

Tut grudgingly left his post, hopped up on the dash-board, and continued growling from his perch.

They came up the pier hand in hand.

Shelly said, "This'll be fun. Just follow my lead. I'm the Captain here."

"Fun? If this is fun, I must be ready for Augusta Mental Health."

Donny slowed his pace, and Shelly looped her arm in his and pulled him along. He was beginning to feel like a banded short lobster in the tank with unbanded selects.

Feeling meek, Donny followed Shelly along the suspended wooden walkway and up the stairs to the dining porch, half-full of members. She walked them past the tables, greeting people as they went, and tried to sit him at a table close to the end. But he finally resisted her, moving to the absolute last table where he could have his back to the wall. They staked a claim with their caps and sunglasses.

"C'mon, let's order."

She took his hand again and led him through the slapping screen door into a single large room with photos of past commodores and race-series winners arranged on the white-painted wooden walls. Back to the right was a counter. Shelly took a chit from a wicker basket and filled out what they wanted for lunch without consulting him.

"Don't I get a say?"

"No."

She signed her father's name at the top of the order form. She got two Heinekens from the fridge in the little closet and handed him one.

"You might need this," she said with a smile.

Donny sat back down at their table and took a long haul on his beer. He looked out across the floats and fancy boats on moorings to the horizon of Seven Hundred Acre Island with the mainland in the distance. It was a pristine sight, perfect Maine, with ripples on the water and white wakes trailing motorboats coming in for lunch or yachty experiences, stuff he knew nothing about. *Pot Luck*, with its nice, clean lines and Tut nudged up on the dash staring right at him, made Donny long to escape to something familiar.

As they waited for the food, Shelly talked of the tennis, sailing, and golf lessons she'd had since she was a little girl.

Donny thought of what he'd been up to in those precise years, all spent just over the islands on the mainland to the west. He'd given up the skiff and lobstering by hand and moved to a 21-foot inboard. He'd been able to haul more traps — and more bales of Jamaican marijuana — from out at the mouth of the bay.

He'd put a lot of money aside and quit before the authorities turned their attention from Florida to the Maine coast. He'd never worried about money since, something he figured he had in common with the people sitting around him.

Shelly's name came over the speaker, and she jumped up to get their order. Since they'd arrived, the tables had filled with families with young children, mostly all fair skinned and light haired. He couldn't help smiling over the good-natured banter among the kids. Donny recognized the easygoing freedom of being with your own kind.

Shelly brought a salad for herself and a cheeseburger for him.

"Good choice," he said and meant it.

Boats came in with people in burnt-orange cargo shorts and colorful T-shirts that had names of exotic places on their backs. Every boater who passed *Pot Luck* stopped and stared at her and then backed away when Tut came lunging towards the waterway, all snarl and bared teeth. Some turned and spoke to the others. He didn't think for a moment they were words of admiration.

A woman in tennis whites stood at the entrance of the grand room with a sign suggesting that all the girls gather at the big eating table to discuss and plan the summer's girls tea.

Donny leaned over. "What's girls tea?"

"They put the tea party idea together when I was little. We were all complaining there was never anything to do. One mother thought of a tea party for the little girls where we could all get dressed up and do it fancy. It turned into an annual event. The first girls, like me, are now in college."

They finished up lunch and drank the last of their beer as a man lay out a wet sail to dry on the inner float.

Shelly got into a conversation with a good-looking mother with dynamite legs at the next table. He watched Shelly and felt a ping under his breastbone. He liked the blonde hair tucked behind her left ear, all soft with peach fuzz. Shelly turned and introduced him, but he was captivated by her crooked front teeth. He wanted to kiss her, so he had to struggle back to the conversation.

He stood and shook the woman's hand, their eyes catching with a little search.

Donny smiled and said, "Pleased to meet you," then sat back down.

A dark-green Hinckley picnic boat came in. While trying to turn and land at the float just forward of *Pot Luck*, the guy didn't judge it right and cut too close. He banged gently up against *Pot Luck*, but rugged *Pot Luck* wasn't at all bothered. Tut came like a rocket off the dash, jumped up on the waterway, ran to the bow, snarled through bared teeth, and followed along as close as he could get without jumping into the water.

The boat backed off and tried again, finally docking. The operator made a careful inspection of his stern, getting down on his knees and rubbing his hand over the fiberglass. He didn't look pleased.

The guy lunged across the bridge between the floats and stopped at *Pot Luck*. When he looked at her stem to stern, he got a foul reaction from Tut. The boater backed off, and Donny could tell Tut was getting yelled at as the guy stormed up the incline. He came up the steps, a young balding guy in a blue-and-white pinstriped shirt with little puckers, yellow shorts, and a nautical belt. He was all bent out of shape, his face flushed as if he had a wicked sunburn.

On the top step to the porch, he called out, "Does anybody know who owns that dog and that lobster boat?"

Donny thought the guy might be about to apologize for the minor crash, but he was mad and looked more like trouble. Donny waited and watched.

"I want to know who put that boat there."

He glared around the porch at the members, who had their heads down, embarrassed by the scene.

Finally, Donny stood up and said, "That would be me. What can I do for you?"

Shelly rose as the man came over, chest puffed out, and got in his way.

"Hi, David, nice to see you again. Are you up for the summer?"

She stuck her hand out, and he took it reluctantly, glancing over at Donny.

"A boat like that shouldn't be here. It's too shallow. It should be out on a further float where the water is deeper. It's a hazard to navigation."

Donny scratched his chin.

"My boat draws three and a half feet," he said quietly, "and last I figured, the tide is coming. There's plenty of water there."

"Oh yeah? Well, who are you and what are you doing here?"

"My name is Donny Coombs." He waited, aware that the whole porch had become an audience. "I suppose you could say I'm a lunch guest here."

Shelly put a hand on David's chest and said, "Do you think you can calm down, David? Why don't you join us, so we can talk this out?"

"I don't want to join you and talk it out."

He pivoted and stormed off.

Donny sat back down and said, "That went well."

Shelly laid a hand on Donny's forearm.

"David's proud of his new boat. I guess he's just getting used to it. Let's get out of here."

Tut went all aflutter, his knob tail going berserk. Shelly untied the bow and stern and came aboard. She came right up to Donny, took his cheeks in her hands, and kissed him, long and hard. She stood close at his side by the helm as they headed out feeling as if they were leaving a scene, dodging out of trouble for now.

Chapter 22

The morning came in with a blanket of bright white light, the sun coming off the horizon and pushing brilliance through the thick cloak of fog. Sounds carried sharply through the damp, chill dawn. The birds in the thick cedars blasted out a symphony of little punctuations in various pitches and then flitted off to another tree, ghosts at the edge of sight.

Tut and Donny pulled the pickup down to the pier, turned off the engine, and listened through the open side windows. Several of the gang had beat them to the docks, and their voices carried clearly in the silence through the fog from invisible boats on their moorings. A distant foghorn blast came off the bay, three seconds long, a freighter coming up from the ocean and heading to Mack Point, the deepwater cargo terminal at the head of the bay.

Higher now, the sun battled to burn off the fog from the water's surface and the edges of land. The sky directly overhead was bluing up, and the day held some promise, though fog had never bothered any man who worked on the water.

Except when somewhere out there, under the cover of fog, someone was hauling someone else's gear, cutting traps down to North Haven. Stanley Maven continued to ignore the messages Donny was sending him.

Messages. It seemed to Donny that they were flying through his life, some subtle and some blatant. The Nelsons would clean up and clear out his yard whether he liked it or not. Stanley wanted Donny's fishing spots and wasn't backing down. Chase Payson wanted him to call it off with Shelly. Some numb nut had bumped his boat and practically challenged him to a duel.

Chapter 22

This was as much pressure as he'd ever come across, mucking up an otherwise fine summer. He wished it would all go away and leave him alone. He kept waiting for it to do just that. If it didn't, he'd have to make some moves which he didn't care to contemplate, let alone carry out.

Tut stood on the forward seat of the punt as they rowed out to *Pot Luck*. They fished through the morning and Donny got lost in the repetition, trap after trap breaking the surface, each with its own flash of promise and, more often than not, fulfillment. He was into the lobsters big-time, and the barrel was filling up good.

The fog had burned off some by mid-morning as he was hauling in past Dark Harbor. A residual mist clung to the island edges, still leaving an indistinct horizon down to Mark and Lasell islands.

Donny circled around a buoy to hook the warp with his gaff, then ran the line through the Davy, curled it around the hauler, and brought the line up taut, spooling at his feet as the trap came up. He concentrated on the water and didn't see or hear the boat approaching on his port side.

Donny jumped when Tut barked and turned quickly, trap forgotten. Chase Payson stood in his Mako, behind the console, one hand on the wheel and the other on the throttle. He was bright yellow in his slicker, which made a nice contrast to his red face and gray hair.

Donny turned to the trap and set it on the rail, slowing his motions so he had time to think.

The Mako came around to his starboard side, and Payson shut off the outboard. Donny did the same, and they drifted together in the quiet.

"Good morning, Mr. Payson."

Donny put a foot up on the rail and leaned on his knee.

"There's precious little good about it, as far as I'm concerned."

Payson came to the edge of his smaller boat and looked like he wanted to come right across the water. It was ugly already. Donny waited. The two men locked gazes.

"I will talk and, you will listen, Mister. I'm going to tell you how it is. I'll not stand for you throwing this in my face. Shelly will not come on your boat ever again, and she won't invite you to any more lunches. That's all over and done with.

"I don't know what angle you're playing at here, but whatever it is, it won't work. You go back to your life, and leave us alone. I'm not in the habit of repeating myself."

Donny clenched his fists and kept one eye on Tut, who looked like he'd happily rip Payson's throat out for him. This high-and-mighty summer dipshit might own half of downtown Manhattan for all he knew, but he was out of his frigging mind if he thought he could push Donny around.

Payson might be wrong about how things were going to turn out, but he sure was serious. Small patches of white spittle were forming at the corners of his mouth, and his face was getting redder.

"Are you listening to me? Am I making myself crystal clear?"

"Yes, you're some clear, Mr. Payson. But I don't know what difference it'll make. I ain't working no angle. You might think you can push me around, and like you've got Shelly's best interest at heart, but that don't change nothing."

Payson seemed to collect himself and then decided on a different tack.

"If it's money you want, I'm prepared to give you cash to disappear. How does five thousand bucks sound? Will that make you go away? Or are you playing it out for more money?"

Tut's ears were flat against his head. His tail was deadly still. He almost seemed to be judging if he could jump from one boat to the other as he stood with sea legs on the stern.

Donny straightened up.

"I can take a lot of insults, Mr. Payson, but you've got some nerve. Fact is, your daughter is one fine girl. She shows a lot more class than you're displaying here. Must get that from her mother. You wanna put your money where your mouth is? I'll take a million dollars. In twenties. Otherwise, if Shelly wants to see me some more, that's her business, and trying to run me off like this ain't gonna stop her. Or me neither."

Payson folded his arms and turned quiet.

"You have no idea the kind of trouble I can make for you, Donny. You best heed my warning, or there'll be real consequences for you. You can take that to the bank. I've said my piece. I'll not warn you again."

He turned the key, and the outboards came to life. He gave her full throttle, cut the wheel hard, and raced off to the north toward his cottage. Donny and Tut watched as he receded into the mist, a line of wake trailing after the diminishing boat.

"Numb fuck."

Donny returned to his trap and scaled an urchin back into the water.

Chapter
23

In shorts, tank top, flip-flops, and a backpack, Shelly rode her bike up to the ferry in the sunshine and came across on the one-thirty boat. She pedaled up Route One and was at Donny's door at ten to two. His boat was still out of the harbor, so her timing was perfect, just right to hang the Tibetan prayer flags along the front porch, dress up the shabby house with a little color, more for decoration than from religious conviction.

She stood back and watched the red, blue, and yellow patches of cloth flutter in the wind and then thought the yard could stand some attention.

She found the mower and gas in the garage, checked the oil, topped off the tank, and it started on the second pull. A miracle. It took her forty-five minutes to circle the house and bring the lawn into submission. She thought it could use some sod or seed in places, not like the flat and even family lawns she'd help mow as a youngster directed by the gardener Miguel, a secret from her father, who was worried about her toes. She'd often conspired with Carla and Miguel to do what was not allowed. By the time she was done, she was covered in sweat and needed a beer.

She found one in the refrigerator, noticing it was clean and well stocked. The kitchen was tidy and the house generally picked up. No feminine touch, but orderly and comfy in a bachelor kind of way.

She hazarded a glance at the bedroom on the ground floor. A comforter had been floated flat across the bed, and it was cool in the room on the shady side of the house. Tut had a bed on the floor by the side table. A novel by Reginald Hill lay upside down and cracked half through under the lamp.

Chapter 23

She took a kitchen chair out to the porch, sat, tilted back against the side of the house, and propped her feet on the rail. She was all settled back enjoying the lawn and her can of Bud when Donny's red truck pulled in the driveway.

He and Tut looked over through the passenger window. Tut wasn't growling, and Donny was at a loss for words, her sitting there right at home.

She raised her beer and nodded her head.

Tut went through the window, landed with a thump and a grunt, and ran up the steps with his stiff gait. Donny opened his side and leaned over the back of the truck.

"Come on over," she said. "Make yourself at home."

He looked over the lawn.

"You had time to do the laundry yet?"

"Woman's work is never done. It was next on my list, unless you have other plans for me."

Donny plucked the cooler out of the truck and came onto the porch.

She said, "Grab a kitchen chair, and come out and join your dog and me."

He did just that, tilting back beside her as Tut splayed out flat at the top of the steps. Donny took a gulp of beer and looked up at the flags.

"Nice touch. You moving in?"

"Not today, but I thought we could go out tonight, do something fun."

Shelly rested her cool hand on his forearm, and it gave him a chill.

"Fun would be nice."

They drank beer and watched the cars drive up and down Route One, mostly summer traffic.

"Good fishing?" she asked.

"Fishing was real good. Came across your father out there in the bay. We had a chat."

"Anything I should know about?"

"You happened to be the topic. You and me, actually."

"Don't imagine it was a pleasant conversation."

"You could say there was some tension. He seems to think that us seeing each other isn't such a good idea and wants it to end."

"He's said the same to me."

"You don't like taking his advice?"

135

"Actually, I'm inclined to do the opposite."

"So, are you making some kind of point by being here? Am I just something to bait your father with, feed your rebellious nature?"

"No."

Shelly smiled, and Donny looked at those crooked front teeth. He leaned over and kissed her, leaned back, and took another sip of beer.

"According to things said, you could bring me a heap of trouble. I don't know if I can stand much more trouble in my life."

"I'll hold your hand."

"You Payson women sure do like to hold hands."

"That's because the men in our lives need handholding."

He said, "This can be like a test, see if my definition of fun matches yours. They could be totally different, seeing as we come from different worlds."

"Let's give it a shot. What are you thinking?"

"Pretty much bowling and drinking."

"I'm not sure about bowling. I've always been scared of wrenching my arm out of the socket if I didn't get my fingers out of those little holes."

"Then you ain't got nothing to worry about. This here's candlepin bowling — small balls you hold in the palm of your hand and ten skinny pins. My grandmother taught me how, and she was real good."

"I'm at your disposal. You're the boss."

"Somehow I think that's an overstatement."

"You can hold my hand, how does that sound?"

"Dangerous."

They sat on the porch and drank beer, and he asked about her rowing and her plans after college. Shelly said she was good with a single oar, and that had gotten her into Harvard, her grades good but not great. She didn't quite know about the future but would take it as it came.

He said, "If we do these fun things, that puts you here after the ferry's done for the day. I'd have to run you and your bike across the bay tonight, but it wouldn't be no trouble."

"You're already thinking of getting rid of me? Let's see how it goes. If the weather gets shitty, or the fog comes back in, then maybe I could get stranded on the mainland. I'm old enough to stay out at night. Of course, I'd have to call home and tell my mother that I'm okay."

"Does your father like to run the boat at night, shotgun cradled in his arms?"

"It won't come to that. He might offer to come get me, but I can tell him not to bother."

"Just the news he wants to hear, I bet."

"Let's play it by ear. You mind if I use your shower?"

"You sit tight while I gentrify the place. I'm not used to female company."

Donny left Shelly and Tut on the porch.

"She's all yours," he said when he came back out to the porch.

Shelly was sitting on the deck rubbing Tut's stomach, the little terror flat on his back with his tongue hanging out, best he'd ever been treated.

"Normally, Tut doesn't take kindly to having his undersides rubbed, not even by me. You seem to have a way with him."

"I like pizzazz. He knows I appreciate him."

She boosted herself up. Tut turned his head and looked like he was shocked the good times had come to an end.

🐚🐚🐚

Donny thought the good times might just be starting as he listened to the shower water run and thought of Shelly naked and soapy in his bathroom. It was a stirring thought tempered by a niggling apprehension. Her father's words came back, and he wondered about how bad an idea this could be. What was the worst that could happen? Pretty bad, he figured.

He peeled the comforter off the bed, dug some clean sheets out of the closet, and quickly remade the bed, putting on fresh pillowcases.

Donny was sitting on the bed when Shelly came out of the bathroom in a short, light-blue sundress with skinny straps and her wet hair pulled back, stunning without any effort beyond who she was. Donny felt a hiccup jump in his chest.

"You sure clean up nice."

"Oh, what the hell."

She sat down on his lap, put her arms around his neck, and kissed him deep and soft, full attention on his lips. It took his breath away. He held her close, and she rested her head on his shoulder.

She said, "You smell nice."

"In a I've-been-fishing-all-morning kind of way?"

"No, in a manly kind of way."

"Well, you best pop off my lap before I get any more excited. I'll freshen up, and we'll head up to Darby's for supper. Then I'll show you how to bowl."

"Promises, promises."

"And you best call your folks and let them in on your plans. I don't think I want to take you back tonight, and we don't need some SWAT team busting in to free the hostage, middle of the night."

Shelly made the call and talked in hush tones into the receiver, hung up and said it was all set, no problem.

Donny took the keys off the peg by the door.

"For some reason, that sounds a bit optimistic."

They left the house and hopped up into the pickup.

"I like your truck," she said. "You don't often see a full seat all the way across."

Shelly lifted Tut across her lap, slid into the middle, set Tut next to the window on the passenger side, and nestled in close to Donny.

They sat at the bar at Darby's, and Donny was proud to introduce Shelly around to the people he knew, which seemed to be most of the customers in the restaurant. They kept the drinking down but the banter up and left in a gale of laughter at a joke that Jerry Darby told them.

Donny had his hands full at the bowling alley. Shelly was new to the game, but she had hand-eye coordination and was smooth on her feet. They were neck and neck until Donny ended the third string with a spare and a strike and tacked on nine pins to finish off. He enjoyed tossing the ball down the lane, but he enjoyed even more watching Shelly's bare legs take her to the line and bend her down to release the ball so low to the wood he could hardly hear the ball fall.

They got back to his driveway a little before ten.

"This is wicked late for me. Especially in the summer when I have such an early start in the morning."

"Maybe you could go in late tomorrow."

"Play it by ear."

The tension finally overcame them and they were on each other as soon as they got through the door. Donny picked her up and carried her to the bedroom. They stripped each other naked. She was smooth and soft, tight with muscle, and had a bikini tan. They fell hungrily under the covers, marveling at the wide expanse of skin on skin.

Donny raised his head and said, "Hold on now. I've got some condoms in the medicine cabinet."

"Oh yeah? How old are they?"

"Old enough."

"Don't need them. All taken care of."

Tut sat on the floor beside the bed and stared at them.

Shelly said, "Turn your head, Tut," then lay out on her back and pulled Donny on top of her.

"Nice and easy, big guy. Yes, just like that, not so deep yet, just right, oh yes, just right, just like that."

She looked into his eyes as he moved deeper and deeper inside.

Shelly reached down and touched herself with her middle finger, looking in his eye. He tore away his gaze to look down at her blonde hair on the pillow, her breasts and her belly heaving, and him sliding inside of her. He cupped her ass with one hand and pulled her up. Shelly's nipples went tight and hard, and her breasts rolled as he went deeper. Shelly moaned and bucked and rose to meet him with naked need and dug her fingernails into his fleshy side. Then she went rigid and flushed up from her chest to her neck and her cheeks. She came in rolling waves crashing across her, went rigid again, and then bent until she snapped at the tender edge, fell back filmed in sweat, and wrapped her legs around Donny's waist.

Donny came with thrusts that reminded him of the water pump on the well dug by his grandfather — pump, gush, pump, gush, emptying into her, swollen, with chills running along the back of his scalp and down his spine to his tensed ass and calves. He collapsed onto her, skin slick and slippery. He lost his breath and had to take in greedy gulps of air in gasping little jerks.

Shelly hugged him close so he couldn't pull away too fast, and they felt their hearts pounding together. Shelly let go a peel of laughter.

"Holy fuck, Donny."

She hugged him closer, and he settled his face into her sweaty neck.

Tut took the calm as a sign and leapt onto the bed and curled up.

They fell asleep like that. Donny woke up in the middle of the night with Shelly in his arms and Tut pressed against his side. He put his nose into Shelly's hair and fell back asleep.

Chapter 24

The bedroom started to lighten up at 4:30 a.m. Tut moved into the small gap between Shelly and Donny, wedging himself in upside down, legs in the air. He sighed and grunted and started to snore.

"Fisherman's hours, oh my God!"

Shelly tried to pull the covers up to her chin, but had to yank because they were anchored by the dog. She pulled on the comforter, and the dog scooted along. She rolled onto her side, facing her new men. Her hand smoothed Donny's hair out of his face.

He said, "Good morning."

"Do we have a plan?" she asked.

"Let's get married."

"How about we play it again, Sam?"

"The name's Donny."

"Donny, then."

Shelly turned on her back and stretched flat, arms to the headboard. "I guess we could take it slow."

"Slow is good. Like going back to sleep? I figure the lobsters can wait until you're back in the bosom of your family."

Shelly pulled the sheet down to her waist.

"Like this bosom?"

Donny reached over Tut and circled her nipple with his warm fingers.

"Yes. I like it very much."

"You better."

"Tut, get off the bed."

Donny slipped his hand underneath the dog and eased him to the floor. Tut growled, but settled back down on his blanket after digging himself a nook in the fabric.

The lovers went at it again, more slowly this time, Shelly flipped on top, the sheet draped over her shoulders.

As they got going, Donny couldn't help but wonder, yet again, how deep a hole he was digging for himself. But soon the sensations of being so close to this lovely girl took over, and he lost himself in her. They finished in a breathless heap of twisted covers, asheen with sweat. She fell on him, and he hugged her close as they caught their wind.

She whispered in his ear, "Was that breakfast, or do you have some food for your guests?"

"Food? What's food?"

They luxuriated and slept again, Tut snoring away contentedly.

Shelly showered, and Donny cooked up some bacon and eggs, toasted some bread, and filled two glasses of cold milk. They ate at the Formica table and looked out through the kitchen window to the Nelson mansion.

"You ever wash your windows? Or are you trying to deny the existence of your neighbors?"

"Actually, I think they prefer my windows dirty so they can deny my existence."

Donny crunched toast and told her about how it was going with the Nelsons. Tut got a piece of crust.

"So, you're an impediment to their Maine experience?"

"Maybe I should suggest they buy my place for protection."

"How much would you sell it for?"

"A million."

The picture of Shelly's father in the Mako, serious as could be, offering money for his disappearance flashed into Donny's mind, and he had the feeling things were about to get even weirder and more out of control.

"You don't seem to be the type to be bought off."

"No, I'm not."

He felt a wave of sadness. By all accounts he should be elated, but all this trouble was complicating what used to be a simple and easy life. He set his plate on the floor, and Tut went to clean it up. The dog then sat and looked up at Shelly, and that made Donny laugh.

"You better give him your plate if you want to be friends.

"I need to haul two hundred traps today if you'd like to come along."

"I'd like to, but I need to run and lift weights, keep up this marvelous physique."

She lifted her arms into an Atlas pose and flexed. Her shoulders and triceps and biceps had better tone than his own.

He reached over and ran a rough hand over her muscles.

"Nice, in an Amazon kind of way."

"Fuck you, and the dog that came with you."

Shelly stooped to gather the plates from the floor and ran warm water into the sink. She whistled an unfamiliar tune, and Donny wondered if the difference in age would mean they couldn't share their favorite music. The sex was good. Hell, it was great. But...

"You go haul, and I'll go over to the island and work out. I've also got a picnic or something my mother planned today. Give me time to do the family thing; keep the skids greased and all that. How about if I come over tomorrow and wash your windows?"

"Is that what you call it? Oh, real windows."

She cleaned up the kitchen, moving as if she knew the place, gliding in her tank top and shorts and bare feet across the linoleum from the sink to the cabinets with the dishes and the refrigerator with the butter.

Donny sat back, sipped coffee, and felt a rare calm in this domestic bliss. He reached over and turned on the VHF receiver sitting on a shelf, connected by wire to the antenna out on the roof, able to pick up all the chatter coming from the boats in the bay.

A boatyard crew boat was hailing their landing craft, asking about arrival timing. A cruiser tried several times to get hold of the harbormaster in Camden, wondering about space for an overnight at the town dock. There was some back and forth insulting, nothing dirty, from some of the Lincolnville lobster gang.

Donny picked up the mike and depressed the switch. "*Little Rocker, Little Rocker*, this is *Pot Luck*."

"*Pot Luck*, this is *Little Rocker*, switching over to channel 13."

Donny punched in the numbers one and three and put the mike to his mouth.

"Hey, Billy. Leaving anything for me?"

"Donny? I thought you gave up on fishing. Boat's on the mooring, and the day's just about gone."

"By my watch, it's eight twenty in the morning."

"Just what I said. And looks like you got some voodoo spiritual thing going on, them little flags on the porch I seen coming by this morning. Bet you're just finishing up on some chanting and stuff, now that you got religion and all."

"How'd you know anything about that?"

Donny looked over at Shelly's backside as she stood at the sink, arms up with palms together above her head. He laughed into the mike.

"I remembered it from school, if you can believe that."

"I don't remember you going to any school."

"I stood beside you at graduation."

"That was you?"

Shelly came over. She sat across his lap, draped an arm over his shoulder and stuck a finger in his ear. It tickled. Donny tried to brush her away, but she was as persistent as Tut, and he got the shivers. He keyed the mike.

"I'll be out a little later. Something came up, and I got my hands full here."

"Anything got to do with that bike in your yard?"

"You don't miss much."

"Speaking of which, I was talking to our constable, and he told me he was doing his rounds down to the dock around two a.m. and thought he'd seen some activity on your boat. What with her going ashore and all, I thought you should know."

"Well, thanks. Keep the wet side down and stuff a few bugs in my traps, will ya?"

"That's a big ten-four. *Little Rocker* over and out and back to sixteen."

"*Pot Luck* over and out."

She hugged him. "It's all so manly, that talk. Just about drives me crazy."

"You were crazy to begin with."

With the bike tossed in the back of the truck, the three of them made it down to the ferry in time for the nine o'clock boat. Donny and Tut sat in the truck on the pier and watched Shelly wheel the bicycle down the ramp, turn, and wave. There was that thing again, that thing going off inside his chest, a bubble bursting, an internal hiccup — felt like coming down fast on a swing, leaving something of yourself behind. Scary and good at the same time.

"She's something special, Tut. Trouble, sure, but special too."

They rowed out together. The boat rode high on the water line, half fuel and no load, looking normal. Donny tossed Tut onto the boat, climbed aboard, and then tied off the punt. He looked around. Everything seemed right, all the gear in its place.

They'd had some trouble with kids coming onto the boats late at night, messing things up and stealing little stuff. But they'd known who it was and had put the fear of God into them, so it hadn't happened again.

Donny engaged the bilge blower for a couple of minutes and then shut it off. He went to the ignition switch and was about to turn the key to fire her up, but he looked down and saw that one of the engine-box clamps lay open and unhooked. He let the key be. He unlatched the other clamp, lifted the box on its hinges, and looked over the engine, old and rusty, but wicked true and always reliable, the guts good as gold.

But somebody had been in there. The distributor cap was unhooked. One hand on the manifold, he leaned over and looked along the near side of the engine down into the bilge. The fuel line running from the aft tank up to the fuel pump and into the carburetor had been unfastened. The bronze nut, a compression fitting, was loose, and the line was hanging off.

He'd have turned the key, and the starter would've turned over. The fuel pump would've pulled gasoline through the line and spilled it into the bilge. The fumes from the gasoline would've spread out along the frames and planks and engine mounts, ripe for some action. A spark from the distributor, unable to get to the plugs, would've flashed in confined air under the floorboards. It would've been a bomb.

Donny stood up straight and rubbed his head, coming to grips with the sabotage. Depending who'd done it, the outcome could have taken two turns. If Stanley had set it up, he'd know that Donny would either notice the unfastened latch and investigate or open the engine to check the oil first thing in the morning. As such, this was a warning. A pretty blatant warning, sure, but without any real risk of harm because it would've all been discovered, as it was.

But if it'd been rigged by someone who didn't anticipate the habits of a full-time lobsterman and the things he was likely to do, someone like Del Nelson or Chase Payson, then he might have planned for Donny to turn the key and blast himself all over the goddamned harbor.

He thought about Payson coming over during the night. He'd have figured out where Shelly was spending the night and would never try to blow up a boat he knew his daughter might be on. He might be an asshole, but he wouldn't kill her to save her. He could pretty much eliminate Chase.

And he couldn't imagine Del Nelson knowing enough to come out here in the middle of the night and unhook the fuel line, though he wouldn't in all honesty put it past Eliza to hire someone to do it.

Whoever did it, this was a real mess. He went below, took a 9/16ths wrench from the toolbox, and wound the fuel-line nut back onto the carburetor. Then he snapped the distributor cap back on, mopped up what little fuel had wept out the open line, and hit the blower switch for the pump to suck the fumes overboard. He turned the key, and the 318 Chrysler came to life, settling into a smooth idle. Finally, he set the engine box back down, fastened her up, and went fishing.

His next move would have to be something big enough to put a halt to this shit.

Chapter 25

T he East Coast was in the throes of a record-setting heat wave, and Donny was amused how everyone was pining for winter. How soon they forgot about the bitter cold and the fuel bills and the cabin fever. Donny had taken the holiday weekend off and was surprised to feel lonely because Shelly had family commitments on Islesboro and was putting in her time.

The heat continued into Thursday, but the onshore winds fanned the sweat, and it was comfortable on the water.

Fishing had picked up, and Donny was averaging about six pounds per trap. His barrel was full right up by the time he'd hauled the last trap at almost dark. The wind had come up from the north, and it was blowing good.

Darkness had descended by the time he headed back to the harbor. From a mile out, he could barely see the boats on their moorings. He caught a glimpse of something floating off his port bow, a hint of trouble. He slowed *Pot Luck* and went astern to get a better look.

Del was sitting in his varnished rowboat, both hands on the gunnels for support, his poodle sitting in the stern, floating out to sea. No oars were in sight, the pretty little craft falling in the troughs and getting bashed by the crests. Donny brought his boat alongside and put her in neutral.

"Where you headed?"

"No place good. I just about tipped the rowboat over getting off my sailboat, and both oars fell overboard. I was about to dive over and try to swim ashore, tow Alex and the rowboat with the bowline tied around my waist. But I had my doubts, it being this rough and all."

"Ever think about swimming for the oars? I think they float. Safer that way. Don't suppose you want a tow."

"I wouldn't refuse one, no. I'm sure glad you came along."

"You'd of probably ended up blowing right past Lasell and down off Matinicus by morning. Someone woulda seen you unless the fog came in. Then there'd be no telling. There's always the dog you could eat."

They let that thought hang in the air then get blown out across the waves.

"Do you suppose we could put our differences aside?" asked Del.

Alex was sitting in the stern and seemed right at home, looking out at Donny and Tut. Tut wagged his stub and gave a small yelp. Alex yelped back.

"Our dogs get along better than we do. They don't have the urge to push and shove," said Donny.

"Yes, well… "

"You want peace? Didn't we have this discussion once or twice?"

"Once that I can recall."

"Right, but I notice them 'No Trespassing' signs haven't been taken down. Also, you want to come clean about anything? I've been having some trouble lately. You have anything to do with any of it?"

Donny put a boot on the rail and leaned an elbow on his knee, settling into conversation mode as they rode the seas and floated out into the middle of the bay.

"I wouldn't know anything about that, Donny. I'll admit that Eliza can get a bit overenthusiastic, like helping you remove your junk truck, but I assure you we want no trouble and just want to be good neighbors. You know we work awfully hard in the community and only mean the best."

"You keep saying that. So I'm to believe you got nothing to do with any of my boat troubles? Not even with my oak tree dying?"

"Believe what you like."

Del had to raise his voice. He was drifting farther away from *Pot Luck* into the night, carried by the waves and wind.

"I'm telling you the truth."

Donny put the boat in gear and pulled in close.

"Toss me up your bowline."

Del took a couple of throws before Donny could catch the line. He pulled the rowboat alongside and then leaned over and held her off as the waves rocked the boats together. Del set Alex on the rail. When she jumped onto the deck, she and Tut went to sniffing at each other. Del came over the side. Donny tied the line to his stern cleat, and they both went to the helm.

"Thank you very much, Donny."

"It's the code on the water. No matter what, you go to the aid of anyone in trouble. Someday you might be in a bind and need some help yourself. Everyone on the water is his brother's keeper."

"Not like on the shore? Where it's dog eat dog?"

"I don't see much need of that either. There seems to be plenty of room for all of us and no need for minding anybody else's business. You might mention that way of thinking to your wife."

Donny pulled into the dinghy float to drop off his neighbor and his neighbor's dog and boat. Tut looked like he was sorry to see them go.

Donny's parting words were, "Say hi to the missus."

"Thank you again, Donny. Can I offer you some money for your trouble?"

"Thanks, but no. I'm sure you'd do the same for me. All I really want is less trouble all around."

🐚🐚🐚

The next morning, Del came down with a new set of varnished oars. The docks were full of lobster boats. Billy was changing the oil in his engine, and Wally had his hydro-slave hauler apart and in pieces on the dock. The day's first ferry run was leaving the pen. It was a little after eight o'clock, the heat wave finally over and a nice, cool breeze coming in from the south.

Del stopped beside the crane as Donny swung the load out over the pier and lowered the bait down to *Pot Luck*.

He said, "I was wondering if we could do something with the juice that's seeping out of your bait containers."

"What do you have in mind?"

"Well, I thought you might hose down the pier after you finish loading your bait tubs, whatever you call them."

"The containers are called Xactics, and we transfer the bait into trays."

149

"Yes, well, once you have your trays all loaded up, all that juice pooling on the decking makes a mess. It smells really bad, and if you aren't careful and step in it, you get your boat all grimy."

Donny looked down at his boots and then glanced over at Del's boat shoes, tanned legs, and crisp khaki shorts.

"Never gave it much thought."

"Would it be so hard to spray that juice over to the side, maybe even off the pier? It would make the ducks much more attractive. I have houseguests coming down for a sail, and it'd be such an improvement."

Donny scratched his chin.

"I guess that would be all right. There's a faucet over there, but you'd have to get a hose."

"A hose?"

"Yeah, so you could do the spraying."

"Me?"

"Sure. I don't think the guys would mind one bit. You could do it anytime you wanted."

Del hesitated, looking momentarily lost.

"Yes, well, it wasn't exactly what I had in mind. I was kind of thinking you guys could clean up your own mess. You know, hose it down yourselves."

"Not going to happen, not in this lifetime anyway. But feel free to do it yourself — anytime."

Del waited a few beats and then said, "There's another thing. I'd like to bring my boat, *Wild Wing*, into the dock and load her up with supplies. I was under the impression that these floats are for loading and unloading. It looks like you lobstermen are taking up all the space, not adhering to the rules."

"Seeing as you're new to town, Del, let me explain something to you. Several years ago, this pier was rebuilt with lots of state money coming from Augusta. It was built wicked rugged, so the bait truck could back down, and we could bring our pickup trucks down with our gear. The money came to support the fishermen first and the other users of the pier second. You and your boat? Second. It don't mean we can't get along and share the pier, but it does mean we have priority."

Del's face flushed.

He said, "Do you have any idea what my tax bill is?"

"No. I do know that the lobster industry is a major contributor to the Maine economy. Your boat is pretty and all that, and I'm sure those guys down to Rockport Maritime are glad you had them build it, keeping them employed. And I guess the people who come down to the beach like to see a nice-looking sailboat out there on the mooring. But I'd bet good money that what really attracts them to stop and eat a lobster dinner is the sight of lobster boats, indicating that right here is the freshest lobster they'll ever eat. But, hey, I'm about to head out, so there'll be room for your *Wild Thing*. But you might think about the tide. What does she draw? Ten feet?"

"Her name is *Wild Wing*, and she draws eight feet, and I thought the tide was coming in."

"You'd be hard-pressed to get that kind of water just yet. Maybe in an hour or so."

Del shrugged his shoulders and then bucked up and turned to go down the incline. Donny watched him set the new oars in his rowboat and then come back up and leave the pier without another word. Donny finished loading and left to fish.

🐚🐚🐚

Del took his time up at his house cooling off and glad Eliza was out shopping for the day's picnic aboard *Wild Wing*. He gathered a spool of hose and wormed it into the Range Rover. By the time he made it down to the pier, Donny was a speck on the horizon, but the other two were still doing their mechanical duties.

Del said a curt hello and then connected the hose and sprayed down the pier, working the juice off the inside edge. The effort and result calmed him down, and he began to look forward to entertaining his guests, showing off his boat.

At least Donny was right about that. The workers at Rockport Maritime were glad to have him as a customer, what with the million or so he'd plunked down to have his boat built. She was a classic: a W-class sloop designed by the late Joel White, a 47-foot modern-day sailer with sweet sheer and graceful overhangs fore and aft. She was made of wood but constructed the modern way. The details had gone right over

Del's head. He was told that she was light and especially strong.

Del worked the hose back and forth, his mind wandering back to his boat. Down below was good carpentry and a nice coat of varnish, and she slept up to four. It was all a lot more complicated than that. If he took the time, he could go through all the bills to find out. But what really mattered was that she was something special.

She had a carbon-fiber mast that sported acres of Kevlar sails, whatever that meant. Add to that the latest equipment and hardware, and she was a show-stopper.

Del was just getting familiar with the boat and learning how to handle her, and he had to admit, if only to himself, that he was scared of her and felt small to the task, intimidated by her capabilities and his lack of skill. Even bringing her into the dock under power made him sick to his stomach, full of fear he'd put a scrape in her topsides, or worse, look inept, or worst of all, prompt a display of disgust from his wife.

He finished hosing down the pier. Maybe, if he was lucky, he could time his arrival for when the ferry was on the Islesboro side for its lunch break so not too many vehicles were in line for the one o'clock run, and the lobster guys were still out on the bay.

Chapter 26

The lobster-boat races were supposed to start at ten in the morning, so Donny and Shelly got out of bed, early for her and late for him, and gathered together a picnic lunch and some cans and bottles of beer and water for Tut. They steamed out of Lincolnville harbor at eight and headed down the bay for Rockland, the weekend's venue in the summer series of boat races.

It was a lazy, hazy, sticky day with a mist hanging over the islands to the east and the Camden Hills off to starboard. They got down to the lighthouse and the breakwater by nine, no reason to push it, enjoying each other's company with a little touching and feeling going on.

The Coast Guard was handy, the big buoy tender anchored off the end of the breakwater. Donny paralleled *Pot Luck* along the granite that led out to the lighthouse just outside the racecourse, which was empty now but would shortly be the scene of some very fast and loud lobster boats racing down the line.

It was early enough so that they had their pick of spots. Donny tossed the anchor right in the middle, plenty of space and a mud bottom. The hook set nicely as he backed down, and it held fast as the westerly wind blew *Pot Luck*'s stern toward the course. He cut the engine, and they settled in for a morning of entertainment.

Off to their right was a 42-foot Duffy on anchor. He waved over but didn't recognize the family onboard and couldn't see the hail on the stern, so he didn't know where she'd come down from. It could be from anywhere along the coast; these races were a popular gathering spot on weekends, a time to leave the hard work and financial pressures of fishing back at home, get liquored up, and have some fun.

There was as much entertainment among the spectating boats as there was on the course, maybe more. Off to their left was a raft of two big boats out of Vinalhaven, a real fishing island just south of its more gentrified sister island, North Haven. Those out of Vinalhaven took fishing as serious business.

Shelly got out the deck chairs and set them up facing out across the transom. She arranged the cooler at their feet so they'd have a footrest. The sun was coming down hot. She did that magic girl thing and snaked her bikini top up underneath her shirt and tied it off in a way that looked impossible, hardly a bit of flesh exposed. Then she unbuttoned the shirt and shrugged it off, adjusted her top, and put her hair up.

Donny was mesmerized. So was a guy from Vinalhaven, and Donny felt a rush of pride blush over him.

Shelly slid her dark glasses over her nose and sat down in a chair as if she owned the boat. She cracked a Bud and let out a sigh.

"This is nice," she said.

"Yeah, it is," was about all Donny could muster.

She pulled over the dog bowl and poured Tut some water, the two of them acting like best friends and Donny just a little sideshow for them to enjoy. That was okay.

He went to the helm, fetched a pair of binoculars, and then sat down beside his girl. *Pot Luck* swung on her anchor, easy on the water in the light breeze. Donny swigged some beer as they watched the Coast Guard's big, rigid-bottom, orange inflatable come along the empty racecourse.

It looked impressive, what with the 50-caliber machine gun mounted on the bow, the crew of four decked out sharp in dark-blue coveralls, sidearms, orange life vests, and dark glasses. They nodded and Shelly waved. Nice boat with the twin 225-horsepower Honda four strokes, his with the pretty girl.

The spectator masses were filling in, almost all serious fishing boats: Hollands, Duffies, Wesmacs, and hulls from Young Brothers — all of them teeming with friends and family. The fishing gear had been left home, replaced with tables and chairs and coolers and gas grills. Someone upwind was cooking, the smell of charred meat in the air, and Donny got to wanting a sandwich, but he held back and enjoyed his first beer on an empty stomach.

The raft to the south was growing, four boats now, and it looked like the start of a really good party, young guys and gals draped across the pilothouse and sitting on the roof, not a one of them without a beer bottle or a bright-red plastic cup filled with ice and rum and Coke, or milk with coffee brandy.

For some reason, Shelly leaned over and kissed Donny. Tut growled.

Shelly said, "Shut up, shithead."

Tut wagged his stump.

"Donny, do you ever race?"

"Boat's too slow, and I'm too cheap. All these racing boats have at least four times the horsepower *Pot Luck* has."

"So then tell me how you guys name your boats."

"Each name will tell you a little something about the lobsterman. Look over there. A bunch of older family guys who name their boats after their kids: *Kimberly Ann*, *Abigail*, *Carter*, *Nicole Lynn*, *Nicholas Frank*, and *Janice Elaine*.

"Some of us are real cute, like *Pot Luck* with the double meaning.

"Then you got the wise guys: *Knights Mare*, *Sea Cock*, *Shitpoke*, and *She's All Wet*.

"And then come the dreamers: *Moon Dance*, *Misty*, *Odyssea*, *Rich Returns*, *Governor*, *Rising Son*, and *Thunder*.

"And they come from all over: South Thomaston, Owl's Head, Boothbay, Stonington, Deer Isle, Port Clyde, and Cape Jellison."

A 46-foot Wesmac, dry-exhaust stack spewing high-horsepower diesel fumes, grumbled into the line on the right and headed into the wind. The skipper threw an anchor off the side and backed down. Donny could see that the neighbor on the other side was as nervous as he was about the proximity until all the anchor lines stretched out, and the vessels behaved in unison.

The Marine Patrol Protector scooted by.

"Ought to have a John Law race against the orange Coast Guard boat, see if them twin two-twenty-five Mercs can match the Hondas," Donny said, almost to himself.

Shelly laughed, looking over the scene.

"I thought you said times were tough with the boat price down and bait and fuel way up. It doesn't look like hard times to me."

Donny gazed down the line at the boats, working vessels every one, hoses poking out the scuppers and pumping glistening water back into the harbor, big numbers along the aft topsides and the paint worn off amidships under the Davy where the traps rubbed the side raw.

Each pilothouse bristled with antennas and upside-down buoys showing their colors, life rafts, big deck lights for baiting up in the dark, and the radar domes: Furuno, Ray Marine, Garmin, JCR, and Raythcon. They were all the tops of serious working machines, testimony to the value and reward of hard, honest work, the harvesting of a resource known around the world as the best there was — Maine lobster, the finest kind.

Donny admired the fleet, all Maine-built hulls, rounded bows, and graceful sheer with not much freeboard. Ninety percent were glass, only three or four wooden ones like *Pot Luck*, old-fashioned and out of favor, but solid and friendly to fish from.

He said, "This here's an industry celebration and a time to forget the troubles, put the giant squeeze aside."

Donny was impressed by the turnout of his brethren, who all got up early and went out no matter what the weather, fishing hard on their feet all day long. Over the VHF radios came a static rendition of the "Star-Spangled Banner."

The races started up.

Four skiffs came down the course, the outboards pushing them hard and fast, all with teenagers at the tillers reminding the crowd where they'd all started: with a small boat and a few traps.

The *Instigator* committee boat proudly flew a big American flag over Maine's own banner, both snapping wildly as she trailed the contestants in the race. They all blew past and churned up a mess of wake that amplified into wave city, rolling out to thrash the spectators.

The fleet of spectator boats were like a live animal, pulling up and circling around and looking for fresh meat or leaving the fold to head down the line to participate in their heat.

The wind was calm, and the sun was hot. Shelly lay back in her chair absorbing the rays.

A noncontesting lobster boat sped from left to right counter to the course and excited law enforcement. The Coasties and Marine Patrol gunned their massive twin outboards and dashed in pursuit, blue lights flashing and arms waving. The crowd sharpened its attention and in a better-them-than-me attitude watched the action as good as the racing, but it was a disappointment, as the boat was waved off with no one arrested.

The races progressed, each heat boasting larger and more powerful boats roaring down the course, some loud and some with a high-pitched whine coming off the muffled stack, their bows high, their sterns low, and their props digging hard into the water, flat out, wide open, right in the corner.

The neighbor raft was getting rowdy, some serious partying going on. Half-naked young bucks with stern-man tans, white streaks of bare skin where the work-time suspenders sloped on dark backs; scantily clad, blanched-white girls, tipsy from the morning alcohol, sought diversion from their own credit-card debt and their husbands' boat payments and underwater mortgages. They'd tied an inflatable woman to the antenna mast, and she looked good.

Barbecue smells drifted across the water on the wind. A schooner in full sail slid around the lighthouse and out the harbor. A wild guy on a slippery jet ski dug donuts and then rocketed out into open water.

A race went by. Wave city came again and threw the rafted boats against one another like links in a slapping chain, cushioned by great, round, orange mooring balls hung over the side, skippers riding the rails and keeping a hand on the neighbor's boat, making sure the fenders did their job.

Just beyond the near raft was an even bigger bunch of boats called Miss this and Miss that, a raft with a theme. They were tied side by side, but bow to stern, and were a good mix of open and closed transoms, all with large beams and massive deck space for working large numbers of traps — serious money for serious fishing. They were having a big lawn party, tailgating on their investment, little kids mixed in with parents and grandparents. All this was reported to Donny from Shelly's lips moving underneath the black tin-can-sized binoculars.

Donny saw a girl go off the stern of a boat in the middle.

"What's happening now?"

"She's retrieving a Ping-Pong ball. Looks like beer pong. Must be their last ball."

"What's a girl like you know about beer pong?"

"A girl like me?"

"You know, sheltered, innocent, hardly legal to drink."

157

"Ha! I've been watching my parents pickle their livers all my life. And I'll have you know, I had the fastest beer at my boarding school."

"You did not. Maybe white wine, but not good, old, cold beer. Too common for the fancy likes of you."

"Are you always so free to display your lesser qualities? I'll show you, if, that is, you have a church key on this miserable tub you call a boat."

"Coming up."

Donny gave her a light-hearted tap on the head and then went below and rummaged through his miscellaneous box of discarded parts and junk. He found a bunch of stuff he'd forgotten, but down deep at the bottom was a church key.

She took it and demanded a can of beer from the cooler.

"And make it snappy, Skipper."

A boat race blew by.

She turned the can over and dug a neat triangle in the bottom. She carefully brought the inverted can to her mouth, tipped it up, popped the top, and guzzled the contents down in one, two, three seconds. Her lips were foamy, her eyes watered, and she smiled and burped.

Wave city hit. Donny rode it out on sea legs and said, "You've got culture, that's for sure. We might have a future."

"You got a Ping-Pong ball and some cups? You know how to play this game, don't you?"

"Oh sure, Tut and I play it every night just before bed. He sleeps tight, and I sleep sober."

A black 32-foot BHM came out from around the lighthouse. Donny locked right onto it as it grew larger, idling along the line, coming closer, squeezing through the sliver of water between the racecourse and the sterns of the spectator boats.

Donny picked up the binoculars and took in the name, *In The Black*, and saw the captain looking over his compass and out the dirty windshield. The man seemed to catch his eye, and *In The Black* turned and headed straight toward them.

Donny said, "Here comes trouble."

Shelly leaned forward in her chair and shaded her eyes, turning toward where Donny was looking. Tut came out of the shade, hopped up on the transom, and stared at the approaching boat.

Chapter 26

In The Black came in slowly, backed down, and floated just off *Pot Luck*'s stern, close enough almost to step from boat to boat. The captain came out of the pilothouse and approached his port rail, course-grained acne-scarred face covered in stubble. His long, greasy hair came out horizontally from around his stained John Deere cap, brown T-shirt stretched tight around a gut that hung over his belt.

"Well, well, what have we got here?"

The cigarette dangling from the corner of his lip bobbed up and down, his eyes squinting in the smoke. He took it out of his mouth, put a foot on the rail, and leaned on his knee.

"If it ain't Mr. Big Shot with his mongrel runt dog and his summertime whore."

Shelly came right out of her chair, long-neck Bud bottle in her hand. Tut bared his teeth.

Donny set the binoculars down on the cooler.

"You're sure a classy guy, Stanley. I scrape stuff off my boot better than you."

"Ooohhh! That's real clever, but I got a warning for you. You move off my gear, or you lose it, simple as that."

"It's you who's camping on my sets, Stan. Believe me, you want to think long and hard, maybe decide to give up fishing altogether, before you get hurt."

"What did you call me?" Shelly was on her toes. "What exactly did you say?"

Tut turned his head and looked at Shelly.

"I called you a summertime whore."

Shelly wound up and scaled her beer bottle right at Stanley's head, a straightaway fastball, right on the money. It took Stanley by surprise, but he was able to get his forearm up in time to deflect the bottle. It had enough momentum to go right and explode and foam against the starboard combing.

Tut started barking his little-bastard head off. Shelly handed the binoculars to Donny, opened the cooler and took out a beer can. She threw it at a port window, but it bounced off the Plexiglas.

Stanley ducked down, crouched his way to the helm, and gunned it out of there.

Donny stood still, working his fists, staring at Shelly.

The Vinalhaven raft exploded in cheers and shouts, clapping into the air.

Shelly bowed and said, "That went well."

Stanley motored off toward the finish line, joining a couple other Islesboro boats down there.

The races wound down. Some of the boats pulled anchor and headed out. Donny pulled his own anchor, steered out around the lighthouse, and headed into the wind that had come around from the north. Tut stood at the bow with his ears flying in the breeze. Shelly came forward and put her arms around Donny's waist, but his mind was on Stanley and the plan for Monday morning.

Chapter 27

I want you to go down there and give them hell. Somebody with brains really must take charge. You need to stress the value of cleaning up the pier, and get together with Jason from the Whale's Tooth restaurant to tell the committee members that we need to attract boaters into town to spend money at the restaurants and the stores. And I can't believe you let Donny talk you into cleaning up his mess!"

Eliza was on a roll, steaming along with her agenda, pressing hard. Del sat back and tried to keep a lid on this stress. He wanted the same things, but he wasn't inclined to be the pressure cooker that blew its top. While he wanted peace, she wanted him to fight a war. He was achieving successes, small ones to be sure, but measurable progress, gaining a little respect here, a little dignity there, by hosing down the pier, trying to do his part to get along.

Eliza wanted action in big gulps, sweeping decrees from the harbor committee that would immediately and forevermore put the fishermen in their place. She wanted to build on the actions from the Town Meeting, wrestle control of the town from the locals who were ruining the place. She thought they had victory within their grasp.

"I think we should go slowly with these people, sweetheart. We may get more support from those in town who are on the fence. Maybe we can convince the lobstermen, bring them along without pushing so hard."

"You don't understand. This is a contest of wills, and the weakest loses. They'll respect a hard line. And if you'll not stand up to them, then I'll come to the meeting and make our points."

Del didn't have the energy to argue.

161

"Okay, come along, if you insist. Why don't we play it by ear? Judge the mood and then make the decision on how hard we push. Maybe it'll all work out."

The eastern sky at 5:30 lit up in layers of depth, the sun illuminating clouds near and far and in between in rims of neon orange before bursting above the closest cloud bank, climbing into the clear, blue sky. From there, it became so bright that with the reflections off the bay, it looked like a thermonuclear event or a welder's torch, too bright to look at directly. The northerly breeze was crisp and cool, a reprieve from the sultry stillness of the night. The boats on their moorings were silhouettes on the rippled surface, little wind-brushed scalloped dents of water catching the reflections of the sun as if life beneath the surface were swirling, awakening to the day.

The day had promise, but not for the lobstermen. It was Sunday, their day off, but there were preparations to make, especially for the upcoming harbor-committee meeting and the clash of expectations and desires.

Eliza filled Del's coffee cup, sat down, and collected Alex into her lap. She let out a deep sigh.

"Del, honey, you need to find your backbone."

"Don't you think it's a little early for contentious accusations? I'm still working on my second cup of coffee. Can't the assault wait for half an hour?"

"Oh, sweetheart, you're so sensitive. I'm just trying to get you to address the fact that your priorities are all screwed up."

Del felt a sheen of sweat break out across his back and under his chin. He stood and opened the French doors to let the fresh morning coolness into the great room. He was comfortable in his life and really didn't need to make war with the locals. He wanted to be left alone, to take *Wild Wing* out into the bay and learn how she handled, to ignore the coming houseguests and their talk of Deepwater Horizon and the oil disaster in the Gulf, the Republican tsunami coming in November, and the current march to socialism led by the Obama cult.

He wanted to be left alone. He wanted to avoid this conversation with his wife. In fact, he wanted more and more to avoid his wife altogether. But Eliza gathered her bathrobe, crossed her arms underneath her breasts and lit into him.

Chapter 27

"We have allies. But none of this'll work if we don't put up a united front. All this talk of the pier being for the lobstermen is hogwash. You can't ignore three-quarters of the town who want a pretty pier and an attractive harbor. And all you want is to sail your new toy. There are more important things in life. We have the Perkins coming up from Boston next week, and we're trying to get invited to that big party on Key Island. You were going to make inroads into the Tarratine Club on Islesboro. How's that coming?"

New toy? Del tried to gather himself and looked over at his wife and felt a wave of resentment, bordering on disgust. Priorities? He wanted to fling his coffee cup against the picture window. He took a deep breath. A screech of seagull noise came through the screen, and Del cringed at the sound, reminding him of his nerves.

Eliza dropped Alex onto the floor and took her coffee cup to the sink.

"I'm going to do my Pilates, then run on the treadmill. You think about what I said. I'll not be bested by these yokels. Go play with your little boat, but try, *please* try to see the big picture. You tend to lose sight of what's important."

Del was silent and glad to see her go. He did think about what she said. The houseguests. Priorities. The important things in life. He looked through the screen to Donny's dying oak tree. This battle of wills with his new neighbor was taking on mission status with Eliza, and he thought she was losing all rationality. He suspected that the resistance to his wife's gentrification battles was much deeper than she could possibly realize, and there was real trouble brewing. The battle was turning into a war.

He sat back down and tried to find calm. He didn't share Eliza's desire to attend the Key Island party or become a member of the Tarratine Club. He had all the boat in *Wild Wing*. All the money he'd spent on her, and Eliza was calling her his "little boat."

She didn't know it, but his discretionary funds were getting low. *Wild Wing* came in over budget and promised to be a real drain, and he struggled to justify to himself the balance of outlay to pleasure. He was now considering leasing her out to some avid sailor who might want to collect those red Mount Gay sailing caps from the West Indies' sailing extravaganzas — the BVI Heineken and St. Martin Sweetheart regattas.

He'd kept the gathering financial pressures from Eliza. Maybe he should reconsider, bring her down into the realm of reality. But then he'd have to deal with the repercussions, the whining, the recriminations, the temper tantrums, the pitched fits. On the other hand, when she learned about the money troubles, maybe she'd leave him. That too deserved some thought.

He went to his desk in the study, pulled out the latest Harbor Ordinance, and reviewed the issues, looking for some opening. Clearly, the commercial fishermen had a leg up on the priority front, but the town pledged its commitment to public access. There had to be something he could use to drive a wedge. He was as big a taxpayer as anyone, but he was so far back on the waiting list for a mooring he'd had to rent one from the harbormaster, who had a stranglehold on them. With *Wild Wing*'s draft, he was relegated to the outer harbor beyond the three guest moorings where it was less protected and got really rough in a stiff southerly blow.

He could press on the lack of action to provide more dinghy space. It seemed that the people in power had little incentive to make progress on the issue — after all, they had theirs. But there was a groundswell of support by the eating establishments that wanted to encourage water traffic for their restaurant tables. And there were some like-minded pleasure boaters who'd come to town and wanted better access to the water.

Eliza wanted him to propose building a private pier off their shorefront, but given the cost, it was out of the question, to say nothing of the lack of protection.

The 30-year agreement that gave the commercial fishermen top priority for the use of the pier ran out in 2020. Maybe they should just wait for that. Yeah, right. Eliza would mate Alex with Tut before she'd wait nearly a decade. He could threaten a lawsuit, and maybe just the threat would be enough. But what if they called his bluff and made him take them to court? The lawyer fees alone would be exorbitant. And even if they didn't, he'd look foolish and vindictive. He'd look to the town the way Eliza looked to him.

Maybe it was time to push the pencil and see what it would cost him to get a divorce. Del smiled grimly. Whatever it amounted to, it was probably worth it.

🐚🐚🐚

Eliza nudged him in the side. Del stood up and walked to the podium.

"You probably know who I am, but in case you don't, I live on Route One just south of the ferry terminal, Del Nelson and my wife, Eliza."

He nodded toward his wife, who gave him an encouraging smile.

"I'd like to register some complaints. But first I have a question about who's in charge here and what motivates those in charge to address these complaints."

Clayton Robertson, the harbormaster, was sitting in the middle of the crescent table at the front of the room.

He said, "Mr. Nelson, could you please speak into the microphone so what you will say will be recorded accurately for the minutes?"

He was flanked by the other members of the committee.

Del slipped the folded pages Eliza had written for him out of the inside breast pocket of his blazer. He leaned forward and at the same time twisted the microphone more toward his mouth. With his free hand, he slid his half glasses onto his nose. He cleared his throat.

"Thank you for hearing us. First, I'd like to point out that the present rules aren't being enforced. I rent a mooring from you, Mr. Robertson, and I have the right to tie my rowboat at the dinghy float. The ordinance says that the other rowboats must have padding on their sides, so they'll do no damage to the boats tied alongside. I've gone down to the float on several occasions to find a plywood monstrosity tied next to my rowboat. It actually has screw heads sticking out of the side, which have ruined the paint and chewed apart the wood on my rowboat. This damage will cost a substantial amount of money to repair.

"The dock is so congested that I can barely find a place to tie up my rowboat. At low tide, the water goes completely out from under the float, so I have to remove my shoes and drag my rowboat in the mud under the incline and out into water where she'll float. The silting in of the harbor makes it impossible for me to bring my sailboat into the dock except at middle to high tide. Yesterday, with the tide going, I almost bottomed out at the float, and I had real trouble powering through the mud to get out to my mooring.

"And then there's the issue of how close the moorings are. When the ferry comes in and the tide is slack, no matter how the wind is blowing, the boats all go helter-skelter. If there's any wake or a swell from the south, then there's danger that they'll come together and damage will be done. This situation is unacceptable.

"When I can get a parking space in the state lot, and the tide is right for me to use my sailboat, then my wife and I have to weave our way around the puddles of bait juice that seep from the bait boxes. Couple that with the smell, and you have a horrible situation down at the docks.

"Which brings me to the topic of who is in control. As I read the harbor ordinance, all rowboats should have protection and should be bailed out. This is not being enforced, and if you don't believe me, just go down there after a rainstorm.

"The waiting list for moorings and parking spaces is too long. There should be more moorings out farther, another float for the dinghies, more town parking, and the town should have the harbor dredged so that the floats are usable at low tide. The pier should have a cleanliness ordinance. I know there're others who would like to see the pier cleaned up.

"You on the committee need to address all these concerns. We are big-time taxpayers in this town, and we deserve respect and attention. Thank you. That's all I have to say."

Clayton Robertson cleared his throat and said, "Thank you, Mr. Nelson, for listing your concerns. They'll all be noted in the minutes. I will not be able to promise you solutions at this meeting, but I can say some things about what you've brought up.

"First off, I'll start with the issue of commercial fishing rights as they're balanced with the concerns from recreational boaters, like you. I admit freely that I'm the harbormaster and a fisherman. I sell retail lobsters and clams out of the house. I have a vested interest in the harbor as a working platform for the commercial fishermen. That said, for the record, I can only comment on the history of the pier and the present priorities.

"In 1990, as the funding was coming together for the reconstruction of the pier, we were soliciting money from the State and the towns of Lincolnville and Islesboro. An agreement was made to secure the state money. This agreement was to be in force for thirty years. In the agreement, it is expressly stated that the top priority is for harbor access for the commercial fishermen. Recreational use of the pier is also mentioned, but it falls second to waterfront access for the lobstermen.

"I acknowledge that at times the bait boxes leak, or some of the juice is spilled when we load our bait trays. I will bring this up with my fellow fishermen, and we will try to keep the mess to a minimum.

"The other items you mention, the rowboat dock, space for dinghies and parking, and the long wait for a mooring: these are perennial problems with no solutions in sight. It's not for lack of thought or desire. Our harbor isn't protected, so moorings farther out might as well be in the middle of the bay. There's no room for another dinghy dock. There's no more land for parking.

"Regarding the silting of the harbor, we've been in constant conversation with the MDOT. They know the ferry stirs up the bottom and is the primary culprit. They have no money for dredging, and we have no money for dredging. Dredging is nowhere in sight.

"I'll personally approach the person who owns the offending punt, and if there are damages, then you'll need to deal directly with him and his or your insurance companies.

"Thank you for your contributions to this meeting."

Clayton was about to move on to other business. Del let out a deep sigh and looked over at his wife. She nodded. Del spoke up again.

"I wonder if there is the will within this committee to really address these issues. You collectively don't have the clout to effect change. I believe I have the clout. I would like to volunteer to be on the committee."

"Mr. Nelson, we would welcome a person of your stature to be on the committee. You're more than welcome to run for the position, and it's highly likely you'll be elected at the next town meeting. Now we will move on to other business."

Del sat down in the molded-plastic chair next to Eliza. She leaned over and whispered congratulations into his ear. He felt like a puppet and wanted a stiff drink.

The next discussion was about law enforcement and the several incidents of vandalism and boat tampering in the harbor. The Nelsons stood up and left.

Chapter 28

T he bay was calm as the sun came up over Islesboro. Donny and Tut worked the gear up by Acre Island. A couple of gulls floated off to starboard. Gilkey Bell gonged as it swayed in the lazy swells.

A human-interest story came over the radio. Donny stopped baiting the trap on the rail and listened. Tim McGraw had been on an early-evening, pre-concert run in Bristow, Virginia, with some of his crew when he jogged past a woman and a little girl, who carried a homemade sign that read, "This is my first Tim McGraw concert. I need a hug."

"I like your sign," Tim said over his shoulder as he went by.

The announcer described Megan Robertson, a nine-year-old fourth grader who'd had more trouble than most people suffer in a lifetime. She'd survived open-heart surgery at the age of three and a mini-stroke a few years later. One of Tim's songs, "Live Like You Were Dying," had given her courage, while she was going through rehab, to relearn how to use the left side of her body.

As the concert began, security ushered the girl, her mother, and their sign up to the front. Tim sang "Little Dancer" down to her and then waved her up. The crowd lifted her to the stage. He sang and danced her around as tears ran down her face. From the wings, Faith Hill waved and cheered. As the song ran down, Tim gave her a big hug and a deep bow.

Later, Megan said, "He's my dream."

Donny turned to Tut. "That just about says it all."

Quicksilver, the only water taxi in the area, steamed by churning up a major wake, loaded down and packed with carpenters and drywallers who couldn't wait for the first ferry run at 8. A boatyard crew boat was leaving the mainland. The summer was half gone.

The lobsters were coming in good. He was averaging more than seven pounds per trap. Donny turned to Tut.

"I just figured it out, at least as far as Shelly is concerned."

He felt stupid talking to his dog, but the relationship fog had cleared up, and he knew she was worth the trouble, that he was getting really serious about the girl. He thought back on his father's approach to these upper class people, full of deference and kowtowing. It was worth a chance; she was worth the chance. So what if they couldn't talk about music, what with the age difference? What was fourteen or fifteen years anyway? That gave him pause.

He'd give her a call when he got to the mainland and accept the invitation to the big party.

"What the hell am I going to wear?"

Tut didn't seem to care.

They headed back at 4:30. He thought of Shelly all dressed up fancy, and his insides took a loop. He took special care to clean up *Pot Luck*.

Donny and Tut rowed in from the mooring. Bert was on the float, sorting the day's catch into several crates.

Donny held the oars in the air and drifted into the dock.

The four thirty ferry from Islesboro was backing into the pen. The ramp came down and clanked on the steel deck.

Bert looked up from his work and then nodded up to a group of people waiting to walk onto the ferry for its last run back to the island.

"Looks like a big to-do over on the rock."

Donny looked over his stern, Tut standing rigid but giving Bert a break for once and not snarling at him.

Local cars and trucks climbed off the ferry and drove past the knot of walk-ons already spiffed up: coats and ties, flimsy dresses on the breeze, tanned thighs, excited chatter, and overnight bags with telescoping handles. Two different worlds gliding past each other, each practically invisible to the other.

Bert pushed a crate over the side. It sank and then floated up flush with the surface.

"The band came over in a big box truck in line for the three o'clock ferry but missed it 'cause of all the party traffic.

They made quite a fuss, waving their hands and shouting at Tom, 'Do you know who we are?'

"Tom told them he didn't rightly care who they were. So they had to wait. Tom comes down and tells me of course he knows who they are, seeing as this is the biggest event of the summer, attracting assholes from all over New England, out-of-state plates on BMWs and Mercedeses and one Rolls Royce from New York."

Donny dipped his oars and spun his punt so he could face Bert directly.

"I heard all about it from Shelly. She said, and I quote verbatim, 'Brahmin families putting guests in breezy corner rooms for the weekend, the whole of Dark Harbor aflutter in anticipation, the caterers taking the late-morning ferries with hoards of staff and vans of food and cases of liquor and mixers. Ice. Ice comes over in giant coolers in the back of pickup trucks.' "

"Christ, you should write a book! Kiss my ass and make it a love story. I thought Brahmins were cows or some shit."

Donny floated and wondered whether to mention he was attending the party. Tut got bored and lay down on the stern seat. Loaded trucks groaned down the ramp. Then the last lucky cars parked along the sides. The walk-ons herded down to hand their tickets to Shirley, the ferry girl.

"You want a report?"

"A report of what?"

"Of the party."

Bert rubbed his whiskered chin, and Donny was close enough to hear scratching.

"What, she invited you over to the party, did she?" He paused to consider. "That'll be a sight, let me tell you. She all sweet perfume and you smelling like fish bait."

"C'mon, Bert. You never saw that movie *Atlantic City?* Where Susan Sarandon, who works at an oyster bar in the casino, goes home and washes all over, and I mean all over, with lemon juice to get the smell off?"

"No."

"Man, you gotta see it. Burt Lancaster watches her every night through her kitchen window."

"And you watch it every night on the VCR, it sounds like."

"I'll loan it to you. For when the wife is out and it's just you and the dogs."

"Sure you will. You got lemons to spare? And tell me something else. What're you going to say when you open your mouth? Tell them how much bait's gone up? And then they ask you what's your opinion of the new stimulus plan, and do you think Apple is a good buy at this price? Gimme a break."

"Jesus H. Christ, Bert, you're jealous."

"No, I ain't jealous of nothing, just smart. Ain't nothing good going to come of this, you know. You know what happens when you get led around by the dick, don't you? Crushed with the shingle spade like the small crabs. You got no business messing with these people. They're out of your league. You'll be like spoiled bait and get dumped over the side.

"And I know it ain't none of my business, but you think her Daddy's going to stand for this much longer?"

Donny set his oars in the water and headed to the dinghy float. As he crossed past the stern of Bert's boat he said, "I don't know why everybody is getting so bent out of shape over it."

"Sonny, it's you who's gonna get bent out of shape. What's the matter with Shirley there by the ferry? Or Helen down to the diner in Camden? Nice-looking girls who know the score."

"Maybe they know the score. But they ain't never seen *Atlantic City*."

🐚🐚🐚

After a shower and a short nap, Donny laid out the best clothes he had: a white, button-down shirt and a dry cleaned pair of khaki trousers. He took out an old pair of boat shoes and rummaged around in the mess at the bottom of his closet and found some shoe polish in the corner.

He only had white socks but thought they'd looked flashy.

He cracked a beer in the kitchen and thought he looked sharp, kind of like a boat captain.

"Say something edgy, controversial," she challenged.

"Why? I don't do edgy."

"Sure you can, just try."

"What did I miss?"

Shelly was standing on the dock in a spaghetti-strap, blue-cotton summer dress that came to mid-thigh, tight around her waist, showing off her leg muscles and her ripped arms. She looked like she could take Donny right down if he didn't do what she wanted. That was a sexy thought, the dress riding up in the melee. A cashmere shawl over her shoulders was tied in a loose knot.

"Well, you missed all the pre-party commotion. The Commodore wanted Mummy and Daddy to host a dinner party, but they talked it over and didn't want to hassle with the caterers and having to make conversation about annoying houseguests, who's in which club, and staffing problems at the flat in Paris."

"That's nice."

"Something edgy, you can do it."

"Your father will sink my boat when he sees it at the dock."

"Don't be silly. He doesn't care that much about you."

She gathered her hair and put up a high ponytail. "Let's take the Whaler. They want to keep the big boat traffic to a minimum, leave space for the water taxis. *Pot Luck* will be fine tied right here to our dock."

"And your father is OK with this plan?"

"Mummy is so busy getting them dressed in their elegant but I-just-threw-this-together clothes, they won't even notice your boat."

"And what planet did you just come from?"

"They're heading over late, so there won't be anything they can do. Mummy'll be worrying about how many cocktails Daddy has already had. She won't let him bother about you and me."

Shelly untied the Whaler's bowline. Misgivings about *Pot Luck* or not, he really did like the Marshal Tucker Band, and he could dance after a couple of stiff drinks. It was a go.

Donny stepped onto the flat bow of the Whaler, and it sank into the water with his weight. He turned the key, and the 40-horse Evinrude came to life. They skipped across the little waves and headed south in the waning light of dusk, no need yet for running lights.

Donny came around the western side of Key Island to land at the southern dock, avoiding all the big-boat traffic coming in on the other side. It was a small island.

They tied off and walked up the incline along the slatted wood pier and then into the woods on a crushed-stone path, their way illuminated by lamps sending smoke into the thicket. It looked like a fire hazard to Donny, thinking some drunk could bump into one and set the whole island ablaze.

The path led them through a flower garden to the lawn that ran up to the three-story yellow house with stout, white columns, every window lit up in soft light. A few guests wandered the lawn, looking around. They said hello as they passed, but nobody was familiar. No surprise there, for Donny anyway.

Most of the activity was around the house and down by the pier in a boxy building right on the shore and a big white tent to the side.

Donny asked, "Do you know the host?"

"I know what he looks like." She stopped. "And you will too. Here he comes."

A neat, trim, and handsome man approached and halted on the grass beside the path.

"Well, well, if it isn't the famous rower." He took her hand in two of his. "Shelly, don't you look splendid tonight."

He turned to Donny.

She said, "Peter, I would like to introduce my friend, Donny Coombs."

They shook hands. He had a good handshake, firm, short pump, and a sparkle in the eye. He was about Donny's age from what he could see in the lamp light, no coat and tie, and Donny felt even better about what he was wearing.

"Donny, this is our host, Peter Thrush."

"Donny, so good of you to come. We've got a really good party brewing. Please go down and grab a drink. I have to do all the host business, so I don't have much time to chat. But Shelly, you absolutely must save a dance for me."

He squeezed them both on the shoulders and strolled up to the house.

"Nice guy." Donny watched him go.

"He's very nice."

"Who is he, and how does he happen to have the Marshall Tucker playing in his tent?"

"I hear he has oodles of money and decided to pick up a lost summer tradition. Back when I was little, the father of the Secretary of the Treasury gave his grown son a yearly birthday bash. He pulled out all the stops — top notch entertainment — and I heard they served catered breakfast at 3 a.m. to fortify the dancers. Probably not that lavish tonight, but it should be a good time."

The bar was in the tent along the right side, sparkling stacks of glass in front of a line of liquor bottles and mixers. The bartender, in a white shirt and black trousers, stood with his hands clasped, waiting for some business.

Donny recognized him, the son of one of the Islesboro lobstermen, but couldn't remember his name. Shelly ordered a rum and tonic, and the bartender poured a stingy inch of Wild Turkey for Donny. Good that it was a hundred proof. Donny reached into his pocket for some cash.

"No, no, the drinks are on the house," the bartender said, then added, "I know you."

Donny upended an empty glass, peeled off a five-dollar bill, and folded it into the glass.

"I fish out of Lincolnville."

"That's right, Donny Coombs. We aren't supposed to take tips."

But he palmed the cash and slid it into his pocket.

"Thanks all the same." He winked.

Donny winked back and said, "This is Shelly Payson. You treat her right."

He said, "Pleased to meet you."

They shook hands.

"Likewise." Shelly turned to Donny and said, "Let's wander."

They weaved through empty tables and chairs and out the flap to the boathouse. Donny finished his whiskey and wanted more of that deep-down glow. He'd have to pace himself, not get shitfaced and insult somebody. Shelly sipped at her drink.

Calling this a boathouse was a good touch, and it probably had been one a long time ago. Now, with the nautical paraphernalia on the walls and hanging from the rafters, it was all for show, more of a museum. A low, empty stage was set up in front of tightly packed vacant round tables covered with cream-colored tablecloths. The wall studs and rafters were neatly whitewashed.

They exited through the back door. A set of short steps led down to the shore. The tide was coming in, and a bunch of locals had crashed the party and were pounding drinks and smoking in the semi-dark. Donny pulled a Camel from his trouser pocket and lit up.

The night was clear skies with tons of stars. A light wind from the south combined with a flooding tide, which was good. The approach to the dock could be tricky at low water, and it would ruin someone's party to run aground in evening clothes. Off to the right, the narrow pier ran out over the water down to two floats hung inside and out. Lit up with lanterns, it made a pretty sight.

The *Quicksilver* water taxi was coming in with a load, showing green-and-red running lights as she came straight in, and then turning to port showing just green. Tom, the captain, beamed the spotlight on the top of the pilothouse to the side of the float. He leapt out and tied off, and the crowd of party people, mostly older judging from the way they moved, stepped carefully over the rail, not wanting to slip on the dock.

The group made its way up the incline, now flat because of the tide, and came ashore along the pier. Tom untied and headed back to the yacht club for another load. Things were picking up.

Shelly looked up to the stars and looped her arm around Donny's waist. He put his smoke-free arm over her shoulder. The young guys looked envious but didn't say anything stupid, perhaps recognizing Donny.

"This is going to be fun. Let's get another drink. Then let's get a table for Mummy and Daddy."

"Can't wait."

The room was filling with chatty summer people: painted faces and big hair, sparkly necklaces above dresses with plunging necklines and some swank gentlemen with wavy locks and silk sport coats and bow ties.

Shelly picked a table tucked toward the back and off to the side, out of the way of the traffic. Work was going on at the little stage: a chair brought in and a freestanding microphone, wires leading to two large amplifiers on the left and right.

The first act was Chris Smither.

A pretty girl in a black, high-neck uniform and white apron circulated with hors d'oeuvres.

"You know anything about Chris Smither?" Donny asked.

Shelly polished off her canapé, wiped her mouth, and said, "Not really."

Donny leaned in close to her ear. He could smell that hint of perfume that made him want to take her clothes off doing its job.

"Dates back to the sixties and seventies folk-rock scene. Singer-songwriter, solo guitarist."

"I'm impressed, Donny. You know your music."

"Before my time, actually, but my dad had one of his albums."

"Well, hello there, you two."

The words came from over his left shoulder, the husky, seductive voice of Cornelia Payson, looking beautiful in a floral-print dress tied tight under her breasts with a hint of cleavage, a great sign of how Shelly would look as she aged.

Donny straightened up, not wanting to look like he was curled over her daughter, and said, "Good evening, Mrs. Payson."

He stood up, and the back of his knees almost toppled the flimsy fold-up chair.

"Cornelia — please."

Shelly stood and leaned past Donny to give her mother an air kiss on the cheek.

"Where's Daddy?"

"Getting more drinks."

Donny slid out a chair, and Cornelia pulled her dress taut on the back of her thighs and sat down.

"Donny, dear, tell me more about your appreciation of music."

She said it with an air of fun.

"I mostly listen to the radio. I don't have a collection or nothing. I like country mostly, and some folk."

Cornelia swiveled her head, maybe looking for her husband.

"I met Chris Smither at the Main Point on the Main Line outside Philadelphia in seventy-four. He'd been playing there for ages. It was a little coffeehouse but hosted some really big names in the folk scene. I was a junior at Bryn Mawr. Chase was there with another group, and we ended up sitting side by side. He was a senior at Haverford. That's the night we met."

Chase came to the table with two clear drinks in each hand.

"Wharton, Goldman Sachs, and then marriage. I don't suppose those names mean anything to you, do they Donny?"

Donny stood up.

"Business school and investment bank, in that order. Good evening, Mr. Payson."

"Oh, for the mother of God, call me Chase."

His eyes narrowed as he stared at Donny. "But I thought I made myself clear the last time we met."

"What are you talking about, Daddy?"

"Never mind."

He waved his hand. He leaned forward and almost lost his balance. Cornelia relieved him of the drinks, and Chase sat down with a thud. He surveyed the room and grunted.

Cornelia distributed the glasses around.

Donny remembered the evening of Painkillers and was glad he hadn't hit the Wild Turkey harder. He kept his mouth shut against both speech and booze.

A woman along the wall waved over at the table. Donny figured it must be a friend of the Paysons, but then he recognized Eliza Nelson in a tight black dress, big hair, and those perfect legs sticking out of the short hem.

Donny realized she was waving at him. He waved back.

Del materialized beside his wife in brick trousers, blue button-down shirt, and a yellow sweater draped over his shoulders. The two of them came over to the table looking at the two empty chairs.

"May we?" Eliza flashed a toothy smile.

Shelly looked at Donny and her parents and then got up and said, "Of course, you may. Let me introduce you to my parents. My mother Cornelia and my father Chase, this is Delano Nelson and his wife Eliza. They're Donny's neighbors in Lincolnville."

The Paysons stood, and handshakes crisscrossed over the table. They all sat down. Eliza jumped in as if silence were a threat.

"And you must be Shelly. We've seen you over at Donny's house. It's just splendid to make the connection."

She beamed at the table and then cast her smile around the room. The men adjusted themselves in their chairs.

"Boats. I have boats, you have boats. Mine are very expensive, and heavens, what about those boatyard bills!" Chase slurred his words.

"But Rockport Marine does excellent work. They just delivered my sailboat, top-notch craftsmanship. Fiberglas versus wood?" Del raised his eyebrows at Chase.

"Someday I might be able to afford a wooden boat too."

Laughter.

Donny watched the two peacock around each other and thought of *Pot Luck*.

Cornelia asked, "Are you new to the area, Eliza?"

"We've just finished our house, and it's so lovely up here, so quaint. Del and I just love it, and we find the Mainers so welcoming and friendly."

She smiled at Donny. He had nothing to add, lips tight in a line.

At the front of the room, Peter Thrush struck a fork to his glass. The crowd fell silent. Eliza and Del twisted around to face the stage.

"I want to thank you all for coming over to this little get-together tonight. It's lovely to see so many friends. I just want to welcome you and to introduce — Chris Smither!"

He swung his arm out, and the room's attention focused on the slim man in black who walked into the light holding his guitar by the neck. The room broke out into applause, and Chris waved his hand and bowed. A cracked and dented face and an honest smile.

Chris took the stage and arranged himself on the chair, strummed his guitar and tuned a string. After a few words, he launched into his set.

Donny let a melody flow over him and decided to ignore everything else. He closed his eyes.

Chris played for twenty minutes and then took a break. The Nelsons spun their chairs back around.

Del leaned way back, hands behind his head, legs splayed, and said to Shelly, "I hear you're an accomplished rower."

Shelly nodded.

Chase gulped the last of his drink, looked as if he had something to say, but didn't. Donny wondered how long he had to put up with this shit. He licked his lips and smiled politely. Chase stood and leaned on the table on two flat palms.

"I'm off to the bar. Can I get anyone anything?"

When no one took him up on the offer, he said, "The music just takes you away, doesn't it, Donny?"

Then he left.

Chase returned with a drink for himself just as Chris Smither came back. He proceeded to wash the crowd in good-time music till his second set ended. The crowd went wild and then quieted down to prepare for the Marshall Tucker Band.

Donny clasped his knees and shifted his weight forward.

"Can I get anything for anybody?"

Nobody was ready yet, so he escaped the table and made for the bar.

"Double Wild Turkey. No ice."

He eased out the back and lit up a smoke with the locals.

Donny reentered the boathouse and looked for Shelly. A crowd was clearing away tables and chairs from the front, making room for dancing. The stage was being set up for the bigger band, a bevy of activity with mikes and wires and guitars on stands, keyboard and drums, huge amplifiers off to the side.

The Marshall Tucker Band came out in ten-gallon cowboy hats and boots, long hair and beards, shirts with snaps and white piping, four guitars, the keyboard and drums to the back, and a guy with a silver flute.

Shelly came out of nowhere and dragged him out onto the dance floor, crowding up as soon as the band struck the first note.

Somewhere along the line, Donny had acquired the ability to turn music into movement right on the beat. And Shelly was a sight: toned, long-fiber muscles under tanned skin and the flexibility of a dancer, sliding left and right, a stomp of feet, jump and twirl, huge smile and eyes for her man. They linked arms and spun around, and he twirled her with a swing move. He lost all orientation. They could have been alone on a distant planet. They didn't sit down but danced and danced.

Donny brought their sweaty bodies together and held her tight. He looked down onto her upturned glowing face and stood still as the song gathered steam, the flute high and clear and sharp.

"Heard it in a love song; can't be wrong," the band sang.

When they started moving again, Donny danced her off in unusual directions, and Shelly followed as if they were one, swaying and dipping and spinning.

"I'd stay another year if I saw a teardrop in your eye."

Cornelia and Chase danced by, and Donny caught a frozen stare over Cornelia's shoulder. Chase looked perfectly pissed off, but Donny couldn't imagine fireworks with this many people.

As the music ended, Chase came over and gave Donny a shove. Nobody noticed in the crowd. Donny almost lost his balance and turned red inside. He trembled and bunched his fists.

He said through clenched teeth, "Don't you ever come that close to me again."

Cornelia slid in between the two.

"I will not allow this."

She got in her husband's face, put her two palms on his chest, and pushed him back — then back some more. Then she spun him and dragged him off.

Shelly was crimson and stormed after her parents. Donny stood alone and watched heated words fly back and forth among the three. Cornelia led her husband out the door by the stage as the band started the next song.

Shelly came over and took his hand. "I need some air."

She took him out the back steps into the cool night air, crisp on his wet skin and damp shirt.

"I'm sorry, Donny. It's my fault. Maybe this is too much for Daddy. He can go off the deep end when he's had too much to drink."

She grasped his neck and planted a hard kiss on his lips. "Let's go home."

The party was over.

Chapter 29

S unday came in all fuzzy, and Donny felt right ignorant. Frank Sinatra's words echoed around Donny's swollen head.

"I feel sorry for all you nondrinkers. When you get up in the morning, that's as good as you're going to feel all day."

He'd dropped Shelly off at her dock, traded the Whaler for *Pot Luck*, and made for the mainland. She'd suggested a cooling-off period, and he agreed, not trusting himself with further confrontation.

Donny worked on his traps in the garage and by noon was feeling a little better. He took Tut for a walk up the mountain trails at Point Lookout, sat down at the top, and looked down on the bay, his place of work. He could make out Shelly's house on Islesboro.

He thought about what Bert had said, the show put on by Chase and Eliza last night, Shelly's friend David who came at him during their lunch at the club, and his father turning down the dinner invitation from the owner of the home he was caretaking.

After snooping around, Tut came over for a pat on the head. He curled up in the sunshine and went to sleep. Donny pulled on a piece of timothy grass. The top came off easily, and he put the tender end in his mouth. He could feel love for the girl, but Jesus Christ, the complications seemed insurmountable.

In the parking lot, his truck started hard and barely made it home before it died in his driveway. It wouldn't turn over the next morning. He called Mike up to the garage and arranged to have the truck towed and fixed. He and Tut had to walk down Route One and cut through the woods on the path to the ferry terminal and the pier.

Chapter 29

His residual anger had dissipated. A crisp north wind had cleared away any humidity, and it was almost sweater weather. Today, he had to tend his southern strings. The haul promised to be good, the lobsters having come into the shallow ledges to shed and now hungry to rebuild their shells.

It wasn't until he got right in close to Acre Island that he became aware of the nightmare. All his buoys were gone.

He got out his binoculars and scouted the shoreline down to the Ensign Islands as far as he could see. Plenty of buoys but none his color. He circled *Pot Luck* around a line of lavender buoys, just where his gear should be.

Donny threw his cap on the deck and grabbed the gaff and smashed it over the rail, breaking it in two.

"Cocksucking, motherfucking asshole!"

He struggled for control. Tut stood up, growled and barked and looked around for the source of trouble. Donny sat down hard on the rail, leaned his forearms on his thighs, and took a deep breath.

He said to Tut, "Hell to pay. You hear me? There's gonna be hell to pay now."

He smoldered and took *Pot Luck* south along the islands, finding the water empty of his buoys. The magnitude of the situation grew the farther he went. He finally came up on one of his neon orange buoys off the Ensign Bell. Half of his southern gear had been cut. On paper, he calculated close to a ten-thousand-dollar loss, enough to justify hiring a diver to work the ledges and retrieve his traps, but a substantial loss of time and opportunity.

He hauled what was left, good fishing and plenty of time to sort things through.

He broke for an early lunch and, drifting in the swells, called Mike on the cell phone Shelly had forced on him to see when his truck would be ready.

"I got good news and bad news, Donny. What do you want first?"

"All I've had is bad news. Let's hear the good."

"Well, I've got a nice truck I can lend you until yours gets straightened out."

"What the hell does that mean?"

"That brings us to the bad news. You're screwed. I hope your deductible is nice and low. It looks like someone filled your gas tank with sugar, and your engine's shit the bed."

Mike waited as Donny absorbed the news. Without another word, Donny pressed the red button and disconnected the call.

He finished up and headed back to the harbor at noon, tended to his meager catch at the dock, and walked north along Route One, Tut heeling at his left ankle.

The weather was still super fine, the day bright, and the sky and bay a deep, rich blue, the waves capping white in the fresh breeze. But the world felt monochrome to Donny, and he carried the dark cloud all the way up to Mike's Align and Repair shop. He took the loaner keys and signed on the dotted line to have his engine replaced. Tut sniffed over the different front seats and then plopped down on the passenger side.

They were third in line for the one o'clock ferry over to the island. Donny only grunted to a surprised Tom, who was shocked that he was using the ferry. Donny pulled off the ferry on Islesboro and took the road south down toward Pendleton Point. Each driver in the oncoming cars waved. Donny gave each one the finger.

He took Gull Road off to the left, wound down along the dirt ruts, and parked beside a stack of worn-out traps and a ramshackle house, peeling paint and rotting wood its major features. He turned off the engine and sat in the silence.

"You stay right here," he ordered Tut.

Stanley's lavender pickup was sitting in front of a pile of stove wood. Donny eased out of the truck and left the door open.

He didn't break stride. He pulled on the screen door with exaggerated coolness and walked into a dark place. The kitchen was a disaster of empty pizza boxes and dishes piled high in a smudged sink. Beer bottles lined the counter.

Stanley looked up from the table, his naked gut hanging over his sheened jeans. He tried to stand. He was pie-eyed drunk. A half-bottle of Evan Williams whiskey sat beside a brimming ashtray, a cigarette wedged in a side notch, smoke curling up into the heavy still air.

Donny took two steps and open-handed him across the side of the head. Stanley fell over and hit the floor hard. He crawled over to the counter, and Donny followed and kicked him in the ass. Stanley grunted and tried to pull himself up.

Donny said, "You're going to pay for this."

Stanley struggled to his feet and reached for a handgun beside a toaster. Donny kicked out and swept Stanley off his feet. He fell empty-handed and banged his chin on the edge of the speckled and chipped Formica counter.

"You're a fucking disgrace."

Donny bent and grabbed Stanley's beard and yanked his head up close, getting a charge of putrid alcohol breath. He slapped Stanley across the face, so hard that it stung his hand. Stanley's eyes rolled back in his head.

"Restitution. You know that word? You're going to make things right with me. You move all your gear off my buoys, nothing closer than two hundred yards. You're going to pay me for the trouble you've caused. And you do all this because I'm your worst fucking nightmare, and you don't want me coming back — ever."

For good measure, Donny kicked him again. He reached over for the Ruger .44-magnum revolver, emptied the rounds, and flung them across the kitchen, pinging off the wall and into the other room.

Donny took a deep breath, walked out, and let the screen door bang behind him. He fired up the truck and spewed gravel as he spun out of the yard and up the drive. Tut came over and licked his cheek and wagged his stub.

Donny ruffled his face and said, "Let's hope that's the end of it."

On the way back, he waved to the approaching cars and got in line for the two thirty boat, plenty of time. Five cars up was a powder-blue Mercedes with Mr. Chase Payson sitting in the driver's seat.

"Great, just great. Might as well make it a convention of assholes."

Donny's presence went unnoticed, a good thing for all concerned, all things considered.

Chapter 30

L ife at the Payson paradise was fractured. Father and daughter weren't speaking. Mummy was trying to mediate the conflict and having no success. An arctic chill ran through the house.

Shelly was in the kitchen waiting on an English muffin in the toaster. She picked up the receiver to dial the Village Market up-island. She heard her father's voice and was about to ease the phone back on the hook, but she held her breath and covered the mouthpiece with her hand.

"Bill? Chase here. I've got some work to throw your way. Look up a guy, Donald Coombs, lives in Lincolnville, Maine. Thirty-five years old, lobsterman, old-time family from here. Dig up whatever you can to bring a shitstorm down on his head. I don't care how you do it, just get it done. Freeze his accounts, ruin his credit, and fuck him up.

"Whatever it takes, but don't leave anything that'll come back to me, of course. The usual fee'll suffice, I presume? I'll have the cash delivered to your office by Wednesday."

He hung up.

Shelly put the phone down. The muffin popped. Ignoring it, she snuck up the back stairs to her room, sat down at her desk with a pad of writing paper, took a number two pencil from the drawer and clicked it on her teeth, thinking over the raft of bad things that had plagued Donny so far this summer.

She listed them: boat cut adrift, oak tree poisoned, *Pot Luck*'s fuel line tampered with. Not much of a list, but certainly a pattern of disruption. Then she added the conflict with a local lobsterman and his troublesome neighbors. When she tacked her father's name to the bottom, the list had doubled in length.

Chapter 30

She started to picture a counterattack, a whole tsunami coming back on whoever was responsible, and it included her father.

Chapter
31

Tut came down sick on Tuesday morning, spewing diarrhea all over the kitchen floor just after he returned from his morning rounds. A dog way too proud to stoop so low, he had to be really bad off.

He took to drooling and vomiting dry heaves and staggering around the house. Donny picked him up and cradled him in his lap as he made the call to the vet up to Belfast.

No, he didn't want to make an appointment. His dog needed immediate attention. Yes, he could be up there in fifteen minutes.

He laid Tut on the front seat and cursed the summertime traffic that kept him waiting for a gap to pull onto the road north.

George came out of his Little River vet shop and carried Tut into an examining room. He took a pulse and temperature and then looked into Tut's eyes and slack mouth.

"Nothing you can point to?"

"Total surprise, no idea."

"Looks like poison. Any antifreeze he could have got into?"

"Not around my place. I know about antifreeze. And anyway, Tut's way too sharp to drink that shit. Had to be something deliberate, you ask me."

George filled a plastic syringe with some white goop and forced it down Tut's throat, too sick to object.

"That should get him to vomit. If that doesn't work, we pump his stomach, shove down some activated charcoal to absorb whatever's left, then give him a laxative."

Donny paced the floor and ran his hands through his hair.

"He's a tough little guy. He'll fight this."

"Donny, my money's on Tut, but it depends on how long this stuff's been in his system."

Tut lay flat on his side on the stainless table and groaned, his side coming up and down with shallow breathing. Then he puked all over the place, bright yellow bile running across the table and onto the floor. He tried to sit up and then slumped back down. Donny laid a hand on Tut's rib cage; his stub tail gave a weak throb.

George said, "That right there tells me he's going to pull through."

He wetted a towel in the sink, scooped up the vomit, rinsed, and finished the cleanup.

"I need him to stay here, do the things I said, and monitor him through the night. If anything happens, I'll call you."

"Thanks, George, but if it's all the same to you, I'd like to hang around awhile."

"You're welcome to stay as long as you want. The room is yours."

George tossed the towel in a hamper and left to gather up the medications.

His hand on Tut's side, Donny stared out the small window on the parking lot. Donny felt very tired, but knew he was up to the tasks ahead.

Chapter
32

Del was standing at the sink looking out the window at Donny's wreck of a house, steam coming off his coffee cup.

"Donny just carried his limp dog to his truck and drove off fast. Do you know anything about that?"

Eliza stroked Alex's head at the dining-room table, sitting in the morning's first sunlight.

"I don't know what you're implying. I had nothing to do with it."

"What were you doing out in the garage?"

"Looking for something."

"Looking for what?"

"What does it matter? And I don't need this third degree, so back off."

Del was used to his wife's dark side, chewing on tacks like they were peanuts.

Still looking out the window, he said, "I think there's a limit to what Donny will take before this little war stops being one-sided, darling."

"He wouldn't dare."

"Oh, I think he would."

🐚🐚🐚

Shelly rang Donny, but he wasn't home. His cell phone was shut off. The cooling period was off, and they needed to talk.

Cornelia was arranging flowers in the mudroom sink, cutting stems, sorting colors, and sticking them into four different vases. Shelly gathered her slicker off the hook.

"Mummy, I'm headed over to the mainland. When I get back, we need to talk."

"About what?"

"Some serious trouble. I'm getting worried, but I don't want to talk about it now."

"Okay, honey. Everything will turn out. It'll be all right. It always is."

"We'll see."

🐚🐚🐚

The ferry was halfway across the bay, and Shelly jumped the wake without slowing down.

Pot Luck was on her mooring. She tossed the fenders over, pulled into the inside of the outer float, and tied off. She took the woods path and then walked along the left edge of Route One into oncoming traffic up to Donny's house. His truck was gone, so she sat on the porch and dialed the cell phone. He answered.

She said, "I'm sitting on your porch. I'll be here when you get back."

"OK, see you soon." He hung up.

Ten minutes later, a strange truck turned in the drive and pulled to a gentle stop. Donny got out — without Tut at his feet. His shoulders were sloped and his head was down. He sat heavily on the chair next to Shelly.

She put a hand on his arm. She said, "Where's the little bastard?"

His voice was small.

"I was up to the vet. Looks like Tut got poisoned this morning, but the Doc says he'll pull through. I've got to leave him there overnight."

"Oh, Donny. That's horrible. You must feel awful."

"I would, if I could feel anything at all."

"Is there more?"

"On Sunday, my truck died. Mike says sugar in the gas tank. That's a loaner."

He nodded at the driveway.

"Half my southern gear was gone on Monday morning, so I drove over to Islesboro and slapped Stanley around something awful. This morning Tut was wicked sick, and I took him up to George. Now, here I am."

"That's more than just a run of bad luck."

They looked out on the traffic going by. Shelly left her seat and folded herself into his lap and put her arms around his neck and rested her head on his shoulder.

"I'm so sorry."

He wrapped her in his arms and squeezed.

He said, "I don't know what to do."

"Whatever it is, we'll do it together."

"I should fish my northern gear, but I feel more like killing someone. And I know exactly who. Problem is, there's too many of them."

"How about we both work your gear? While we're out there, we can figure out who dies first."

The boat seemed empty without Tut on the dash. Shelly filled bait bags, and Donny tended to the culling and banding. The catch was good, but the mood was dark, and they mostly worked in silence. Donny was lost in thought, and Shelly waited as they worked.

He tipped the freshly baited tailer trap over the side and watched it sink. The line played out, came taut, and pulled the main trap along the rail and off the stern. Donny brought *Pot Luck* around to starboard and turned south to the next buoy.

Shelly stood at the top bait tray, in an orange bib and blue rubber gloves, stuffed whole herring into a yellow-net bait bag, cinched it tight, and tied it off.

"I have some ideas, if you care to hear them."

"All ears."

"It all depends on what you want."

"I want things to go back to the way they were. Simple. I mind my own business; everyone else minds theirs."

"You have to be more specific."

Donny slowed the boat, bent over, and gaffed a buoy with his back-up gaff, a little shorter than the one he'd broke. He looped the line over the Davy and into the hauler plates, warp spooling on the deck.

"I want my neighbors gone. I want Stanley to back off. I want money for my lost gear, or at least enough to pay for a diver to recover the traps. I don't want to fight with your father. I want everyone to get the fuck out of my face and leave me alone. Except you."

The trap broke the surface. Donny spun it around and pulled it onto the rail, opened the door, and began tossing little lobsters over the side, plopping in the water, a tail flash and a dive down into the depths. He divided the crab into their fatal pails.

Shelly shook out the old bait and tied in a fresh bag. She moved the main trap forward to make room for the tailer. Together, they tended that one working side by side, quietly.

"I've got the beginnings of a plan," she said, "but it may be a little drastic. I figure the Nelsons killed your oak tree and poisoned Tut. To my way of thinking, that's so low-down, it about justifies anything short of murder. You've got to handle the Stanley thing, but it seems like you have a head start there. Regarding my father, I'm very sorry to have to tell you this, but he's called in some shady professional help."

Shelly told him about the phone conversation she'd overheard.

"Great, just great."

But his mind went further, and he wondered how much of his worries he ought to reveal to her.

"If your father has some private eye digging into my history, messing up my credit, freezing my money, he can really hurt me."

Donny took a deep breath. He brought the throttle back to idle and put *Pot Luck* into neutral. They drifted with a bit of forward momentum.

"Back in the nineties, I got to running bales of dope from mother ships out in the Gulf back into the shore here, little coves and big box trucks. I did real good and put away some serious money. I stopped when I got scared about all that cash. The business has moved off now, and there's no trace anymore. But I think if anyone wanted to dig deep, well, they might find something there, evidence of some money laundering, stuff paid for in cash, too good a standard of living, that kind of thing."

"Christ, Donny, that was fifteen years ago. How bad can it be? What kind of money are we talking about?"

"A little more than a million dollars."

Shelly stared at him.

"A million dollars?"

"Yeah."

"Holy shit!"

"Yeah."

"Where is it?"

"In a safe place." He smiled. "Then I own the car wash in Rockland and the coin laundry in Belfast, all real proper and such."

They hauled some more gear in silence. Shelly swept a lock of hair off her face with her forearm, smudging her cheek with some herring grime.

"Well, we'll just have to get Daddy to back off, simple as that, though it may be a little harder than dealing with your neighbors."

She outlined her plan for the Nelsons. Donny was stunned by what he heard.

"Don't you think that's a bit extreme? And where'd you get this criminal mind all of a sudden?"

He took off his glove and removed the bait from her face.

"Extreme is as extreme does. And I watch those crime shows. With a little curiosity and the internet, even you could become a master criminal. Look, nobody gets hurt, and they leave town in disgrace. What's better than that?"

Donny thought a bit.

🐚🐚🐚

They put the Mako on one of Donny's inside moorings. Shelly called home, spoke with her mother, and stayed over Tuesday night. Tut's absence was palpable. They went to bed early and spooned naked.

Tut recovered nicely and was almost himself by Wednesday. He came home and took a nap on the kitchen floor.

Shelly spent some of the morning looking out the kitchen window over at the Nelson house deep in thought. She went to a pad of paper on the table, added to her list, and then returned to the window.

Offhand, she said, "This should be a movie."

Chapter 33

It took Donny by complete surprise. He acted on pure instinct, not a single ordered thought in his brain.

He was standing by the rail, ready to snag a buoy. Next thing he knew, he found himself down on his knees, ducking low. It'd been an instinctive reaction, like dipping your head a fraction just before the bug hits your forehead — would have been your eye on the highway on your motorcycle. The portside window blew out, followed by the crack of a rifle shot.

Donny crouched there, disoriented, looking at the window, shards of splintered fiberglass stuck in the frame. The boat rocked in the swells. He peered out into the thick fog. Off the port bow, he could just make out the spruce trees on the island. Toward the west was smooth rolling sea and a steady mist. From the way the Plexi blew out and into the water, the shot must have come from the west.

He'd been watching the radar and there'd been no return on the screen before he pulled the lavender buoy, warp, and lobster trap. Just the blip from Gilkey Bell and the shape of Seven Hundred Acre Island and to the north the tip of Islesboro where the ferry came in.

The thought of physical danger hadn't crossed his mind. He was in the middle of molesting Stanley's traps, the ones where his were supposed to be. Donny was systematically pulling the traps, opening the doors, and leaving them loose and unlatched. Before he set them back, he pulled offshore into deeper water and tied two half hitches into the warp about halfway down, so they'd get fouled in the hydraulic hauler.

Of course, he wasn't doing all this in broad daylight. Stan had the reputation of being whiskey soaked and trigger-happy.

Donny looked up to the radar screen mounted on the ceiling, angled toward the helm. A blip registered just south of the Bell. When the next sweep came around, the blip was closer to the Bell. It was moving away fast.

He shoved the trap off the rail, spun the wheel, and pushed the throttle all the way forward. *Pot Luck* cut a sharp swath. Her stern dug into the water. Donny straightened her out, and she rose up and settled down on a plane till her bow flattened for the chase.

The tide was half out and going. The wind was five knots from the north. Stanley had a slightly bigger boat, but a smaller engine. *Pot Luck* was faster.

The blip turned east toward the ferry landing and then south toward the Gut, the slip of water between Seven Hundred Acre and Warren Island.

Donny knew Stanley was headed to the spot where at low tide they could both walk from one island to the other without getting their feet wet. An hour on either side of high tide, either one of them could run a boat that drew four feet through without any concern. But the lower the water, the dicier it got, especially if the tide was going.

All this swirled through Donny's mind. The blip kept south and entered the Gut. *Pot Luck* turned in a sweep and followed, coming up on his wake. The shores of each island made solid green brackets on the screen. The fog was so thick he couldn't make out the banks on either side. Stanley's blip stayed steady down the middle.

In clear weather, a rock on the west side acted as a gauge. When it was anything more than half visible, there wasn't enough water. Local knowledge went a long way. Donny didn't look for the rock in the fog but figured he might have enough water. Stan's boat drew less than *Pot Luck*.

Donny kept his boat at full throttle, and he was gaining. They were approaching the pinch where the islands were closest and the water shallowest. Here, the bottom was mostly soft, especially slightly to the east. Stanley was roaring through, his wake growing more pronounced, churning up white froth, and Donny knew he was close. At any moment, Stan's transom would fill the windshield.

Donny swapped looks between the fog and the radar screen. Stan had almost made it.

He looked forward, and Stanley's stern loomed out of the fog. Until now Donny had no plan, but for Christ's sake, the bastard had shot at him. *Pot Luck* was built rugged, and her oak stem could take a collision no problem. That was the plan, and Donny braced for the impact.

Then two things happened at once. Stanley, whom Donny could just make out, lurched forward as his skeg scraped bottom and then almost fell aft as his boat came free. And *Pot Luck* ran aground. Donny was thrown forward as his boat lost momentum.

If the bottom was soft enough, and he had just enough momentum, and he kept the prop churning, he might power into deeper water. Time slowed as *Pot Luck* strained against the mud. If she stopped, she was dead.

She stopped.

Donny shouted a string of swear words directed at Stanley. He pulled the engine back to idle and shut her down. The sound of Stanley receding into the fog was replaced by the dampened sound of their wakes hitting the shore on either side. From above, a seagull squawked what sounded like a laugh. For some reason it made him think of Tut, recuperating on the mainland.

Donny had work to do. When the tide went out from under the boat, she would list so far to port or starboard that when the water came back in, it could pour over the waterway, flood the deck, and sink her. While she was still upright, he could prop her up.

He shook off his short boots and got his waders and a short saw from down below. He pulled the hip boots up all the way, set the saw on the rail, and let himself over the side into three feet of water.

"Damn it!"

The water was too deep. Of course. It poured in over the top of his boots, soaked his jeans from his waist down, and flooded his socks. Donny sloshed to shore, sat on a rock, and raised his legs one at a time letting the water drain out.

Then he scavenged three stout pieces of drift lumber. He brought them back to the boat and measured with his body the distance from the bottom at an angle to the toe rail. He sawed each to length and wedged them at amidships, bow and stern on the port side.

His watch read just past eight-thirty in the morning. Two hours until dead low water and at least another two for the water to come back in enough to float *Pot Luck*. He was at the northern reach of Cradle Cove on the eastern side of Acre Island. He started to walk along the shore, west and south. On the other end of the cove was Dark Harbor Boat Yard, hot coffee, and a dryer.

Chapter 34

T he heat wave continued into late August unabated and without the usual offshore breezes that generally brought relief to the coastal region. Like the early, warm, and especially dry spring, nature was conspiring to accelerate all things good and bad about Maine in the summer.

The water was warmer sooner, so the lobsters came in more quickly to shed. Lawn's growth slowed and had to be mowed every nine days instead of midsummer's four to five. The leaves were changing color, and the Canada geese honked overhead in formation, landing down by the shore to rest before their trek farther south. The blueberry and apple harvests came early too and caught the field and orchard owners scrambling for early field help.

The heat came so early, stayed so long, and was so oppressive that the talk in the convenience stores was all about the relief coming with the winter snows. As temperatures soared, tempers flared. Summertime traffic always frustrated the locals, but this year their passive grumbling about those from away gave way to angry outbursts.

Donny sat on the porch, cold beer in his hand, and Tut asleep at his feet as the pre-Labor Day traffic filed past his driveway, nothing but out-of-state plates. He wasn't happy. He'd replaced his lost traps, was landing record pounds of lobster, and the boat price was coming up. Otherwise his life was in shambles.

The fact that Stanley could have killed him in the shooting incident, coupled with his certainty that he was behind the sabotage of *Pot Luck*'s fuel system, shook Donny out of his easy-going way of letting things cool down and settle themselves. He'd come to acknowledge that it was a war, and it wasn't going to end without more violence.

He could have chalked his disagreements with the Nelsons up to an irritant, but he figured them for pouring sugar in the Ford's gas tank, poisoning his tree, and trying to kill Tut. He was under no illusion; it had been Eliza who had fed Tut some poison. He could abide by a lot of shit, but the words "attempted murder" kept ringing in his head. They'd gone over the line, way over.

Chase Payson was the wild card. They knew he'd hired some dirty-tricks investigator to unearth his old deeds. And there was simply no telling what lengths a father would go to protect the supposed honor of his daughter.

Shelly had gone back across the bay. She was due to head down to Cambridge and finish her college career. They hadn't discussed anything about the future or whether it was possible to continue a relationship with a four-hour truck ride.

He loved her. She loved him. They brought out the best in each other, but then there was the reality of different classes and ages with different prospects and different ways of looking at the world. Exceptions did happen, but the obstacles were steep. Donny had to allow that Chase and Bert might be right. But now Shelly was involving herself in his fights, and she didn't seem inclined to leave the summer behind.

He had to smile. His insides continued to do flips at the thought of her. And boy was he glad she was on his side, what with the plan she had for the Nelsons. He'd never shrunk from shady dealings. Sitting there on the porch with his beer and dog, thinking it all out, it seemed the risks were small compared to the benefits. His neighbors would only get hurt in the pocketbook, though they deserved far worse for attempted murder.

🐚🐚🐚

Shelly came off the float and strolled up the lawn to the sun porch. She wasn't sure how to play things out with her father, and she didn't know how much to involve her mother. She opened the refrigerator, removed a plastic jug of lemonade, drank down deep from the neck, and wiped her mouth with her bare arm.

Shelly found her mother in the garden weeding. It was out of the sun and probably cooler than anywhere in the state. Without a word, Shelly knelt down beside her mother, started to pull spiky green shoots, and laid them on the growing piles of wilting green leaves and root dirt.

They worked together in silence. Cornelia was used to letting the quiet gradually give way to conversation when her daughter was ready.

"Mummy, I love Donny."

"I know."

"What am I going to do?"

"Start by telling me what you want. Then we can go from there."

"There are complications, and I'm not only talking about all the things you and Daddy keep saying. I think Donny and I can transcend those things, at least give it a fair try. But these other things are really big, and I don't want to do anything wrong and maybe make things worse for him."

"That doesn't tell me much."

Cornelia sat back on the stone path, gathered handfuls of dying weeds, and tossed them into the wheelbarrow.

Shelly got off her knees and sat beside her mother.

"I want to put off going back to Harvard, at least for a semester, and maybe for the whole year."

The news didn't surprise Cornelia. She'd seen this coming for weeks.

"Your father won't like this plan."

"I know, and there's more, much more."

Shelly rubbed some perspiration off her brow and told her mother about the extent of Donny's troubles with Stanley and the Nelsons, the story gaining momentum until she ended in a rush.

🐚🐚🐚

Cornelia watched and listened to her daughter and thought how much she'd grown up, but also how young she remained.

Cornelia could see the effervescent effects of young love, the anguish of having a lover in trouble, and the maternal desire to protect and lash back. She still had similar feelings for Chase.

"And how do you see yourself in this narrative? Are you going to just stand by his side, or are you in there swinging?"

"Swinging. But Daddy is involved too."

"How do you mean?"

Shelly told her mother of her father's phone call, leaving out the shit storm that could come down on Donny if his past was revealed.

Though deeply unsettled by the news, Cornelia maintained the poker face she'd perfected over the many, many years of hearing similar shenanigans about her high-powered husband.

Eventually, she said, "And I thought that all the really hard part of parenthood was behind us."

She let out a short humorless laugh. "Let's go back to weeding, and I'll think a bit."

They finished up the path and gathered the piles of weeds. Shelly pushed the wheelbarrow over to the compost pile, upended it, and dumped the load. They went back through the mudroom into the kitchen. Cornelia poured two glasses of lemonade, and they sat at the counter.

"Let me handle your father."

"To what extent?"

"The whole kit and caboodle."

She downed her whole glass, another gulper in the family.

"It'll be a fight with no guarantees, but your father is a reasonable man at the core. He respects my advice, and when I point out that he's at risk of losing his only child, he'll back down.

"You still haven't answered about how you're going to play this out, and I actually don't want to know. You're resourceful and smart, but you also see things through young eyes. That vision isn't always accurate. But life is a learning ground, and you'll gain valuable experience from your mistakes.

"I do ask one thing, two actually, and I want to be able to tell your father these things, Shelly. I want you to tell me that nothing you're planning will involve any physical harm to anyone and that your actions won't land you in jail."

Cornelia observed closely as Shelly played with the condensation ring from her glass on the marble counter top and then said with a perfect poker face, "Nothing I plan will hurt anyone, and I will not go to jail."

Cornelia took a deep breath and smiled inwardly; her daughter would make a fine partner to a high-powered man.

"That said, I want you to be very careful. I've always thought that the more responsibility I give you, the more responsible you'll become. I truly hope that I'm not misplacing my trust in you."

She took her daughter's face in her cold hands.

"I love you very much, and I know I can't protect you from yourself. I believe I've raised a smart and caring girl. Now I have to test my faith. And if you ever get in too deep, you can always come back to me. For that matter, you can come back to your father. He loves you as much as I do and only wants what's best for you. He has an overly protective streak and often doesn't see the detrimental effects of too much control, but he's learning too. You can trust the both of us."

Shelly began to cry. Cornelia wrapped her in her arms, and they cried together. The tears gave way to a sense of the absurd, and they started to laugh.

Chapter 35

The heat wave was over. The air was turning crisp, fall coming early this year.

Shelly returned to Donny's house with a borrowed laptop. She spent all of Friday morning on the Internet trolling all kinds of sites for information on Coastal Conservators, arson-investigation techniques, and Red Cross blood drives.

Over lunch the two of them went over the dovetailed plans for Stanley and the Nelsons. In order to pull off these twin setups, the timing would have to be perfect.

She was more than a little worried about the plan for Donny to disappear. How could he leave without a trace? And what suspicions would he leave in the wake?

Friday afternoon, Shelly had driven Donny's borrowed truck all the way to Augusta. She entered the hardware store with a baseball cap over her bunched-up hair and dark glasses and bought latex gloves, a gas can, candles, contractor trash bags, and some twine. She paid with cash and attracted no undo attention.

She filled the gas can at Irving's and added a diet Coke and some Dentine chewing gum. She paid with a twenty-dollar bill.

She was back to Lincolnville by six o'clock, the last half-hour of the trip filled with Maine Things Considered on the local NPR radio station.

The summer people had returned to their metropolitan responsibilities, leaving transplants from away like the Nelsons time to plot and plan how to preserve Maine's pristine beauty from the absurd freedoms allotted the local people. Coastal Conservators was holding its first fall luncheon meeting on Saturday in Camden.

Chapter 35

Hurricane Earl was a bust, at least for coastal Maine. The storm had moved up the eastern seaboard and churned out to open water. But its slashing rain continued all through early Saturday morning. Most of the working boats in the harbor had stolen away to more protected waters across the bay and into little island coves. The wind was minimal from a hurricane standpoint, so the precautions were unnecessary. But the weather provided good cover.

Shelly and Donny sat at the kitchen table watching and waiting for the Nelsons to leave for their meeting. Bands of rain swept across Route One giving way to breaks of drizzle and clearing skies.

At noon on the dot, the garage door powered up, the Nelson Range Rover slipped out onto the slick, black asphalt, halted for a single lobster bait truck coming up Route One from Rockland, and headed south for Camden.

Donny drove down to the public landing to the pay phone. He dialed the White Hall Inn, which was hosting the lunch, and left a message with the receptionist in a thickened up Maine accent.

"Would you mention to the Nelsons that their pretty sailboat looks to be a bit low in the water, and a backstay seems to have come loose?"

Donny couldn't be certain that both of them would come running to rescue the boat, but he put enough trouble out there that Del might want a hand. And their absence at the beginning of the meeting meant they'd have no alibi when the investigator dug deep.

Shelly lifted the folded bath towel from Donny's table, patted Tut on the head, donned her slicker, slipped into her Boggs boots, and walked across Donny's lawn onto the Nelson property. She stopped under the grand-entrance overhang and pulled on a pair of latex gloves. She didn't look around. She peeled up the corner of the doormat and came up with the front door key. She unlocked the door and left the key in the lock.

Alex came over yapping furiously but calmed down when Shelly offered one of Tut's biscuits. The dog clicked her toes on the hardwood floor and settled back down on the day bed in the dining room. Shelly heard the first crunch of small teeth breaking the hard crust of the dog treat, but her attention quickly went to her task. She spread the towel on the foyer tiles, shrugged off her slicker, and slipped out of her boots.

She found the filing cabinets in Del's office. She wasn't surprised that not one drawer was locked; it was typical in a region known for its lack of crime. She played her fingers over the carefully labeled files and extracted the insurance and real estate folders. She set them on the desk, jiggled the mouse, and awakened the desktop computer.

She tried not to hurry. She pictured the Nelson Range Rover dashing past the house and down to the docks, the two of them rowing out in their rain gear in the rough water to check the boat, discovering it was a false alarm, and then returning to Camden to make the rest of the meeting. She prayed they didn't want to stop by to give Alex a treat.

At the Knowles Agency website, she clicked on the Contact Us tab. She typed in a request to increase the amount of insurance on the house, signed off as Eliza Nelson, then followed up with the phone call since the coverage could not be bound via email.

It was twelve thirty on a Saturday. The summer was over. The principal players would be taking the weekend off or, at the very least, be out to lunch. Secretaries and receptionists would be manning the phones. No one could think Eliza didn't sound like herself over the phone.

Shelly dialed the insurance company and asked for Robert Strong. The girl said he was out, but would she like his voice mail? No, she would not. She would like to speak to an agent so she could bind an increase of coverage on their house.

After a minute on hold, a syrupy female voice came on the line. Yes, of course she could handle the increase. Shelly referred to the file and said she thought the insured amount of $900,000 was inadequate, that they had actually spent a good deal more than that on the construction, and would she please increase the coverage to one-point-two million dollars. Shelly smiled at the amount taken off the top of her head, the same amount of cash that Donny had invested and hidden in the cellar.

The agent said yes, of course, she would bind it immediately. The increased premium would be reflected in a bill that would arrive the middle of next week. She thanked Mrs.

Nelson for the business and wished her a dry and safe week-end.

The Downeast Real Estate website was flashy and polished. Shelly flipped through the file folder and found the name of the agent who'd handled the purchase of the raw land. Shelly emailed him directly from the site, inquiring about the state of the market, how prices were holding up in the Great Recession, and how realistic it would be to list their new house if it was priced right. Eliza said she'd call soon.

Shelly called the real estate company. The agent was out of the office until Monday but could be reached immediately by cell phone. Would she like the number?

Shelly asked the secretary to leave a message for Tim Jones. She'd sent him an email inquiring about the state of the market and the possibility of listing the house. Oh, and she'd be boating all next week, so she'd call back the week after to chat. No real hurry.

"Yes, of course, Mrs. Nelson. Goodbye."

Shelly replaced the files, set the computer back to the way she found it, and let it go back to sleep. She went over to Alex and made sure she'd eaten up all the crumbs. Shelly re-dressed for the wet weather and wiped any moisture off the floor. She let herself out the front door and returned the key to its hiding place.

It was amazing how, when you put your mind to something, invariably essential items fell into place. It was happening for Shelly and Donny. The Red Cross was having a blood drive up in Bangor on Sunday.

Chapter 36

S helly snuggled in close to Donny on the bench seat in the borrowed pickup.

She said, "You know, once it all starts, it'll take on a life of its own."

Donny downshifted for the slower traffic coming through Searsport.

"I'm ready. I suppose it could all come apart at any time, but I'm all in."

Tut got up from his nap on the right passenger seat and growled at pedestrians walking toward the Penobscot Marine Museum, then fell back with a thump, curled up with a sigh, and went back to sleep.

They took Route 1A up through Winterport and into Hampden, caught 95 north past Bangor, and exited at Stillwater Avenue and the Mall.

At Walgreens, they bought three throwaway cell phones for $40 apiece. Each had 60 minutes of call time and a toll-free number. They didn't have to fill out any paperwork, and they paid with cash.

American Red Cross was on Union Street, and the parking lot was half full of cars, a moderately subscribed blood drive. They sat and watched the entrance. A few people drifted out and looked no worse for their loss of blood. More cars pulled in. The time was right, and they both got out the driver's side.

Shelly wound down the window a crack and said, "Guard the car, you little bastard, but don't make a spectacle of yourself when all the people come rushing out."

She grabbed the recycled Hannaford grocery bag and slammed the door.

The reception desk was right in front. They approached a woman, and Shelly said in her most affectionate voice, "We're here to donate blood. This is our first time, so could you please explain the procedure?"

"We're so thankful to you both."

She focused on Donny over the glasses on her nose and gave him a big smile. Then she turned and surveyed the open room to her back.

"On the left is the waiting area. You may have to wait fifteen minutes or so. You can use the time to fill out these forms."

She handed two clipboards to Shelly, looking over Donny again.

"Return the paperwork over there," she gestured with a nod of the head, "and when your name is called, go back to those chairs and relax. The nurses will take care of everything else, and you'll be out of here in no time. The restrooms are on the right, down that hall. Enjoy."

Donny took Shelly by the hand and led her to the last row of chairs.

"Enjoy? What does that mean? Makes it sound like we've just been served the ten-dollar breakfast at Denny's."

"Shut up. We need a plan."

"I thought you had a plan."

They settled in the seats and looked the place over. Shelly started to write drivel in the blank lines on her form and then gazed right toward the restrooms. Donny watched as people submitted their completed paperwork, names were called, and donors were matched with a blood bag stacked like overstuffed envelopes in an open tub. The donors were escorted to a La-Z-Boy and side table by an attending nurse.

Donny pretended to fill out his form.

"The blood bags are just on the other side of the desk, but how do we steal one without getting caught?"

Shelly, still looking down and busy with her pen, said, "I may end up in jail, which would then be a sign that what we've got planned for the rest of the week isn't such a good idea after all."

She let out a laugh that caught the attention of a flannel-shirted fat man to their left. Shelly smiled back, cursing herself for creating a memorable moment. She toned down her voice.

"You go out to the truck and wait. And when I come out, don't do anything foolish. No peeling out."

"I look numb to you?"

Shelly looked him over.

"Jesus! Want to let me in on the plan?" he inquired.

"No. It'll be self-evident."

Donny walked out the swinging doors and disappeared. Shelly watched for women coming in and out of the ladies' room. She waited. A rail-thin woman with a scrawny little boy on her hand went in, took five minutes, and came back to her seat.

Shelly stuffed the clipboards into the grocery bag and went down the hall to the bathroom. Just before the door, on the wall, she placed all four fingertips on the fire alarm and pulled down. The siren blasted out as the bathroom door eased shut behind her. The noise was almost too loud, even as she crouched up on the toilet seat inside a stall. She put her hands to her ears and could hear her blood pulse, thinking it was a good sign, given what she was about to do.

🐚🐚🐚

Tut had come all unglued when Donny pulled open the door and sat down behind the wheel. But after a face lick, he put his front paws on the dash, turned his attention to the front doors, and then looked back to Donny.

"She'll be out shortly."

They waited.

The fire alarm must have had outside speakers because it was deafening and surprised the hell out of Donny. Tut started to bark but settled down when he got slapped on the ass. People poured out the front doors: regular folk still clinging to their clipboards, then official bloodsuckers, the nurses in white slacks and colorful tops or knee-length lab coats. It seemed to Donny as if they did this every day, calm as they were. The exodus stopped, and everyone milled around looking for smoke or down the road for the fire trucks.

🐚🐚🐚

Shelly cracked the door and looked down the short hall. It was empty. It was anyone's guess about around the corners, but she didn't have any extra time. No one was in the main room. She trotted down the carpet, slalomed the chairs and tables, plucked a blood bag from the tray, slid it into her bag, came rushing out the front doors, hand over her heart, "Oh, my God! A fire! Oh, my God!"

She ran over to a clump of people.

A woman took her in her arms and told her, "Honey, it'll be all right."

Shelly hugged her back and said, "Oh, thank you! Thank you!

When they all turned their heads toward the sound of sirens coming from down the street followed by red flashing lights, Shelly slid over to the pickup and settled into her seat.

The fire truck took a wide turn into the parking lot, firemen hanging off the side.

Donny pulled out and headed slowly toward downtown.

"Holy shit! What a fucking rush!" She slapped the dashboard with the flat of her palm.

She pulled out the blood bag. "This is perfect. See here, Donny, it's got the tube and needle and even some anticoagulant."

She was all flushed from the excitement and success. Donny smiled.

"Ever consider a life of crime? Might make more financial sense than going to Harvard. It sure beats fishing in the thrill department. And you've got a wicked wheel man."

"I'll give it some thought."

They picked up 95 south and pulled into Dysarts for trucker food to go. Tut got a bacon cheeseburger. Shelly wanted him to celebrate, too.

Chapter 37

After breakfast on Monday morning, Shelly tied a tourniquet around Donny's right bicep. She slapped the purple nub of vein on the inside of his elbow, and when it bulged, she swabbed it with rubbing alcohol. She unsheathed the #16 needle and looked into Donny's eyes.

"This is going to hurt you more than it's going to hurt me," she laughed.

"I hate needles. Do you know what you're doing?"

Donny closed his eyes.

"Not a clue. I'm a rower."

She steadied her hand on his forearm, took a deep breath, and then slipped the needle in under the skin into what she hoped was the protruding blood vessel.

"You've got good veins, sweetheart."

"Really?"

"Hell, I don't know. But isn't that what the nurses always say?"

She unfastened the tourniquet. The blood came into the clear tube and made its slow way into the bag.

She said, "How much do you suppose we need?"

"Well, the last time I did this, it was overkill. Jesus, Shelly, how do I know?"

Shelly watched the bag. "Well, we want it to look real but not like a bloodbath. And then maybe we should leave enough in you so you don't die."

"Sweetheart."

She leaned over. He looked down her shirt to the swell of her breasts and started to get hard.

"Want to fool around?"

"You got some sense of timing. It's not the time for your little head to compete with the donation."

But she put her palm on his hard-on and squeezed.

"Later, big guy. We've still got a lot of work to do."

She took some gauze from the medical kit and held it over the needle as she pulled it out.

"That's got to be enough. I don't want to ruin our sex life."

"Press on it, here." She held up the bag. "Half a pint should do the trick. Now what? Put it in the fridge or let it cool down on its own?"

"I vote for the fridge."

Chapter 38

Donny opened the kitchen side door and went into the cellar. Shelly listened as he rustled around, the sounds of heavy items being moved and stacked. Then he came up with a plastic Rubber Maid tote and set it on the table.

"Ever seen a million dollars?"

"Yesterday, when I needed some cash for the disposable phones. But my box was bigger."

"A million dollars in hundreds weighs a little less than twenty pounds. And it fits into less than four-tenths of a cubic foot, in case you're wondering about the box I got from the post office."

He pulled out the collapsed-flat cardboard box, white with the red-and-blue of the United States Postal Service. He folded it open, taped the seams, top flaps hanging out, and then popped open the tote and placed the contents next to the beer cans: a big brick of light-green bills wrapped tight in translucent shipping cellophane.

Shelly ran her finger over the top and picked up a corner to heft the weight.

"Is this all there is?"

"One million two hundred thousand in hundred dollar bills. Cold hard cash."

"Can we spread it out on the floor and fool around?"

"Yes and no. I need some traveling money, and we can fool around later."

"You're absolutely no fun."

They unpacked the money and stacked it on the table, setting aside a $10,000 brick for traveling. The rest went into the Postal Service box a sleeve at a time side by side, no longer wrapped in plastic so they could breathe.

"Like fine wine?" Shelly asked.

"Why not?"

There was room for more, so Shelly stuffed crumpled newspaper along the edges so there'd be no shifting.

"If it fits, it ships. What a country. Flat rate for twenty pounds. No wonder the Post Office lost seven billion dollars last year."

It cost Donny $14.40 for postage to send the package to himself in care of the Beachcomber Hotel, Saint Thomas, U.S. Virgin Islands, no insurance. He told the clerk that the package contained just books. But he didn't send it. It was too much money to be floating around if the plan didn't work. And he could always drop it in the mailbox just before running like hell.

Chapter 39

They watched from the kitchen window as Del and Eliza loaded sail bags and a cooler into the Range Rover, Alex in a little dog tote with screen windows. They pulled out onto Route One and headed down to the beach.

"Wait here while I make sure they're off the mooring."

Donny and Tut ran out to the truck and sped off.

Shelly gathered the gas can. She took three trash bags out of the box and slipped one inside the other and then again. She smoothed them out, now a triple-layered container, strong and resilient.

Donny came back in and said, "Good to go."

He hefted a five-gallon jug of heating fuel from beside his boots in the mudroom.

Tut got shut in the house. They made their way over to the Nelson's. Shelly let herself in the front, replaced the key under the mat, and relocked the door from inside. She opened the back-porch door for Donny. They set to work.

Shelly started in the pantry, splashing the heating fuel on the floor and Persian rugs. She worked through the dining room, the living room to the parlor, and into the office, pouring the accelerant onto love seats, sofas, and armchairs. She shook out the last dribbles onto the desk.

She opened the file cabinet and pulled out some financial and insurance records. On the right wall, in the bookcase, she found a line of photo albums. She stuffed them all into the sling bag she carried over her shoulder.

🐚🐚🐚

Chapter 39

Donny had gone to the basement and opened all the slit windows. The room was full of packing boxes, spare chairs, and a set of studded snow tires for the Rover. He shifted some boxes and the tires over to a spot along the load-bearing wall and then dug into his front pocket and found the single 16-penny nail. He picked an open floor joist above his head and drove the nail true with the hammer from the loop on his left leg. With the twine, he put a quick clove hitch over the head and let it dangle loose toward the floor.

He knelt beside the fuel tank and loosened the compression fitting with a crescent wrench he took from the deep leg pocket of his cargo pants. Fuel oil began to seep and pool onto the concrete floor.

Shelly made it down the cellar stairs.

"Jesus, it stinks. You sure we're not blowing ourselves up?"

She tossed the empty jug onto a chair.

"I wouldn't think so, but you never know." He surveyed the room and their work. "I worry about the last step, though."

He took a deep breath. "Let's do it."

He held the triple garbage bags open and Shelly carefully poured in a gallon of gasoline. She set the half-full jug on a box. He twisted the neck, carried it over to the twine, and strung it up, so it dangled and swung about three feet off the ground. "Bring over one of them boxes, will you, honey?

Shelly manhandled a box over, placing it directly under the bulging trash bag. The heating fuel from the tank had made its way to the pile of tires, and the fumes were making them both feel sick.

"Let's set this grand finale in motion and get the hell out of here." Donny held the garbage bag off to the side as Shelly took a candle and a lighter from her pocket. "Here goes."

She looked Donny in the eye.

He nodded.

She flicked the lighter to flame. "So far, so good."

She lit the candle, tipped it on its side, and pooled wax onto the box top. Then she planted the candle.

"Before I let the bag go," Donny said, "Why don't you open up the cellar door to the backyard?"

She weaved through the mess and pushed the metal door up and out. Donny eased the bag back some more and then released it so that it oscillated back and forth over the flame. He made it quickly for the door.

They each sat down on the step outside and pulled off their new disposable rubber boots. He gathered them in one fist and tossed them deeper into the cellar. He shut the doors. They walked back to his house and then hightailed it down to the Whale's Tooth.

They embraced in the truck.

He gave Shelly a long hard kiss and then said, "See you in the islands."

She had tears in her eyes and couldn't say a word.

He and Tut drove down to the docks.

The rest of the plan was simple: splatter blood, implicate Stanley in foul play, and let *Pot Luck* run aground empty.

Then, with Bert's help, he and Tut would disappear.

Chapter 40

I t had taken Del and Eliza 45 minutes to get off the mooring. He motored his prized boat out around the ferry berth and then south into the wind and down toward Camden. He noticed that Donny was hauling late today, pulling out with *Pot Luck* just after they cleared the ferry dock.

The plan was for an easy sail. He wound the main halyard around the deck winch and raised the mainsail. It flapped in the light breeze. When the line came taut, the boom pulled out of its crutch. Eliza stood aft and caught the crutch before it slammed down on the teak deck.

"I'm getting the hang of sailing, darling. It's starting to be fun."

Del offered a weak smile to his wife. Alex looked out from her little bag, wedged between the cooler and the bulkhead.

Del raised the jib and brought in both sheets for a close haul down the bay. He shut down the engine. *Wild Wing* caught the wind and heeled over on a starboard tack, off with a swirl of wake toward the southern tip of Acre Island.

"Del, you do look mighty pleased with yourself."

She sat on the windward side of the cockpit with her feet braced on the port seat.

"I love how you look just now, your graying hair tussled in the breeze, the smile on your face."

"This is what it's all about," he said. "Peace and quiet, just the three of us."

Eliza freed Alex, who nestled in her lap and looked around, uncertain about her surroundings.

The sharp edges on his wife's face had disappeared, and he thought she was really quite beautiful. He smiled and then looked down the bay and hoped the fog coming in wouldn't cut their sail short.

They tacked straight over to the biscuit, the shallow water between Acre and the Ensign Islands, came about to a port tack, and pointed up to Camden.

Eliza stayed on the leeward starboard side, down close to the water, her right arm slung over the combing.

Del eyed her as she looked back to the mainland. He knew she was seeking out the big field and their fabulous house.

"Del?"

"What is it, baby?"

He squinted to where she was pointing, concentrating on the smudge of smoke wafting into the southerly wind and blowing up to Ducktrap River.

He said, "It can't be our house. It's probably someone burning brush."

But he was far from convinced. He eased the sheets, and they took a broad reach back toward Lincolnville.

By the time they were close enough to the shore, their house was entirely engulfed in flames. Fire in great sheets of yellow and orange rose into the blue sky, and gray smoke swirled northward.

Chapter 41

The bag had swung left and right, back and forth. The flame wavered slightly as the plastic went by. The oscillations slackened and finally gravity settled the contained gasoline smack dab over the candle. Heating fuel had flooded most of the cellar floor. The candle's heat started to melt the black plastic. It stretched and then finally broke, spewing the gasoline down onto the flame. It caught with a whoosh and ignited the fuel on the floor. The boxes caught and then the tires.

The fire climbed the naked wall studs and licked at the floor joists. It spread across the floor, oxygen feeding in from the open windows, and climbed the cellar stairs to the kitchen.

The fire was hungry. In thirty minutes, flames shot out the second-story windows.

It was a spectacular four-alarm fire. The Lincolnville fire department was first on the scene, but with no hydrants this far up the road, there was little they could do. The Camden and Belfast departments came in with their water trucks, but by then it was like drizzle on a conflagration. The Hope fire department put in an appearance.

This was one to remember.

Chapter 42

P *ot Luck* had been set to go, loaded up with bait trays and the blood bag down below. Donny waved to *Wild Wing* as it idled into the wind, though he could see neither Del nor Eliza.

This next part of the plan was the weakest, but as predicted on the weather channel, the fog was coming in.

Bert had the third phone, and once Donny had pulled enough traps to make it look like a working haul, he'd swing by Stanley's *In The Black* mooring and drive *Pot Luck*'s port side into her bow. Then he'd move offshore, splatter his own blood, set a course for Acre Island, meet with Bert, then abandon ship forever. It all depended on the fog.

And that wasn't the only uncertain part of this harebrained scheme. Bert had instinct too, and he didn't buy into any of it. He'd pushed Donny to report the loss of gear and the shooting incident, get Jack between him and Stanley before someone got hurt or killed.

Both he and Shelly were uneasy about this final stage too. How would the authorities look upon the empty boat? Would they really think he'd been killed? How hard would it be to pick up his trail if they really tried? And how would he look when they found him in the Caribbean paying for everything in cash? He'd made it under the radar for so long. Would this be the knife blade that opened up the long-buried can of worms?

And how could he ever come home again? What would he say? Amnesia? No one in Maine would believe him if he claimed that he'd panicked and run away after the violent confrontation with Stanley Maven on *Pot Luck*.

He'd look guilty as hell. Lame and numb!

Bert was right. It wasn't in him to run away. He had the confidence to face Stanley straight up, come what may. This was the life he knew, and the outcome of this little war would be remembered far into the future by anyone who might consider doing it to him again.

He relaxed into the routine of his life. He settled into the motions and still felt the thrill as his traps broke the surface. The keepers came in strong, and his lobster barrel was filling up nicely. He worked his way along the Ensign Islands and over to Lime. In this close, he could just make out his next string through the fog. He didn't have to refer to his radar and chart plotter.

He was leaning over the starboard side to gaff the next buoy when *In The Black* came out of the fog at ten knots.

She rammed *Pot Luck*'s port side just aft of the pilot-house. Donny flew across the sole and landed on his ass over by the culling table. Tut was thrown off the dash and landed on a twisted and snapped front leg next to Donny.

Her black bow rode up onto *Pot Luck*, splintering and crushing the boat's toe rail. The broadside did little damage to Stanley's boat, but *Pot Luck* listed severely to starboard and was pushed sideways through the water and fog.

In The Black backed down and came in along *Pot Luck*'s port side. Donny watched Stanley throw his amidships line over *Pot Luck*'s stern cleat and leap onboard, Ruger in his hand. He was clumsy on his feet, but it wasn't because of the seas. He was obviously into the whiskey, his eyes aflame. The vein in his forehead was swollen and pulsed.

Tut stood his ground, but when he tried to put weight on his broken leg, he whimpered in pain. Still he bared his teeth, growled, and advanced on Stanley.

Donny looked from his dog to Stanley waving the revolver. The irony that Stanley had accomplished the broadside that Donny had planned to manufacture himself wasn't lost on him.

"Cat got your tongue, asshole?"

"Fuck you, Stanley."

Stanley managed a vicious grin, half-revealing his stained, crooked, and broken teeth. He had his eyes on Tut, hopping toward him on three legs and getting ready to sink his fangs into whatever he could reach.

"They shoot horses, don't they?"

Stanley brought the pistol up and pulled the trigger, his aim good for being drunk. The thunderous sound consumed the pilothouse as the gun bucked in Stanley's hand. Flame leapt from the barrel, and smoke rose in the thin, still air.

Tut's head exploded, spraying the helm with blood and brain and coarse, brown fur. His body collapsed in a heap. Stanley shuddered. But then he smiled and swung the muzzle of the revolver over, lining the front sight up on Donny's chest.

But he was two beats too slow.

By then, everything for Donny had turned a bright, boiling red. He didn't think of a next round — of self-preservation or even of Tut. He pushed himself up from the sole of his boat, and his right hand landed on his gaff. He gripped the tail end and swung it wildly in an arc at Stanley's left leg. The hook end pierced the denim and embedded itself in the soft flesh of his calf. Donny yanked and Stanley came off his feet.

The gun went off again, the bullet flying nearly straight up as Stanley crashed onto his back.

Possessed, Donny pounced.

There was no contest. He slammed his fist on Stanley's gun hand and then slammed it again and again till he let go. Then Donny took the heel of his hand and drove it up under Stanley's nose. It could have been the fatal blow, sending shards of cartilage from the nose up into the brain.

Even if it was, it didn't matter. Donny grabbed the sides of Stanley's unconscious head and slammed it down onto the sole of the boat, once, then twice.

Dead is dead, and Donny knew it. It all came clear to him in a flash of insight. He staggered back. The war with Stanley was over, and it was a clear-cut case of self-defense. The money was safe in a box in the basement. The Nelsons had been repaid in kind. If he ran now, it would be an admission of guilt to every bit of it, and he'd be a marked man for the rest of his life. And how long would Shelly want to be around someone like that?

The back of Stanley's skull had collapsed and his head was deflated.

Donny was fascinated by the pooling blood that slowly ran out the scupper.

Donny vibrated in the biggest adrenaline rush of his life. But after a minute, as the shock and hate and exertion overcame him, he nearly collapsed right next to Stanley's body.

He managed to grope his way to the stern, sit on the transom, put his hands on his knees, and look the length of his boat at the aftermath, his heart close to exploding, his chest heaving, and his breath coming in desperate gasps.

He was covered in blood.

Stanley was only a fat slob of a body, lying on its back.

He felt empty and dizzy and numb. He looked at what was left of Tut and was overcome by a wave of tenderness. He began to cry, then was wracked by sobs.

Both boats drifted in the fog, tied together at different angles. Their engines idled softly in the mist. *Pot Luck* was damaged along the port side, but she was still seaworthy.

Donny looked down on Stanley. He searched himself for remorse but found only elation. He felt just fine about the bloody piece of shit lying in his boat. He took some deep breaths and began to think.

Now he had to deal with the complications. Stanley had just provided all the answers.

He could wrap Stanley in chain and sink him to the bottom where the lobsters and crabs would eat him for lunch. That would be fitting. There was deep water out in the east bay, in and among some ledges that the scallop draggers avoided for fear of getting the drag hung up.

Donny looked over at his dog and a wave of sadness crashed over him.

"Ain't no better dog anywhere, you little bastard. A fighter till the very end. God bless you, Tut."

He began to cry again and just let himself go. Then he thought how ridiculous he must look. He took a deep breath to collect himself again.

It was all evidence, even Tut, especially Tut.

Donny found his regular cell phone, looked up to the number penciled into the paint above the right windshield and dialed.

After two rings a voice answered, "Jack Milton, Marine Patrol."

"Hi Jack, this is Donny Coombs. I'm floating just west of Lime Island. I guess you might say I'm sitting in the middle of a crime scene. I think you ought to get on out here as soon as you can. Stanley Maven is lying dead on the sole of my boat."

There was a pause.

"You sit tight, Donny. We'll be right out. I don't need to tell you not to touch anything."

Donny ended the call and then dialed the number of his attorney, Martin Buber up to Belfast. There was no answer, so he left a message.

After tying a shackle to the blood bag, he let it sink out of sight.

Finally, he sat on the starboard rail and waited, the two boats idling in neutral, rising and falling together in the swells, alone in the fog.

Time was of no consequence, but it seemed really quick that he heard the whine of the twin Mercury outboards on the Marine Patrol Protector coming fast.

Jack emerged from the fog and pulled in along the starboard side. There was a Maine State Police officer in the stern. Donny took the line and tied them together amidships.

Both lawmen leaned over and looked at the scene, neither prepared for the extent of violence.

Jack said, "Holy shit, Donny. What the fuck happened?"

The state cop put a hand on Jack's forearm and said, "I'll introduce myself in a bit, but Donny, you have the right to remain silent. Anything you say or do will be held against you in a court of law. You have the right to an attorney. If you cannot afford an attorney, one will be provided for you. Do you understand these rights?"

"I do. But it's really pretty simple. Stanley broadsided my boat, came aboard, shot my dog, aimed at me and— "

"Hold on, Donny."

The state cop took out a recorder and spoke his name, time and date, and that he was talking to Donny Coombs.

"Okay, go ahead."

Donny told them of the escalating tensions with Stanley, him camping on his gear, the increasingly clear messages that went unheeded, and then about all his traps that got cut.

"Then someone sabotaged my fuel line. I can't prove it was Stanley, but it sure was him that took a rifle shot at me up by Gilkey Bell."

"Did you report any of this to the authorities?"

Donny looked at him as if he were crazy.

Chapter 42

"Who else knows about all this? Why didn't you report any of it? Why didn't you let the Marine Patrol and State Police intervene? That's our job, not yours."

"Right. If we called the cops every time there was a little beef, we'd all be in jail. We handle this kind of thing ourselves."

The cop looked over at Stanley's body.

"And how has that turned out for you? Anything else to add?"

"Just what I said before — Stanley rammed my boat, shot my dog, aimed the gun on me, and I killed him.

Donny's cell phone rang.

"Excuse me a moment."

He took the call and listened.

"Yeah, they're here now. Yeah? Okay."

He cut the call and looked over at Jack.

"I've been advised to remain silent."

Chapter 43

Donny spent the night in the Knox County jail while the authorities tried to figure out what to do. The next morning, he and his lawyer were ushered into an interrogation room, met by two men dressed in gray suits, white shirts, and conservative ties.

They shook hands all around.

"My name is Art Wilson, and I'm a detective with the Maine State Police. This is Andrew McGrath, the Knox County District Attorney. I'll fill you in on what's happened since you were taken off your boat. Then Andy will discuss what'll happen next.

"Your boat and the boat belonging to Stanley Maven were towed to the Coast Guard Station here in Rockland. The incident happened in this county, so all legal actions will be centered here.

"The State Police CID team processed the crime scene, your boat, and then the boat of Mr. Maven. You made a detailed statement before being advised by Martin to remain silent. Concerning the death of Stanley Maven, that statement was that Mr. Maven rammed your boat in the fog, came aboard with a loaded handgun, shot your dog, and then turned the gun on you.

"We've found evidence that may support your statement, but it's early in the investigation. We still need to question the other fishermen about your contentions of earlier confrontations. The body of your dog has been taken to the morgue and will be released to you after we've conducted additional forensic examinations.

"Andy?"

"Mr. Coombs, I've talked with Martin here, and he tells me that you'll be claiming that the death of Mr. Maven was a result of actions you took to defend yourself. It's too early for any conclusive forensic evidence to support your story. The ballistic results won't be back for a few days.

"There's a range of charges that can be brought, from premeditated murder down to accidental or self-defense manslaughter.

"As Art has said, the initial findings seem to confirm your story, and self-defense is apparent. I must say that I'm troubled by the level of violence you inflicted on Mr. Maven.

"Level of violence?" Martin interrupted. "What are you referring to?"

"Mr. Maven's face was flattened and the back of Mr. Maven's skull was crushed."

"My client was fighting for his life—"

"Yes, yes," he said. "This will all be argued at the trial."

"Trial?"

"Mr. Coombs, I'm charging you with manslaughter. Because of your previous standing in the community and a clean record, I am judging that there's no flight risk. I'm releasing you on your own recognizance. You're not to leave the state.

"A grand jury will convene within a few days and issue an indictment. You'll then be arraigned, and conditions for your release or incarceration will be issued. You'll go to trial in this county, probably next spring. Do you have any questions?"

"When can I bury my dog?"

"We'll let you know."

Chapter 44

Bert and Shelly were extremely concerned about Donny's disappearance. When there was no call from Donny to Bert, and the day turned into night, Bert called Shelly on their throwaway phones.

The mystery was solved when they watched the evening news in the small parlor off the kitchen in Donny's house.

Bert took Shelly across the bay, where they pitched their phones into 133 feet of water. He dropped her off at her dock.

Shelly came clean to her parents about her involvement in the plot to have Donny disappear. Chase and Cornelia believed her when she claimed absolutely no knowledge of what had happened to Stanley Maven.

Chase said, "And I suppose you know nothing about the Nelson's house."

Shelly remained silent.

Chase held his anger and disappointment in check. Shelly was adamant about postponing college for a semester but assured her father that she'd go back after Christmas. Cornelia buffered her daughter and her husband and had some stern words for Chase in private. An uneasy quiet reigned over the house.

Father, mother, and daughter put on a unified front as they closed up the house, and Chase and Cornelia prepared for the trip back to Cambridge. All the boats were due to be hauled, and the float was scheduled to be decommissioned and stored by the Boat Yard.

Chapter 45

Del Nelson was quiet, but Eliza was livid. Del stood back, observing as the arson investigator from the insurance company watched his wife rant while she paced the ruins on the scorched blacktop, half-melted and buckled, close to where the garage had been.

She said, "This is outrageous! Someone obviously burned down our house, but it sure as hell wasn't us! We were out on our fucking boat, for Christ's sake!"

"Please calm down, Mrs. Nelson."

Del thought the investigator sounded like the last thing he wanted Eliza to do was calm down. He was either enjoying the show, or sizing up a perpetrator, or both.

"We're not jumping to any conclusions here. This interview is just a formality. We'll examine the site and determine the cause of the fire. It's all very scientific. We'll get to the bottom of this, rest assured."

"I'll tell you who did this. That bastard Donny Coombs is who."

"Why would he burn your house down?"

"To get even."

"Really? Even for what?"

Del looked over at his wife and wondered what she'd say. Then he noticed the investigator glance at Donny's yard and stare at the dead oak tree.

She paused and then said, "He's been such an irritant, just a really bad neighbor. We've had some disagreements, and he hates us. Doesn't he, Del?"

She didn't wait for any response. "Ask anyone in town."

She took a breath. "He did this, I just know he did. You catch him and fry his ass!"

The investigator rubbed his chin. "When was the last time you saw your neighbor?"

Eliza bored her eyes into the investigator.

"Yesterday afternoon. He was leaving the harbor the same time we were."

Del watched Eliza bear down on the investigator.

"What are you thinking? That that clears him? You can't seriously think we did this! It has to be *him*! I know it!"

"Mrs. Nelson, please don't take this personally. We're gathering evidence, and all these inquiries are routine."

Chapter 46

Martin pulled over on the shoulder of Route One and dropped Donny at his house. Shelly watched from the bedroom window where she'd been waiting.

Donny slumped to the mudroom door and let himself in. Shelly gathered him in her arms and began to cry.

For a long moment, neither said a word.

Outside, traffic moved along the road. The VHF crackled with sporadic communications from boats on the bay. The refrigerator hummed. They sat at the kitchen table and held hands.

Shelly said, "I'm so sorry about Tut."

Donny stood up and got two beers from the icebox. They popped the tops.

"That's the only bad part, I think. All the rest will work itself out."

Shelly got up as Donny slid his chair back and sat in his lap. She wrapped her arms around his shoulders, resting her head on Donny's chest. He held her too.

She said, "It never would've worked, would it?"

"I don't think so."

"And it worked out for the best?"

"Except for Tut and Stanley, but he gave me no choice."

"And you never sent the money, did you? You always had your suspicions."

"It's down cellar."

Shelly lifted her head and smiled.

"Can we spread it around the floor and fool around now?"

"Not the first part."

Donny stood from the chair with Shelly in his arms and carried her to the bedroom.

Epilogue

The grand jury indicted Donny for manslaughter. He was released after posting a $25,000 bond. The trial was set for April, the first available slot.

Shelly was the spark during those first weeks. She insisted that they paint the house. The two of them scraped and sanded, replaced rotten siding, and laid down two coats of dark-red barn paint. They trimmed out the windows in cream.

The Nelsons gave up. They left Maine under a cloud of suspicion. The arson investigation was still pending, but the fact that there were no remains of photo albums or financial records in the debris was causing the investigator to examine them more closely. Also damning was the fact that they took the dog out sailing on the boat for the first time.

🐚🐚🐚

Bert, Donny, and Shelly hauled all of Donny's gear and stacked it alongside the garage. The season was over.

Shelly returned to Harvard in January for her second-to-last semester. Even after taking the fall semester off, she managed to capture back her seat on the women's eight, which went on to win the national collegiate regatta in March.

Donny went on trial April 16. Shelly came up for the proceedings, which took two days.

The prosecution presented forensic evidence of excessive violence and a witness, a Maven cousin who testified about the confrontation in Stanley's kitchen.

Then the defense called up each member of the Lincolnville lobster gang to testify about the escalating conflict. Bobby

234

Wentworth was also called. He showed up sober and was surprisingly eloquent.

Donny took the stand and told the same story that the prosecution was using as his confession.

The prosecution could not overcome the ballistic evidence. It was clear that Stanley had shot Tut and that he presented a clear and present danger to Donny. That was enough for each member of the jury.

The jury took an hour to return the verdict of not guilty to the charge of manslaughter. Some of the jury, in statements made after, felt they too would have smashed Stanley Maven's head to smithereens.

Tut's body was released, and Donny and Shelly dug a hole out by the dead oak tree in an afternoon mist.

Melancholy hung in the air.

Each shovelful of earth seemed heavier than the last. No words were spoken. There were too many roots, but it didn't matter to the big, old tree. They sliced through them with the spades. They put Tut's blanket in first, smoothed it out, laid him into the ground, tucked him in, and then shoveled dirt gently over his body.

After they were done stamping the earth flat, Shelly walked back to the driveway, passed *Pot Luck* up on jack stands and still damaged on the port side, and got a block of granite out of her car.

It was heavy, so Donny met her halfway back and took the stone, held it out and read the inscription.

"King Tut, the best there ever was."

Donny placed the headstone on the grave, wiggled it down firm, and gave it a pat.

"Yeah, he was."

Donny walked Shelly back to her car.

"You gonna get another dog?"

"Too soon. He'll be impossible to replace. You all right to drive back?"

"I'll be fine. Just four hours of heartbreak."

"Take it slow, and you'll be all right."

"You mean about life?"

"You always were moving on. Your parents were right, even your father. But I wouldn't have traded this past year with you for nothing."

He swept her into his arms and kissed her hard. He felt like he was standing on the edge of a cliff, with no sight of the bottom.

Tears streamed down Shelly's cheeks, and she couldn't let go of the embrace, as though she wanted to remain in this frozen moment forever.

Donny pulled them apart and opened her car door.

"You drive careful now."

He watched her pull out onto Route One and head south. He waved until the car was out of sight. He turned and fished a smoke from underneath his sweater, fired it up, and stared at *Pot Luck*.

note to readers :

Literary Wave Making 101 —

1) love it y you'd write a brief review for Amazon, and

2) y you liked the book, please share a recommendation with friends.

"Once Upon a Nightmare" coming out in the Summer of 2014

Thank you, Thank you

[signature]